Praise for the Ivy Meadows Mystery Series

"This gut-splitting mystery is a hilarious riff on an avant-garde production of 'the Scottish play'...Combining humor and pathos can be risky in a whodunit, but gifted author Brown makes it work."

– *Mystery Scene Magazine*

"Vivid characters, a wacky circus production of *Macbeth*, and a plot full of surprises make this a perfect read for a quiet evening. Pour a glass of wine, put your feet up, and enjoy! Bonus: it's really funny."

– Ann Littlewood,
Award-Winning Author of the Iris Oakley "Zoo-dunnit" Mysteries

"This gripping mystery is both satisfyingly clever and rich with unerring comedic timing. Without a doubt, *Macdeath* is one of the most entertaining debuts I've read in a very long time."

– Bill Cameron,
Spotted Owl Award-Winning Author of *County Line*

"Funny and unexpectedly poignant, *Macdeath* is that rarest of creatures: a mystery that will make you laugh out loud. I loved it!"

– April Henry,
New York Times Bestselling Author

"Brown mixes laugh out loud observations about the acting life with a witty and intriguing mystery. Consider yourself warned. *Oliver Twisted* is a fast-paced addictive read impossible to put down until Ivy has caught the killer."

– D.E. Ireland,
Agatha Award-Nominated Author of *Move Your Blooming Corpse*

"A definite delight...sit back, wait for the curtain to rise on this one, and then have a whole lot of fun figuring out whodunit."

– *Suspense Magazine*

"The setting is irresistible, the mystery is twisty, and Ivy is as beguiling as ever, but what I really loved was the depth and complexity of painful human relationships right there in the middle of a sparkly caper. Roll on Ivy #3!"

– Catriona McPherson,
Agatha Award-Winning Author of *The Day She Died*

"It is not easy to combine humor and murder, but Cindy Brown does it effortlessly. Who else would think of combining *The Sound of Music* with *Cabaret* with a serial killer? The result is such fun."

– Rhys Bowen,
New York Times Bestselling Author of *Malice at the Palace*

"A fun and rollicking mystery at sea with a delightfully twisty plot and a heartfelt heroine who is as entertaining as she is soulful. I highly recommend this series. More please!"

– John Clement,
Author of the Dixie Hemingway Mysteries

"This novel excels at operating at several different levels. While it is endlessly entertaining and full of humor, the author is not afraid to tackle serious topics and confront contemporary issues...One of the greatest joys of reading this series is watching Ivy grow up before our eyes...a masterful blend of mystery and the entertaining fun of the theater world."

– *Kings River Life Magazine*

"The mystery kept me glued to the pages...had me roaring with laughter...A delightful read and I can't wait to see what happens next in this amusingly entertaining series."

– *Dru's Book Musings*

"For true Dickens fans, theatre lovers, and mystery buffs everywhere, it is indeed the best of times. Please sir, I want some more!"

– *Broadwayworld.com*

KILLALOT

The Ivy Meadows Mystery Series
by Cindy Brown

MACDEATH (#1)
THE SOUND OF MURDER (#2)
OLIVER TWISTED (#3)
IVY GET YOUR GUN (#4)
THE PHANTOM OF OZ (#5)
KILLALOT (#6)

KILLALOT

AN IVY MEADOWS MYSTERY

Cindy Brown

HENERY PRESS

Copyright

KILLALOT
An Ivy Meadows Mystery
Part of the Henery Press Mystery Collection

First Edition | November 2018

Henery Press
www.henerypress.com

Cover art by Stephanie Chontos
Author Photograph by AJC Photography

Trade Paperback ISBN-13: 978-1-63511-430-0
Digital epub ISBN-13: 978-1-63511-431-7
Kindle ISBN-13: 978-1-63511-432-4
Hardcover ISBN-13: 978-1-63511-433-1

Printed in the United States of America

To all of the wonderful folks
who've helped with my launch parties,
with special thanks to Annie Bloom's Books
and O'Connor's Café and Bar.

ACKNOWLEDGEMENTS

I owe a huge debt of gratitude to all of the people who turned my launch parties into theatrical events—I wish I could have named all of you in the dedication. Thanks to: Portland Actors Ensemble (Patrick Cox, Michael Godsey, Curt Hanson, Sarah Keyes Chang, Brian MacEwan and Jennifer Zubernick), Sam Mowry and The Willamette Radio Workshop, Paulette Rees-Denis and The Harmony Ranchers, Amelia Ford, Beth Kahlen, Michele Mariana, Cindy McGean, Becca Stuhlbarg, Brian Tennison, Autumn Trapani, David Withers, and especially Bruce Miles, who has been in every show and makes an awesome Uncle Bob.

I also want to thank:

Holly Franko, Janice Maxson, John Kohlepp Jr., Lindsey Nyre, Shauna Petchel, and Autumn Trapani for being amazingly helpful first readers.

John Kohlepp Jr. for providing me with cool custom swag (Ivy Meadows coloring pages!), Orit Kramer for her fab graphic design, and Ruth Barrineau-Brooks for being a wonderful proofreader.

Sir Bil Woodford of the Imperial Knights, who is generous not only to mystery writers who want to know about the finer points of jousting, but to the horses he rescues.

John Hopper of JB National Investigations, who's knowledgeable about everything PI and a nice guy to boot.

Barbara and Dale Fiedler, for being gracious and generous to a writer in need of a quiet space, and to Pam Harrison, who makes nice things happen.

My writers' group for giving me the support (and the kicks in the butt) I need on an ongoing basis. Thanks to Ann Littlewood, Doug Levin, Evan Lewis, Marilyn McFarlane, and Angela M. Sanders.

My other writer friends who provide support, feedback, and sometimes wine: Lisa Alber, Gretchen Archer, April Henry, and Martha Ragland.

The team at Henery Press, who always makes my books so much better. Thanks to Kendel Lynn, Stephanie Chontos, Maria Edwards, Art Molinares, Christina Rogers and Meagan Smith.

All of my FB friends who gave me ideas for belly dancing troupe names, especially Michael Mooney, who supplied Gimme Shimmie.

And especially to Hal, for giving me a happy ever after.

Chapter 1

"*Ow.*" It hurt when Riley hugged me. Partly because he was strong. Partly because he was wearing chain mail. But mostly because he was wearing chain mail in the Arizona sun. I craned my neck to look at my upper arm. "I think I actually got a burn from your armor."

"That's 'cause I'm hot." Riley grinned over his shoulder at my boyfriend to show him he wasn't flirting with me.

But Matt didn't notice. Maybe it was because he hadn't been noticing much lately when it came to me. Or maybe he was distracted by the unicyclist in the kilt. Or the earthbound fairies flirting with landlocked pirates, the knights in homemade armor ogling sun-tanned damsels, or the witches mingling happily with hobbits and dragons and Storm Troopers among cactus-lined roads. Yeah, I had to give him a break. The Phoenix Renaissance Faire was a pretty distracting place.

"No, seriously," I said to Riley. "How can you stand to wear that?" It was only March but already ninety degrees in the shade—and there wasn't much shade at the faire, it being in the desert and all.

"I dunno. Sometimes I pour water over my head."

"I think a lot of people are hot," Matt's glasses glinted in the sun as he turned to watch a man wearing nothing but a Conan the Barbarian-style fur diaper. "That would explain some of the costumes."

"Nah, it's this way at every Ren faire. Isn't it great?" Riley bowed to an elfin-looking woman wearing a headdress made of antlers, and then stepped around two underage pirates dueling with wooden swords. "It's like heaven." He bowed again to a woman whose breasts nearly popped out of her cinched-up bodice. "With boobs."

I smacked him on the arm, even though he didn't mean it in a sleazy way. An old theater friend, Riley was a big curly-haired Irish Setter of a guy—happy, harmless, and good-naturedly goofy.

"I've never seen anything like it." My brother Cody stood next to his girlfriend Sarah, staring at the scene in front of us: merchants hawking their wares from half-timbered storefronts, kids riding on a giant swing shaped like a swan, and hundreds of costumed people thronging the dusty roads. The far-off sound of bagpipes competed with laughter from an open-air theater and the shouts from a nearby axe-throwing booth. "This is so cool." Cody continued to stare. A few people stared back, probably because he was really handsome, like a twenty-something Brad Pitt. "Why have we never been here before?"

"I don't know," I said, but I did. The faire wasn't cheap, and Matt was still paying off student loans, Cody and Sarah could only make a little bit of money at their jobs since they were both on disability, and my acting gigs and part-time PI work barely paid the bills.

"Riley?" Sarah dipped her head in that shy way she had. "Thank you for giving us tickets."

"Thank you, indeed," I said.

"My pleasure," said Riley. "Let me show you the lay of the land before I have to go to work. Ha! I get to call jousting 'work.' This way." He started to lead us toward a group of Tudor-looking buildings, but was stopped by a little boy wearing dragon pajamas: "Are you a real knight?"

Riley did look impressive in his silver armor. He knelt down next to the boy. "What do you think, small sir?"

The boy chewed his bottom lip. "Do you have a horse?"

Riley nodded. "A gray one. He's back in the stables."

"And a sword?"

"Indeed I do." Riley stood up and unsheathed his sword from

the scabbard that hung on his side.

"Wow."

A roundish middle-aged fellow wearing a short, hooded cape stopped to watch Riley and the boy. He looked vaguely familiar—an actor I'd worked with? I was trying to place his face when Cody gave a shout. "Turkey legs!" He took off running toward Fryer Tuck's Faire Fowl booth. Matt followed, taking his wallet out of his pocket.

Riley bowed to the little boy and his mom, sheathed his sword, and said to me, "I'm going to go get them a discount." He hoofed it up to the booth where the guys were placing their orders.

Sarah drifted over to a table full of jewelry in front of a faded red gypsy caravan. I followed and joined her in perusing necklaces of crystals hung on silver chains. An old woman dressed all in black pushed aside the curtain that served as the door of the caravan. "Tell your fortunes, miladies?" she asked in a heavy Slavic accent.

"No, thank you," said Sarah.

"What about you, my dear? The crone knows all." She put a finger beside her nose. It was supposed to be spooky but made me think of that poem about Santa Claus. "And laying his finger aside of his nose," I whispered to Sarah, "and giving a nod, up the chimney he rose." Sarah giggled.

The fortuneteller must have heard. "I wouldn't be so cavalier if I were you." She pointed over my head into the faire behind us with a shaky finger. "Death is near."

Chapter 2

"Oh no." Sarah's bottom lip trembled. Her disability made her take things literally. "What should we do?"

What I wanted to do was smack that crone upside the head for scaring Sarah, but she'd skittered back into her caravan right after her pronouncement. "Nothing." I put an arm around Sarah's shoulders. "That woman is just an actor, like Riley, like me. We just make stuff up. It's all just pretend."

Still, I looked over my shoulder to where the old woman had pointed. Nothing any more out of the ordinary than we'd already seen: a knight in black armor, several top-heavy wenches, a juggler, lots of people in T-shirts and shorts, and the little pirate brothers, who were still dueling in the road a few feet from us. The smaller of the boys turned his back on his brother, who scowled, then swung his wooden sword over his shoulder like a baseball batter about to swing. At his little brother's head.

"No!" I leapt in between the two boys. *Crack!* The sword caught me in the shoulder and I fell down in the dirt.

"*Boys.*" The kids' mom didn't look up from her cell phone, just pulled them away from me and continued walking down the road.

"Are you well?" The knight I'd glimpsed earlier knelt down next to me. He wore black armor, but no helmet over his thick blonde hair.

I sat up. "I'm fine. The fall was more about my leaping than the kid's sword. Though a 'thank you' would be in order!" I shouted at the boys' mom's back.

The knight stood up and held out a hand to me. He was big—muscled and maybe six four, with a bristling red beard. "It is held that valor is the chiefest virtue, and most dignifies the haver."

I took his hand and let him help me up. I nearly curtseyed. Don't know if it was the effect of the Shakespeare line, the knight, or the Ren Faire in general.

"Thank you," I said. "Sir...?"

"Angus Duff," he said in a deep baritone. "At your service, milady." He stepped closer and looked into my eyes. His were green, like mine. "Hear my soul speak," he said quietly. "Of the very instant that I saw you, did my heart fly at your service; there resides, to make me a slave to it."

I nearly melted. I loved that line from *The Tempest*.

"Ivy," Matt said behind me. I turned to see him holding two turkey legs; Cody and Sarah, also with turkey legs, right behind him. "What happened?"

"Well, there was a fortune-telling witch, a hostile pirate, and a gallant knight." I turned back to Angus, but he had disappeared into the crowd.

"Sounds like a typical day at the Ren faire." Riley joined us.

"Is the fortuneteller always that creepy?" I took the turkey leg Matt handed me.

"Nah, she's usually cool. In fact, she told me I'd be the most famous jouster at the faire. Speaking of which, I should get going. Gotta get ready for the joust—you know, prepare physically and mentally. It's not easy riding a horse while wearing a hundred pounds of armor and carrying a big stick."

"Is jousting dangerous?" asked Cody.

"You bet. We're riding big animals at a gallop, head to head, and trying to hit each other with lances. It's very dangerous. Deadly sometimes."

"Really?" said Sarah.

"Oh yeah," Riley said. "You know how to kill a jouster?"

"How?" asked Cody.

"Take away his beer. Ha!"

Cody laughed. "Take away his beer!"

"Is that funny?" Sarah whispered to me.

"It is to Riley," I whispered back.

"Squire Riley!" Angus had come back. Maybe he'd quote some more Shakespeare. Instead he smiled at me and said, "We meet again, milady," then turned his attention to Riley, punching him on the shoulder in a sort-of friendly way. "What have you done with my helmet, thou artless apple-john?"

"I haven't seen your helmet," Riley said. "I'm not your squire today."

"Zounds!" Angus's face grew red. "Some lackey must have made off with my helmet. Can you bloody believe it?"

"I can," said Cody. Angus frowned at him, and Cody stepped back, unsure if he'd said something wrong.

"It's okay," I said to my brother. "He was asking a rhetorical question." Cody looked even more unsure. "I'll explain later."

"He was just asking God," said Sarah. That was actually a pretty good definition.

Angus's face looked like a pot that was trying not to boil. "The joust begins in half an hour." His Ren faire accent—sort of British Shakespearean—was gone. "What the hell am I supposed to do now?"

Cody began to open his mouth. "He's asking God again," I whispered, and he shut it.

"I'd let you borrow mine," said Riley, "but—" He stopped as a young woman ran toward us, long brown hair streaming behind her as she wove through the crowd. She skidded to a stop and held out a black knight's helmet. She didn't say a word, probably because she was trying to breathe. The run, plus the dust, plus her tight bodice would have made talking pretty tough.

"Bianca, thank God." Angus took the helmet from her outstretched hands. "You're as brilliant as you are beautiful," he said. She was amazing-looking—young and strong and tall, dressed in an "Amazon warrior meets Renaissance villager" sort of costume: a leather bodice and knee-high boots over a hip-length poet blouse and leggings. "Did you bring the gorget too?" he asked.

Bianca stood up straight, put her hands on her hips, took a

deep breath, then coughed. Really dusty out here. She shook her head.

"Doesn't matter. Gorgets are for cowards. Thank you." Angus grabbed Bianca's face and kissed her on the lips. I loved it when Matt kissed me that way. It seemed like it'd been ages.

Bianca didn't appear to feel the same way. She pulled away from Angus, glowered at him, and ran off. Riley stared after her, his back unnaturally stiff.

"I'll see you at the joust," Angus said to Riley. "Prepare to meet thy doom." He flashed a smile in my direction, then strode off down the road.

"That's the guy who helped me up," I said. "He was great."

"He can be." Riley kept his eyes on the path Bianca had taken.

"What's a gorget?" asked Matt.

Riley shook himself like a dog after a bath. It must have helped him shake off whatever was bugging him, because his sunny nature returned. "It's a piece of armor that protects the neck."

"Is it important?"

"All armor seems important to me."

"Why did he call you an apple-john?" Cody asked Riley.

"It's an insult from Elizabethan times," I said. "It means "withered apple."

"It does?" said Riley. "I always thought it had something to do with Johnny Appleseed."

"Johnny Appleseed was cool," said Cody.

"Right?" said Riley. "Right?!"

"So you're friends with Angus?" I asked. The energy between the two men was strange—a mix of camaraderie, competition, and something else I couldn't put my finger on.

"He's kind of my friend," said Riley. "He's also kind of an asshole."

Cody's eyebrows drew together. He was obviously confused about why someone would be friends with an asshole. I couldn't say.

"I'm his squire," Riley continued. "He trained me. Normally I'd be helping him, handing him lances and stuff, making sure he has his effin' helmet. But today I get to joust and they thought it'd be cool if I went up against him. Angus doesn't know it yet, but I'm going to tickle his catastrophe." Riley grinned. "That's Ren faire speak for 'kick his ass.'"

Chapter 3

"See you at the arena." Riley jogged away.

"Break a leg," I yelled after him.

He turned around but kept running, backwards now. "I get to joust!" he shouted, grinning wider than the sky. "I still can't believe I get paid to be here."

"Did he just jog in chain mail?" asked Matt. "In ninety degree heat?"

I rubbed my shoulder where the boy had hit me. His sword may have been wooden, but it packed a wallop. Again, Matt didn't notice. I wished I knew what was on his mind.

We'd been doing fine—better than fine—until just this last week or so.

Except for a fight last month about me possibly going on tour and not telling him. Could that be it? We'd made up, but maybe my equivocation still bugged him.

I grabbed Matt's hand as we all walked into the jousting arena. He gave my hand a gentle squeeze, but didn't look at me like he usually would. *Stop it, Ivy.* He was probably just checking out the place.

The jousting arena looked like a dirt soccer field ringed with bleachers, the middle divided by horizontal "fences": wooden stanchions topped with railings, like the barriers they use to keep people in line. Several entrances broke up the bleachers: the wide public walkway we'd just entered, and two open gates—one that led to the desert and the other to a staging area. The bleacher areas were divided into four sections, each marked with a different color. We climbed into the green section, as Riley had instructed, but didn't find four empty seats until almost the top row. Sarah sat down, then jumped back up again. "Ouch!" She frowned at the aluminum bleachers and tugged at her shorts. Matt spread his faire map across the hot metal seat for Cody and Sarah. I did the same for us. We rustled when we sat.

Cody nodded at my turkey leg. "Are you going to eat that?"

I shook my head. The tension with Matt had stolen my normally voracious appetite. I handed Cody my untouched turkey leg. Matt frowned at me. "I'm fine," I lied. I was not about to spoil this outing with my emotional insecurity.

A bugle blasted through the desert air. Across from us, people dressed in royal-looking Elizabethan costumes filed into a theater-style box covered by an awning.

"I think that's the queen," said Sarah.

"Ladies and gentlemen!" said a man who stood next to the royal box. "Are you ready to meet your knights?" A roar from the crowds. "Presenting Squire Riley, jousting for the first time today!" The gate opened and Riley rode out on a dappled gray horse, carrying a banner with a green and white coat of arms that matched the cloth covering his horse's flanks. He stopped in front of the royal box and bowed to the queen, who acknowledged him with a wave. He straightened up and galloped around the perimeter of the arena, the banner streaming behind him. As he rode past the green section, the crowd stood up and cheered. Riley stopped in front of us, raising an arm in greeting. He was helmetless and his grin infectious, even from up high in the bleachers. "Oh my God," said a young woman near me. "I want that knight for Christmas."

The announcer introduced two more knights, then said, "And now, the most notorious—I mean *victorious* knight of them all, the Knight of the Black Death, Sir Angus!"

"Really?" Matt said. "He named himself after a plague?"

A huge black horse burst out of the gate, hooves pounding the dirt. The knight on his back carried a tattered black banner.

"That symbol on his flag," whispered Cody. "It's made of a skull and bones."

"It's creepy," Sarah said.

Huh. The courtly knight I'd met earlier did look creepy. Angus had added some pieces of armor so that black spikes jutted out from his shoulders, like a dragon's hackles. He stopped in front of his section of the crowd. "Arrr!" he yelled, arms in the air. Angus's section responded in a tribal sort of roar rather than the good-natured yell that had greeted Riley. I reminded myself that the men were just actors playing their parts, a Renaissance riff on good cop, bad cop.

The announcer introduced two more knights. After all of them had left the field, he explained the rules of the joust, then said, "First on the field of battle: Sir Evan the Blue Knight, and Sir Collier the Red." The two knights, now helmeted, rode out on horseback, their audience sections cheering wildly. "The rules of chivalry apply. You may salute your opponent."

The two men did so, then steered their mounts to opposite ends of the arena. Squires handed them long lances and shields.

"They have to carry both of those?" said Cody. "How do they stay on their horses?"

How indeed, I thought as the knights' steeds flew toward each other. *Crack!* The blue knight's lance smacked Red's shield so hard that the tip of the lance shattered. "Huzzah!" shouted the blue section.

After a few more passes, it was determined that the blue knight had won that round. The crowd went crazy. You would've thought their team had won the Super Bowl.

"And now," the announcer lowered his voice, "the most feared knight in Christendom: Sir Angus, the Black Death." Angus thundered into the arena. He'd painted a slash of black across his helmet so that his eyes looked like bottomless holes. "He's like a Ringwraith from *Lord of the Rings*," whispered Matt.

"I was thinking about a horseman of the Apocalypse, but Ringwraith works too," I whispered back.

Angus raised his visor. "My squire, whom I trained, dares to challenge me!" he shouted. "I will meet the challenge of this dissembling peasant and put to rest his perfidy, once and for all!"

The crowd hushed. Angus was some actor, making you feel his intensity even when you couldn't see his face. His squire handed him his lance.

"Where is he?" shouted Angus. "Has he run off to hide like the little boy he is?" His horse reared up, then raced around the arena, pulling up just a few feet in front of a squire dressed in green and white. "Where is your master?" shouted Angus. He shook his lance at the sky. "Come and face me, coward!"

Riley appeared in the gateway to the staging area, suited up in his silver helmet and armor, his shield and lance already in hand. His squire began to run toward him, then veered off as Riley tore around the arena on his gray horse, passing Angus, whose horse reared again, whether on purpose or not I couldn't tell. Riley stopped at the opposite end of the arena, facing Angus. He and his horse were a head shorter than Angus. A thrill of fear went down my back. How much of this joust was a drama played out for the audience, and how much was a real blood sport?

"Commence!" said the announcer.

The horses rocketed toward each other, the knights' lances pointed at each other. *Crack!* Angus's lance glanced off Riley's shield.

"Did you see that?" Matt whispered. "It looked like Riley pulled up his lance at the last minute."

"I saw."

The two horsemen faced each other again. Angus's monstrous black horse pawed at the ground.

"Commence!"

The horses ran straight at each other. Once again, Angus bested Riley. "He pulled up again," said Matt.

"I know." Was this part of the act? Or was Riley scared to go up against Angus? It'd be natural, his first tournament and all.

"Last pass," said the announcer.

Horses and knights lined up again. "On to victory!" shouted Angus. His section of the crowd roared with him.

"A cheer for the green knight," said a wench dressed in Riley's colors. Our huzzah sounded puny next to the primitive yell of Angus's crowd.

"Commence!"

The horses charged. Riley stampeded toward Angus so fast he was almost a blur.

"Now he's going for it," I said.

Crack! Riley's lance slammed into Angus's head. Angus's shield and lance went flying. His body followed. It landed in the dirt with a thud.

"What happened?" asked Sarah.

I didn't reply. I was too busy watching Riley ride out of the open gate into the desert beyond.

Chapter 4

Angus lay in the dirt. He didn't move. His squire ran over and knelt beside him.

"Don't worry," I said to Cody and Sarah. "He's just acting." But I didn't take my eyes off Angus. None of us did, but it didn't matter how hard we stared, he didn't move.

"Is there a doctor in the house?" the announcer asked. "If so, could he or she please proceed to the arena? Everyone else, please exit the jousting area in an orderly fashion, beginning with the first rows of bleachers."

People surged out of their seats. They didn't exit but crowded together at the guardrail, straining to see through the small ring of people that now surrounded Angus. The squires and costumed wenches who'd been leading the cheers tried futilely to keep order. Our little group couldn't move.

"Riley hurt him," Cody said.

"I think so," Matt said.

"But why?" Cody asked.

"I'm sure it was an accident."

"But why did he ride away?" I said. "And why isn't anyone going after him? Hey!" I shouted as loud as I could. "Shouldn't someone go after Riley?"

Even my actor-voice wasn't loud enough to cut through the hubbub. "Hey," I tried again. "Hey!"

Finally the red squire looked my way. I pointed at the open gate. "Shouldn't someone go after Riley?" I must've gotten through to him because he turned toward his knight, when a hush fell. The crowd turned like one body toward the gate that led to the staging area—where Riley stood in his chain mail. "What's going on?" He stumbled into the arena, rubbing his head. "Where's my helmet? And my horse?"

For a moment, people stood still, unsure where the greater drama lie. Then a few of them rushed toward Riley. I joined them, leaping over bleachers. Snatches of conversation hit my ears: "What the hell?!"

"Who was that jouster?"

"Is the other guy dead?"

I finally got close to Riley. "What happened?" I asked.

"I don't know. I was almost ready. I had just put on my helmet and...that's the last thing I remember." He rubbed his head again. "My head hurts." He pointed to the ring of people surrounding Angus. "What's going on over there?"

I didn't answer. Riley's eyes looked glazed. "Sit down for a minute, okay?" I said.

Riley began to sit, then collapsed. He lay there sprawled in the dirt, smiling up at me as if this kind of thing happened every day.

"Could we get some water over here?" I shouted to the crowd. "Some medical attention?"

A woman ran up with a bottle of water. "I'm a nurse."

"I think he may have been hit on the head," I said. "Can you check for a concussion?'"

"Do you have a headache?" she asked Riley.

"Yeah."

"Feel like vomiting?"

"Now that you mention it..." Riley began to heave and I turned away, not just to escape his barf but to check out the staging area. Lots of footprints and hoof prints, but no sign of anyone, nothing that could tell me what happened.

"I think he should get checked out," the nurse said to me. "Someone called 911 for, uh," she motioned toward Angus. "We'll have them take a look at this knight too."

"Riley," I said. "His name is Riley McFarlane."

"What?" said Riley. "You rang?"

I watched the nurse cover Riley's vomit with a faire map, but my mind was busy elsewhere. Something was wrong. But what? So much was wrong, the addled Riley, the too-still Angus...ah. I intercepted the Red Knight who was walking past. "Hey," I said. "Did you catch the fake Riley?"

"*That*'s what my squire was trying to say." The knight turned around and ran toward his horse and jumped into the saddle. "I will catch him!" he called to me, and rode his horse out of the gate into the desert.

Matt came up next to me. "I sent Cody and Sarah back to the faire. Told them we'd call Sarah's cell when we were ready to leave." We rejoined Riley's group, where an EMT was shining a penlight in his eyes. "You probably have a mild concussion. Did you lose consciousness?"

"For a minute or two."

"And it looks like you vomited." The EMT nodded to the lumpy place in the dirt covered by the map.

"Yeah," said Riley. "But it could've been the steak-on-a-stake I ate right before the joust. Or the funnel cake. Or the fish and chips."

"I think we should take you in to the hospital, just to be sure," said the EMT.

"No. No way. I heard how much that costs."

"Riley," I said gently.

"Seriously, I've been hit on the head way harder than this." That could explain a few things. "No hospital."

"All right." The EMT stood up and brushed the dirt off his knees. "But can someone check on you every so often, just to make sure you're okay?"

"Yeah. Bianca can."

"The woman we met earlier?" I asked

"Yeah. She's my girlfriend."

"She is?" This was the first Riley had mentioned a girlfriend. I remembered the woman running in the dirt street, Angus kissing her on the lips, the tightness in Riley's face as he watched them.

"Yeah. We live together, in her fifth-wheel. It's cool. Much better than my tent."

Right then, Bianca appeared at the entrance to the stadium, disheveled and panting. She stood there, looking back and forth between Angus and Riley. Finally, she ran toward us. "I was doing my show," she said. "I just heard—" she looked over her shoulder at the medical personnel surrounding Angus. "What happened?'

"Hi babe." Riley grinned at her affectionately. "Not sure. I think someone hit me on the head."

"Are you okay?"

"Yeah. I got a head like a rock."

"And what about...?" She turned again toward Angus. We'd kept Riley's back to the spectacle, not saying anything about it. Better for him to find out when his head was clear.

Riley followed Bianca's gaze. Hope his head was clear enough now. "Wha?" His mouth dropped open.

The EMTs lifted a stretcher. Angus lay on it, his head and neck in a brace, his face covered by an oxygen mask, his body uncannily still.

"Oh, Riley." Tears spilled onto Bianca's cheeks. "What did you do?"

Chapter 5

Riley waved at the stretcher. "I didn't do that." The EMTs loaded Angus into an ambulance parked at the gate where the jouster had escaped. "Right? Right?"

"No. You couldn't have done that." I explained what happened, to him and to Bianca.

"Bastard." Riley stood up and turned in circles like he was trying to figure out where to go or who to fight. "He stole my helmet." He held up his bare hands. "And my gauntlets. That's expensive shit. Bastard." He stopped turning, stricken, and sat back down in the dirt. "And my horse. Oh my god, he stole Thunder. We have to get him back."

My cell rang. Cody.

"What's going on? What's happening?" My brother's voice was high, stuttering, veering toward losing control. "Is the knight dead? Where are you?"

Then, "Ivy, I think we should go now." Sarah's voice. She must've taken the phone from Cody.

"Yeah," I said. "Everything's under control here." Riley was being tended to by one of the EMTs. Bianca knelt next to him, rubbing his back. "Meet you at the car."

Ten minutes later, Matt and I caught up with them in the parking lot. Cody's brain injury caused mood swings, and he was crying big, gulping sobs. Sarah held his hand and whispered to him, her face close to his. I went to him and hugged him until his chest stopped shaking and he pulled away. "Is he dead? Is the knight dead?" he asked.

"No," said Matt.

"Are you sure? How do you know?"

"When they took him to the ambulance, he had an oxygen mask over his face. They only do that if you're alive."

"Oh." Cody got his breathing back under control. "Okay. But what happened?"

"We'll tell you about it on the way home," said Matt.

He and I explained the scenario as well as we understood it on the drive back to Phoenix, then Matt turned on Cody's favorite Beatles station on Sirius and we rode the rest of the way back without talking.

Once we'd dropped Sarah off at her apartment and Cody at his group home, Matt said, "My place?"

"Sounds great." We could talk over beer and pizza, maybe get whatever was bugging Matt out in the open.

Okay, confession time: It wasn't just Matt who was on edge. I was uptight too—had been ever since a head cold cost me my last theater job. It had only been a little over a month since then, but aside from two commercial jobs (which you really couldn't call acting), I hadn't gotten any work and had none lined up. My ego and my pocketbook were smarting, but more than that, I was worried. Acting was a big part of my life, of who I was. I was grouchy when I wasn't working on a show and especially grouchy when I was worried that my career might be stalled. Sure, it sounded dramatic—a cold killing my career—but I didn't handle the situation particularly well, and the theater community is small. Actors are expected to deal with things like illnesses. The show must go on is not just a saying. It's a rule.

And though I was not comfortable with straight talk about important things ("Skirting the Issue" was my family motto), I couldn't take much more of this weird tension, so I decided to take the emotional bull by the horns.

Sort of. I couldn't make myself jump right into the conversation, so once Matt and I had beers in hand and the pizza ordered, I said, "Did you think that was weird?"

"Which part?" Matt sat down on his couch next to me. "There

was so much weirdness."

"Riley," I said. "He was upset about his armor and his horse, but..."

"Yeah. He didn't say anything about Angus. Then again, he probably had a concussion. Or maybe it was more about denial."

I understood denial, especially when it was about being involved with someone getting hurt. Denial was my main survival tool after the accident that caused Cody's injury. The accident I sort of caused, well, did cause through my neglect and now made my brother sob in parking lots and...

Matt must have known I was on my way to that dark place. "I think Cody's fine," he said. "Things like this are tough on anyone. He just processes it differently than the rest of us. Maybe more honestly."

I loved Matt. And he had just given me an opening. *Here goes nothing*. "So...speaking of processing things honest—"

The doorbell rang. "That was quick," Matt said. He got up and opened the door for the delivery guy. Once he'd tipped the guy he put the pizza on the coffee table in front of his couch, and then went to the kitchen for paper plates and napkins and a shaker of red pepper flakes. "You must be starving," he said, "since you didn't eat at the faire. Want another beer?"

Had he not heard me? Or didn't want to talk? I didn't know, but I did know that all my emotional courage had been used up for the day. "Sure," I said. "A beer sounds great."

I was such a coward.

Chapter 6

I berated my cowardice through a mostly sleepless night, then dragged myself into the Duda Detective Agency office the next morning. Yeah, it was Saturday, and yeah, I wanted to lie in bed all day, but I had the day off yesterday to go to the Ren faire, so the office it was. At least Uncle Bob would be there. He usually came in when I did, even on the weekends. He always said it was because there was work to be done, but I think it was because he liked the company. I did too, and was especially glad to have him around today. I always felt comforted around my uncle. He was like a big bowl of mac and cheese.

"Eleven forty-five?" he said when I walked in. "Nice."

Well, some days he was more like a small bean burrito: a little stinker.

"I did say I'd be in this morning, and I am a woman of my word. Is there coffee? Please tell me there's coffee." I'd already had a few cups, but not enough to lubricate my little gray cells. "Though looking at your shirt might work better than caffeine."

"Thanks, Sunshine." Uncle Bob's shirts were always XXL and they were always Hawaiian, but rarely were they neon yellow and fuchsia. He waved at a half-full pot sitting on the ancient Mr. Coffee Maker. "Thought you might be late, so I saved you some."

I walked across the tiny shared office space to the "coffee station" (the top of a metal filing cabinet) and grabbed a mug that said, "There Might Be a Margarita in Here." As always, I checked the inside of it before pouring coffee. More likely to have old coffee in it than a margarita, but I never gave up hope.

"I read about the accident at the Ren faire. Were you there?"

"Right there, unfortunately. We saw it happen."

"Is Cody all right?" For all his gruffness, Uncle Bob was a big sweetie, and way more than the typical uncle to my brother Cody and me. He was the unconditional love in a family where even conditional love was scarce.

I'd called Cody on the drive in to work this morning. He was still upset but not emotional. "It was tough on him—would have been tough on anyone, but he's okay." I gave Uncle Bob the rundown on the joust.

"Huh," he said after I'd finished. "The faire must have some really good PR people. The article called it an accident."

"Not hardly. In fact, it seems like it'd have to be pretty well thought out."

"Premeditated, as we say in the biz."

"Yeah. Was there an update on the jouster who was hit?"

"Critical condition."

"Oh no." I saw Angus's green eyes again, heard his voice and Shakespeare's words—"Hear my soul speak. Of the very instant that I saw you..."

"Neck injuries," Uncle Bob said.

"Oh my God." I choked on my coffee.

"Sorry. Shoulda told you that coffee's been there a few hours. Made it for my niece who was coming in this *morning*."

"It's not that." The coffee was horrible, but I wasn't going to give him that satisfaction. "The gorget. It's a piece of armor that protects the neck. Angus—that's the jouster's name—he couldn't find his. He was talking, well, shouting about it in the middle of the faire. Anyone could've heard him and realized he was vulnerable. What do you call that in the biz?"

"Dunno. A crime of opportunity?"

"A premeditated crime of opportunity," I said. "Sounds like a super villain."

"Sounds like something you should keep your nose out of. You said you're friends with the other guy?"

"Theater friends." Riley and I met a few years back during an ill-fated production of *Macbeth* but lost touch when he began traveling the Ren faire circuit. He'd kept his Phoenix agent, though, so I'd run into him during a commercial shoot for Castles and Coasters. We caught up between takes of us hitting golf balls through windmills, and he offered me comps to see him joust at the faire.

"Is he doing okay?"

Dang. "I haven't talked to him since yesterday. I had to get Cody home, and then..." And then I spent a weird tense night with my boyfriend, sensing that we both wanted to talk but didn't. I pulled out my phone, searched for Riley's number, and dialed.

"Hello?" said a woman's voice. Probably Bianca's.

"This is Ivy Meadows, looking for Riley."

"Just a second. I'll wake him."

"Oh, you don't have to do that."

"Yes I do. I really need to get to work. It'd be good to see him awake and alert before I leave. Well, awake. Alert is too much to hope for."

A moment, then "Hey, Ivy." Riley's voice was rough with sleep.

"How are you?" I asked.

"My head hurts like hell, I slept like shit, and my horse is still missing. Other than that, I'm awesome."

"They haven't found your horse?"

"Not since last time I checked, around eight in the morning." A murmur in the background—Bianca's voice. "No, still missing. I'm really worried about him. What's he going to drink out there in the desert? I can't believe some stupid shit stole my horse."

And hurt Angus. I didn't say it out loud.

"A bunch of guys have mounted a search party...Hey, didn't you tell me you were a PI? Maybe you can find him?"

"Um..."

"There's a reward."

"Really?" The Riley I knew was always broke.

"Yeah, people here helped raise it. They get it, you know, how much a trained jousting horse is worth. Horses in general don't like running at full speed toward each other. They want to veer off, you know, avoid a head-on collision. Took me a year to train Thunder."

"I'd like to help, but it seems like your friends out there might be more likely to find him than me," I said. "Unless Thunder has an online profile."

"He does have a Facebook page, but yeah, I see your point." Riley sighed. "At least they found my armor."

"Who, the police?" Maybe they dusted for fingerprints.

"Nah, some hiker spotted a fire and went over to check it out. Stupid guy stole my armor then set it on fire."

"Can you set armor on fire?"

"That's why he's stupid. Burned up a couple of bushes and blackened my armor, but that's all."

I wondered if the thief set the fire to destroy any fingerprints. I wondered if that would work. I wondered if the thief was cruel enough to—No, I was not going there. But Riley was. "I just hope to hell he didn't hurt Thunder. If he did, I'm going to track him down and kill him."

Chapter 7

I got off the phone with Riley and was trying to figure out a way to dump the horrid coffee without Uncle Bob noticing when the phone rang. "Duda Detectives," I answered.

"May I speak to Ivy Meadows?"

I hesitated. Ivy Meadows was my stage name. I used my real name, Olive Ziegwart, at work, and tried to keep the two personas separate, mostly because I did undercover work every so often. "May I ask who's calling?" I said.

"This is Doug from Time and Tankard Entertainment."

"Just a moment, I'll see if she's available." I put the caller on hold. My uncle raised an eyebrow at me. "They asked for Ivy," I whispered, even though the caller was still on hold.

"Ivy Meadows got any outstanding warrants? Any debts? Anybody after her?"

I was pretty sure he was teasing me, but I shook my head anyway. I wasn't lying. Olive Ziegwart had a few debts, but Ivy didn't.

"Then I think you're safe." He went back to his computer screen.

I took the caller off hold. "Hi, this is Ivy. How can I help you?"

"Didn't you just answer the phone?"

"That was my sister," I said. "We're a family business." Uncle Bob chuckled.

The man cleared his throat, a "tell" that he didn't really want to have this conversation. "Well," he said—another tell—"You may have heard about the accident at the Phoenix Renaissance faire yesterday."

I decided to let him have the accident bit. “Yes,” I said. “Is the jouster going to be okay?”

“We hope so. Anyway, the sheriff’s office is looking into the matter, but we have some concerns about...liability. Basically we want to make sure that our environment is safe. We’d like to hire you to investigate the incident.”

Incident, not accident. At least he was getting more honest as the conversation progressed.

“I see. May I ask who referred me to you?” It seemed weird that they’d take a recommendation from Riley, being as how he was involved in the trouble. I didn’t know anyone else who worked at the Ren faire.

“I understand you did some work for Gold Bug Gulch last fall.”

Work? I’d gone undercover at the Western theme town, where I solved a murder, nearly got myself killed, and kicked some ass. I guess you could call it work.

“Arnie Adel recommended you.” Ah, that explained why Doug asked for Ivy. Arnie, who was part-owner of Gold Bug Gulch, was also the producer for Desert Magic Dinner Theater and had known me as an actor before hiring me as a PI. “We would love to have you help us with this...little problem. Will you do it?”

I thought about it. I’d been working at my uncle’s PI firm for a couple of years now. I knew that cases like this were never as simple as insurance scammers or cheating spouses, and took way more time. I knew it was tougher to investigate cases where friends were involved, and though I wasn’t close to Riley, I did like him. I knew cases like this could be dangerous: I’d been poisoned, shot at, and nearly drowned on other investigations. And I knew that a Ren faire in the middle of the desert held myriad dangers: swordsmen and ax-throwers and scorpions and snakes (not just the reptile variety). I knew the whole thing was probably not a good idea, that Uncle Bob would probably balk and Doug might, too, if he knew I was a friend of Riley’s.

I said yes.

It was curiosity, of course. Uncle Bob said it was what made me a good PI. It was also the reason I was always getting into trouble. Oh well, I'd always gotten myself out of trouble too. So far.

I agreed to meet Doug at the Ren faire at six thirty, after it'd closed for the day, to sign the contract and get some background info. Once I hung up the phone, I said, "Isn't there a restaurant you like out in Apache Junction?"

"Lord, yes. The one with that broasted chicken." Uncle Bob nearly salivated. "Broasted. I don't even know what that means, but damn it's good."

"Broasted..." I Googled it. Curiosity again. "Best I can tell, broasted means cooking chicken in a pressure fryer. This says that broasting keeps the fried chicken juicier—"

"Stop. You're making me hungry."

"Then let me treat you to dinner tonight."

Uncle Bob squinted at me. "You, treat?" He didn't mean I wasn't generous. He meant I was usually broke.

"I can write it off," I said. "Since it's a business day-trip. Well, evening-trip."

"To the Renaissance faire?" My uncle was a master eavesdropper. "With all of those weird people in costume?" A master eavesdropper who thought most theater folk were crazy. "Plus this is about the jousting accident, right? You know what I think about investigating friends."

"I know. That's why I want you on the case with me, to keep me objective."

"I don't know..."

"Plus I have the feeling this will be a tough case. I'm going to need the help of my favorite PI. Who just happens to love broasted chicken."

"All right." My uncle grumbled but his eyes were smiling. "I am such a sucker."

I texted Matt to let him know I'd have to work that night.

"I understand" was his response. I understand? That was it?

Wasn't he going to miss having a Saturday night with me?

Nothing I could do about whatever was going on with Matt right now, and Uncle Bob was paying me by the hour, so I put my boyfriend woes aside and got to work investigating Angus. I began with the PI tool of the trade—the Internet. I learned that Angus Duff was born, raised, and graduated high school in Casper, Wyoming. He was thirty-five years old, his parents were both deceased, and he had no siblings. He'd worked at a convenience store for a few years after high school, and in the North Dakota oil fields for a few years after that. He began working in Ren faires when he was twenty-four. He'd been jousting for nearly ten years, and was considered a headliner. He had a car loan on his pickup truck and one black mark on his criminal record, for assault. Digging a little further, it looked like the charge was the result of a drunken brawl when he was working the oil fields. It was a lot of information, and it helped me not a bit. "So unless whoever he hit in North Dakota fifteen years ago somehow followed him here *and* learned to joust, I've got nothing."

"Uh huh." *Tap. Tap.* Uncle Bob was painstakingly typing something. Not an invoice or client correspondence. He usually asked me to do that.

"I need to know how he was viewed at the faire, who were his friends were, who hated his guts. But how can I do that when lots of people know I'm Riley's friend?"

"It does complicate things." *Tap, tap...tap.*

I snuck a look at Uncle Bob's screen. Looked like an email. "And word travels fast in a tight-knit community like that," I said. "I wouldn't be at the faire more than a few hours before almost everyone knew I was asking around about Angus. It'd be easy for people to decide what stories to tell—to protect someone they liked or to blame somebody who stole their girlfriend or something."

"Girlfriend what?" Uncle Bob's ears turned pink.

Ah. I bet he was composing an email to his girlfriend, Bette. They maintained a long-distance but loving relationship. Hmm. Maybe I should email Matt. Would that be weird?

Uncle Bob sat up straight, now engaged with the Ren faire problem. "I think we should go undercover: me as a tourist, you as an employee, like we did on that cruise ship. That worked out pretty good."

"Except for me nearly getting killed," I said. Uncle Bob always looked at that cruise ship job through rose-colored glasses, probably because it was where he met Bette. And yes, emailing Matt would be weird.

"Yeah, but you're smarter now, right?" said my uncle.

"I don't see how I can go undercover this time. Some of the Ren faire people have already seen me, and it's not exactly a secret that I'm a PI. No one knew me on the SS David Copperfield. As far as they knew, I was just a new actor onboard."

"That's it." Uncle Bob's grin outshone the neon yellow of his shirt. "That's the ticket. You're an actor. And a good one."

Aw. "Thank you."

"So you can act like someone else. You know, disguise yourself enough so that no one knows it's you."

"Oh...I don't think...it might work on TV, but..."

"C'mon. I think you can do this, I really do. Just consider it the greatest acting role of all time."

Chapter 8

The Renaissance faire was out in the desert east of Mesa. It was easy to tell when we were near, because a slow and steady stream of cars passed us going the other way, back into town.

"All these people were out here for the faire?" asked Uncle Bob.

"They get twelve thousand people a day." I'd done a bit of research. "And there are four hundred employees and two hundred and twenty-three artisans."

"Artisans?"

I pulled off the highway onto the dirt road that led to the faire. "You know, potters, woodcarvers, glassblowers, that sort of thing."

"And everyone's in costume?"

"All the employees and vendors. And a lot of the people attending too."

"So we have thousands of suspects, most of them in costume?"

"That's why I need the best PI in the world."

"Not in the whole world," Uncle Bob said modestly. "Just in Arizona."

The road ended at an enormous parking lot, mostly empty now since the faire was closed. We parked close to the entrance and walked underneath an arch with Olde English lettering welcoming people to the Phoenix Renaissance Faire.

"Big place," said Uncle Bob.

"Thirty acres."

He shook his head. "Whoda thunk it?"

We walked past a few half-timbered shops to a small Tudor-looking building with mullioned windows: the administration office.

Walking into the office was like time travel. Outside, Jolly Olde England (plus cactus) held court. Inside, sleek Ikea-type desks and computer monitors prevailed. The office was empty except for one person, probably because it was after business hours. The man, tall and stooped with thinning hair, looked up from his monitor, and then stood. "You must be Ivy Meadows." He walked toward us, extending a hand. "I'm Doug Agravaine."

"And this is Bob Duda," I said. "He's going be helping us."

"Oh." Doug took a step back. "I'm not sure we can hire—"

"Twelve thousand people a day come here," I said. "Plus you have four hundred employees and two hundred and twenty-three artisans. That makes thousands of suspects, most of them in costume." I was glad Uncle Bob and I had had that little talk on the way in. "You need more than just me." My uncle shot me a look—sort of surprise mixed with admiration. I was getting better at this PI stuff.

"You're right," Doug said, but he wrinkled his nose like he'd been served a bad piece of fish.

He invited us to sit. I looked over and signed our contract while Doug told Uncle Bob what he basically told me on the phone—that the faire wanted to find out what had happened, but very quietly.

"By the way, we're going to handle this undercover," I said.

"Really? Isn't that a bit much?"

"From what I understand of Rennies, they're a tightly knit group. I think we'd learn more if they didn't think of us as outsiders."

"True," Doug said grudgingly. "Okay, if you think it best."

"And you should know that I actually saw the joust where Angus was injured."

"Well." Doug drew his head back, like a turtle who'd spotted a rock in the road. "That's fortunate, though a little coincidental."

"I was there because I know Riley."

"Oh. That's not—"

"I've talked it over with my associate here and I can promise you I won't be swayed by my feelings. I know Riley, but we're not close. Plus I may be able to get more information."

"I don't know—"

"That's the other reason Mr. Duda is on the case," I said. "To make sure objectivity is maintained."

Doug looked from me to Uncle Bob, who looked the picture of PI professionalism, having changed into a more subdued Hawaiian shirt. Doug nodded. "All right. You did come highly recommended." He stood up. "Unfortunately, I don't have time to show you around tonight, but I suspect you'll both want to see the jousting grounds. Let's walk while we talk."

We went outside and headed down one of the faire's dirt roads. "So," Doug said. "We only run Friday through Sunday, ten thirty to six thirty, March first through April thirtieth, plus a few special days for schools. We make all of our money for the year in just that time. As you can imagine, we can't afford to close or have a light crowd for even a day. The police are of course dealing with this incident—"

"What jurisdiction are you under out here?" asked my uncle.

"Pinal County."

Uncle Bob nodded and looked at me. We both knew that the county sheriff's office covered an enormous amount of land with not a lot of officers.

"As I was saying—" If the stiffness in Doug's voice was any indication, he did not like being interrupted. "We'd like this taken care of quickly and quietly. And I want daily updates, in case we need to take any action. Ah. Here we are."

The three of us walked into the jousting arena. "Wow," Uncle Bob said. "This is a lot bigger than I'd imagined."

"And it's full, or nearly full, almost every joust. We have two a day, at two o'clock and then again at five." He looked at his watch. "I'm sorry, but we just have a few minutes. I need to leave and I can't let you stay unaccompanied on the grounds when the faire's closed. Insurance issues."

"It's okay," I said. "Can we look at the staging area, where Riley said he was hit on the head?"

"Of course."

We followed Doug. "What's your take on Riley?" I asked.

"Popular, but ah, a little short in the brains department. I'm almost positive he was just the fall guy. I don't think he could have pulled off a stunt like this."

We arrived at the staging area. The dirt had been churned up by many feet and hooves. "No chance you preserved any of this as a crime scene?" asked Uncle Bob.

Doug winced. "No. The police are allowing us to go ahead with the jousting, and we need to do it. It's one of the reasons people come to the faire."

Uncle Bob looked around the staging area. There wasn't much to see besides the high wooden walls and the two gates that bookended the area (one led to the stables and the other to the arena), but my uncle was a pro. Maybe he'd notice something I didn't. "They find the horse?" he asked.

Doug shook his head. "And that's a tragedy. Those horses are extremely valuable." He wiped the dust off his brow. "I just hope it's being treated well, not just left in the desert." We all knew what would happen to a horse abandoned in the desert. There was no water for miles.

Doug looked at his watch.

"I think we're good for now," I said. "Could you send us a list of all the employees?"

"Sort of," said Doug. "I can send you *lists*. There are several categories of employees: local employees who staff the restaurants and such, professional entertainers who travel from faire to faire, vendors who basically own their own businesses and rent our facilities, and local volunteers."

"Could you call out anyone you think may have had a beef with Angus?" I said. "Mark them on the list or something?"

"That would be difficult." Doug looked me in the eye, letting his professional demeanor slip. "Angus was an asshole."

* * *

"Not sure I want broasted chicken after that," Uncle Bob said as we walked to my truck.

"Really? What's wrong?'

"You put me in the mood for a burger."

"I did?"

"Yeah, an Angus beef burger." Uncle Bob grinned. "Get it? From when you asked if anyone had a beef with—"

"Stop right now or I won't buy you dinner." I unlocked my pickup doors. "It's funny: Both Riley and Doug called Angus an asshole, but he was really nice to me. Sweet, even."

"Maybe he's a ladies' man."

"Oh. Maybe." I got into the truck. "You know, I've never heard 'ladies' man' used in a complimentary way before."

Uncle Bob climbed in beside me. "Who said I was being complimentary?"

Chapter 9

The broasted chicken place appeared to have been taken over by jolly bikers. The décor of the newly renamed Mother Cluckers Tavern relied heavily on Harley Davidson memorabilia, and its menu boasted dishes like Righteous Ribs, the Bad Ass Burger, and Who You Callin' Shrimp? (along with broasted chicken, of course). Most of the clientele wore leather vests and long beards, but they all looked too happy to be scary. Good food and cold beer can have that effect.

"You weren't kidding about a tough case: an unsecured crime site, thousands of suspects, and a good number of them traveling entertainment types," said Uncle Bob. "Good thing there's broasted chicken for sustenance." He sighed happily and sat back in his seat in the restaurant booth, under a wooden sign that said, "We do not serve women. You must bring your own."

"Mm hm." I licked the chicken grease off my fingers, in a ladylike way.

"You think Bette would like it here?" My uncle's face shone with happiness (and a little chicken fat).

Bette was wildly intelligent, well-traveled, and sophisticated; an investigative reporter who was the brains behind the news site "All Bets are Off." She was also crazy about Uncle Bob. "I'm sure of it," I said. "Hey, maybe you want take some chicken home? You could play a few games of pool while you waited for your order."

"Since I am Arizona's best PI, I noticed that you said 'while I waited.' And what will you be doing?"

"I thought I might stop by the hospital, see how Angus is doing." I held up a hand to head off the objection I saw in his eyes.

"I know they probably won't let me see him, but maybe I can find out a little bit. I have my ways, you know." My ways usually involved asking someone, but hey, it often worked.

"Actually sounds like a good idea," said Uncle Bob.

"The hospital visit, the takeout chicken, or the game of pool?"

"All of it," he said. "And being the apprentice to the best PI in Arizona, I bet you knew that."

"Hello." I smiled at the woman staffing the reception desk. She gave me a disapproving scowl that made me wonder if I had chicken stuck in my teeth. I soldiered on. "I'm hoping you can tell me what room Angus Duff is in."

"Macduff?" she said. "Is this some kind of a joke?"

"No, *Angus Duff,"* I over-enunciated.

"Anus Duff?" She pushed her glasses up on her nose, the better to glare at me. "You kids. Think you'd have something better to do than come down here and—"

I caught a glimpse of a familiar figure down the hall behind the receptionist. "I'll call tomorrow," I said, then hightailed it down the corridor after the swinging ponytail, moving as quickly as was appropriate for a hospital. "Bianca? Hey. Is that you?"

The young woman turned. When she saw me, her face crumpled. She bent over, wracked with sobs. I went to her and rubbed her back until her crying had subsided. "What is it?" I asked gently, though I thought I knew.

"Angus," she said. "He's dead."

Chapter 10

I squealed into Mother Cluckers' parking lot (well, I would've squealed if the lot wasn't dirt), jumped out of my pickup, and ran into the bar. Uncle Bob was bent over a pool table, eyeing the eight ball. I knew better than to say anything at a moment like this, but my mouth was ahead of me, so I just said. "Uncle—urp," right as he hit the ball, of course. My uncle straightened up, frowned at me from across the room, then watched as his ball rolled into a pocket, and said, "Pfa!" which meant, "Hey, I won the game in spite of my stupid niece." The bar erupted and a few guys clapped him on the back. Uncle Bob made friends wherever he went. His opponent, a lanky guy with too-long hair shoved behind his ears, pulled out his wallet and slapped a few bills into my uncle's palm. Uncle Bob waved his winnings in the air. "A round for the house, on me." A bunch more claps on the back as he made his way to the bar.

I met him there. "How much did you win?"

"Thirty bucks."

"No way thirty bucks is going to cover a roun—" Oh. Sometimes I forgot that Uncle Bob was not just the best PI in Arizona, he was also one of the most generous guys in the state.

"It's okay," he said. "You can write off dinner, I can write off this round. I got some important information."

"Me, too. Angus died," I said.

"They found the horse," Uncle Bob said

"What?" we said together.

"You first." Uncle Bob took a swig from the beer the bartender had placed in front of him.

I quickly sorted the information in my head into two

categories: questions and facts. On the question side was: Why was Bianca at the hospital instead of home taking care of Riley? And why was she the only one from the faire at the hospital? Where were all of Angus's friends? I mentally filed the questions for later and gave Uncle Bob the facts: Angus never recovered consciousness and died of his injuries—a broken neck.

"So we're looking at manslaughter or homicide," said Uncle Bob. "The police will definitely step up the investigation. I'm not sure how the Ren Faire will manage to keep it quiet."

"Especially with all of those witnesses. Hey, witnesses. Maybe we could contact them; put something on social media or—never mind. That would be sort of the opposite of keeping it quiet."

Uncle Bob nodded and looked at me intently as if waiting for something. Hmm. There was something...something I wanted to ask...I almost had it when the bartender slid me a beer in a frosted mug. I took a drink. Ahh, it felt great going down. I didn't realize I was so thirsty. But then I had been trooping around in the desert—that was it. "The horse," I said. "You said they found the horse."

"Yep, he'd been through the desert, that horse with no name."

"What? He has a name. It's Thunder."

"You don't know America?" said one of the guys at the bar.

"Well, yeah. Founded in seventeen seventy-six, fifty states..." They laughed. "Plus Puerto Rico, Guam and some other islands," I said, maybe a touch defensively.

"America's a band," said Uncle Bob said. "I think I got an album at home somewhere. I'll play it for you sometime."

"Okay, but for now, tell me about the horse."

"You're gonna like this. It's right up your Tin Pan Alley." Uncle Bob chuckled.

"If you don't tell me now I'm going to eat all your takeaway chicken on the drive back."

"All right, all right." Uncle Bob took a big drink of his beer. "You ever hear of a guy named John Robert Turner?"

"Of course. He's half of the Broadway team Turner and Toe. They had a huge hit with *Hello Dolly Madison*." My uncle looked at me to see if I was kidding. I wasn't. "But what does that have to do with Riley's horse?"

"Seems this Turner guy recently bought a ranch down here."

"A ranch?" I tried to conjure up a picture of John Robert in my mind, but all I got was a snapshot of Turner and Toe together, arms around each other, standing side by side on a New York street in front of a theater marquee. "He left Manhattan to live on a ranch? With his partner?" John Robert Turner and Lewis Toe were in their fifties or sixties and were partners in every sense of the word. One was short, white, and balding; the other was a trim African American with a pencil-thin mustache. I couldn't remember who was Turner and who was Toe. They'd been together forever.

"Don't know about that," said Uncle Bob. "Don't know what he wants to do on a ranch either, train pygmy horses to dance for all I know."

"That'd actually be cool. They could do *Guys and Dolls*. You know..." I sang, "I got the horse right here, his name is Paul Reve—"

"All I know" —Uncle Bob had to talk loudly to be heard over my singing—"is that this guy lives way out in the desert, about twenty miles from the Ren faire."

I'd gotten so excited about the news that John Robert was in town that I'd forgotten we were talking about the Ren faire. And Riley. And Angus. I sobered up quickly. "And?" I asked.

"And Riley's horse—which is fine, by the way—somehow ended up at this guy's place."

Chapter 11

We were just pulling onto the highway to go home when my cell buzzed.

"Can you look at it?" I asked Uncle Bob. I didn't want to stop, and I wasn't dumb enough to text and drive.

He picked up the phone from its place in my cup holder. "It's from Matt. He wants to know if you can come over tonight."

"Really?" It was nine forty-five.

"Yeah..." He peered at my phone. "It looks like you missed couple of texts from him earlier. All asking you to come over tonight after work."

Not good. "Okay. Can you text him back saying I just saw his messages and I'll be there around, um, eleven?"

Uncle Bob did so. "He says, 'See you then.' He must really want to see you tonight."

"Yeah." He must. And I was afraid to know why.

Since we'd come straight from the office, I dropped Uncle Bob off near his car, then swung by a Circle K for a six-pack and bag of Cheetos. I didn't want to arrive at Matt's empty-handed. Nothing to do with procrastinating, because I wasn't worried about why he wanted to see me. Not a bit.

"Hey." Matt kissed me hello and the knot in my stomach loosened a bit. He wouldn't kiss me right before breaking up with me, would he?

"Sorry I didn't get your texts, but..." I blamed my distractedness on the noisy bar rather than the good chicken.

Gluttony wasn't usually a selling point in relationships.

"No worries." He took the beer and Cheetos from me. "Thanks for the hor d'oeuvres. You want a beer?"

"Yes, please." I took the one he handed me and walked over to the couch. "So...Angus died." I found myself tearing up. Guess I was finally processing what had happened. I wiped my eyes surreptitiously. Didn't want Matt to see me crying over another man, even if it was about the other man's death. "And they found the horse." I told him about John Robert, hoping I sounded like a PI instead of like someone trying to not have a conversation about her relationship with her boyfriend. Matt sat beside me, his arm stretched along the back of the couch, his hand absently playing with my hair. I took that for another good sign, until...

"So I know it's a little weird to ask you over so late," Matt said. "But—"

His phone rang. He looked at it. "I have to take this. It's my mom."

My first thought was "Oh, great." I swear Matt's mom psychically knew when we were together and decided to call then. She lived in Grand Island, Nebraska, and was...difficult. At least when it came to me. Maybe it was because she thought I was a stoner (it was skunk she smelled on me, I swear). Maybe it was the fact that she really wanted Matt to marry his high school sweetheart. Or maybe it was her insistence her son should really be back in Grand Island, helping his dad out with the farm. Or...

Then my second thought hit: It was after midnight in Nebraska. Not a time when she'd call just to talk.

Matt sat up straight on the couch, listening. He didn't say anything for minutes, then just, "Of course." He got up off the couch. "I'll be there as soon as I can. Thanks for calling."

He hung up, then walked to the window and looked out at the darkness. "That wasn't Mom."

I had the feeling it wasn't. "Thanks for calling" wasn't something he'd say to his mom.

"It was Katie." The high school sweetheart. "They'd all been at some church supper. My mom was helping to clean up afterward and..." Matt swallowed and looked at me. "She had a massive stroke."

Matt packed while I went online and found the next flight to Omaha. "Five thirty a.m.," I said. "Do you want that one? The next one's at nine thirty. You could maybe get a little sleep if—"

"Book me on the five thirty flight. I wouldn't be able to sleep anyway. And just one-way for now. I don't know how long I'll be there. Crap. I need to call work and ask for family medical leave."

Once the ticket was booked, the bags packed, and the messages left, we had just a few minutes before we needed to leave (Matt always liked to be at the airport two hours before a flight). He sunk down on the couch. I sat close beside him, and we stayed like that, in silence, until it was time to go.

I drove him to the airport. "Katie said my dad's sort of shell-shocked." It was the first thing Matt had said for twenty minutes. "He may run the farm but my mom runs everything else. I don't think he's cooked a meal or paid a bill or made a doctor's appointment on his own since he got married." His voice cracked. "He'd be lost without my mom."

I put a hand on his thigh. He stared out the windshield as if there was something big and bad on the horizon. "You okay?" I asked, to give him a chance to talk.

"I don't know. I don't think I can go there right now. I don't really want to think about this until I have to."

I ached for him, but I also understood. Uncle Bob sometimes called me Cleopatra because I'm "the queen of de Nile." It's true: I've survived on a steady diet of denial ever since I was eleven, when Cody got hurt. You could even say it was denial that caused his accident. I was annoyed at being forced to take my little brother ice skating and so ignored him in favor of my girlfriends. If I hadn't denied his existence that day, maybe I would've seen him skating toward the open water. Maybe I would've shouted to him about the thin ice. Maybe he would've turned back before the ice cracked and the dark water swallowed him whole.

Denial became my friend after that. It seemed like hope. If I didn't acknowledge that Cody's brain injury was permanent, maybe he'd get better. If I didn't think about my parents blaming me for the accident, maybe they wouldn't. If I pretended nothing had changed, maybe everything would go back to the way it was before.

I now knew that living in denial was no good, but I also knew that it was a valuable tool, a way of putting off the tough emotional work until you were strong enough to tackle it. So I didn't try to make Matt talk. Instead, I let him borrow my tool—but not before I used it once more myself. "I think everything will turn out okay."

See? Hope.

Chapter 12

Even night owls are tired when they get home at three thirty in the morning. And I slept badly. Not only was I worried about Matt and his family, but Angus's death sat heavy on my heart, partly because I'd met him right beforehand, partly because we'd actually seen the killing blow, and partly because any death weighed on me. It was one of the toughest things about my PI job. I didn't know how cops and firemen ever slept.

Still, I dragged my exhausted ass out of bed at nine o'clock the next morning. I had work to do. It actually wasn't that hard to get up, because as soon as consciousness crept up on me, my mind began to ask questions. Not about the important things like love and life and death (loved that denial tool), but about the new case: How did Riley's horse get to John Robert Turner's house? When did it get there? If the horse was fine, had it been there since the day it disappeared? If so, why didn't John Robert report it earlier? And what was a Broadway playwright doing on a ranch in the middle of the desert anyway?

I made a pot of coffee while I booted up my laptop, keeping my phone in sight on the kitchen table. I didn't want to miss Matt. He'd promised to call when he could. I was itching to contact him but didn't want to do so at a bad time. And anytime could be a bad time.

So instead I Googled "John Robert Turner and Arizona." Nothing. "Broadway and ranch." Still nothing. I tried real estate news. Nope. I thought again. Why would a playwright from New York move to the desert? Hmm. I tried "playwright and desert." A hit. In a year-old article on Broadwayworld.com, John Robert had said, "I have always done my best work in the desert, under that huge cloudless sky. Its barrenness clears my mind, like a Santa Ana wind." Huh. Seemed to me that he'd never experienced an Arizona wind, which was sort of like being in a giant blow dryer. A photo of the playwright accompanied the article: Ah, he was the pleasantly round Caucasian half of the team. He was also somehow familiar. Well, duh. Even though I didn't visit theater websites very often, he was a famous playwright.

That said, it was odd there was no mention of him buying a ranch in Arizona. Still, I trusted Uncle Bob's information. John Robert must have been able to keep his move a secret. I suppose you could do anything if you had enough money. Still, I suspected someone in town would probably know what was up. I decided to go to my best source. "Buy you brunch at Gay Denny's?"

"Err," said Timothy, which I translated as "it's too early to call." Then my friend/fellow actor/drag queen said, "How many cups of coffee have you had?"

"Four. And a half. Why?"

"Err," Timothy said again. "You know better than to call me before noon."

"But I'll pay." I could write off brunch, too. "A Grand Slam on me. See you at eleven?"

"Urrmm," Timothy said, then hung up. It was a slightly different sound, an affirmative-sounding groan, so I got ready to go. I planned to go straight to the Ren faire after brunch, so I sorted through my closet for anything that could help with the disguise I'd decided upon. I found dangly earrings, flat sandals that laced up my calves, and a long chestnut wig I'd worn during a recent production of *Twelfth Night* where I played the twin of a brown-eyed brown-haired actor. Hey...

I walked the few feet to my bathroom (my apartment was *small*) and pawed through the medicine cabinet. Yes. I still had a pair of dark brown costume contacts left over from the show. I grabbed them along with some makeup that suited a brunette look, stuffed everything into my duffle bag, hoofed it down the stairs to my apartment's parking lot, and got into my truck. I swung by Bert Easley's, a costume shop that'd been around since the 1940s, tried on a couple of outfits, rented two of them, and got to the restaurant by eleven.

Gay Denny's (aka Genny's) was pretty much what it sounded like. For whatever reason, Phoenix's LGBTQ community had been hanging out at the 24-hour restaurant since sometime in the eighties. If you came in late on a Friday or Saturday night, you'd often see a group of drag queens holding court at one of the corner tables. Mostly families and oldsters were there when I arrived. I slid into a booth and checked my phone.

Still no word from Matt.

I broke down and texted him while I waited for Timothy. All during the time I'd been working, the maelstrom of emotions that had kept me from sleeping continued to buffet my soul like one of those hot Arizona winds. Another feeling had been swept into the mix, no—two feelings: relief, and guilt over being relieved. Maybe Matt's weirdness over the past couple weeks had nothing to do with me—maybe he knew his mom wasn't well and all of the tension came from that. That was the relief part. And since I was relieved about something that was bad news for everyone involved, well, that was the guilt.

Ping. A response from Matt. "Sorry I didn't call. It's been crazy. Mom's holding her own. Talk tonight?"

Phew. "That'd be great. XXOO to all."

The waitress stopped by. I ordered two Grand Slam breakfasts and two cups of coffee (sure, I'd already had a pot, but it was a small one). The coffee was already on the table waiting when Timothy arrived a few minutes later. He wore dramatically dark sunglasses and pouted at me. "This better be good." He sat down.

I explained about the horse and John Robert. "But I can't find anything about him being in Arizona. And everyone knows that you know everything." A little smile broke through Timothy's pout. "So," I continued, "I thought I'd see if I could get the info straight from the horse's mouth. Wait that's not right...straight from the horse's mouth would be from John Robert, right?"

"I think you meant to call me a stud," said Timothy. "Because you'd better be calling me something nice, or I won't tell you what, oh, everyone who's anyone knows. I mean, have you been living under a rock somewhere?"

"Did I say horse's mouth? Maybe I should have said horse's a—"

"Uh, uh, uh, Miss Ivy. Be nice to the hand that feeds you tasty tidbits of gossip, or I won't—"

The waitress dropped off our Grand Slams. The smell of bacon and sausage must have soothed Timothy (I know it did me), because he gave a contented sigh. He pushed his sunglasses up on top of his head, poured syrup on his pancakes, and said, "All right. So here's the scoop on John Robert..."

Chapter 13

"Turner and Toe split?" I put down my coffee. "Haven't they been together forever?"

"I know." Timothy poured more syrup on the last of his pancakes. "They were a golden couple. It's the saddest news in the world." That seemed a bit dramatic, even for Timothy, until he continued. "Together they gave us *Singin' on the Train*, *The Look of Mormon*, *Best Little Storehouse in Texas*, and of course, *Hello Dolly Madison*. But singly? Nothing."

"Well they haven't been split that long, right? It's got to take time to create—"

"The word on the street is that this has happened before. They get into some lovers' tiff or creative disagreement and they each go off on their own. Do you remember *Dribbler on the Roof*?"

"How could I forget that one? Didn't it close after opening night?"

"Written by John Robert using a pseudonym. And it closed *on* opening night. At intermission."

"Really?" I was pretty sure Timothy was exaggerating. Pretty sure. "Anyway, now that I've kept my end of the brunch bargain..."

"Wait. Bargaining involves two parties. You just told me to be here."

"You're not going to tell me what John Robert is doing here?"

"Of course I am. I just want you to feel bad for waking me up."

"And I do. Now tell."

Timothy leaned close. "The way I hear it, John Robert was dying to do a solo project, but couldn't come up with an idea. He decided to retreat to the desert—"

"So he bought a ranch? Couldn't he have just gone to a spa?"

"—Where he bought Slim Littlewood's old place, Harmony Ranch."

"Slim Littlewood, the cowboy?" Slim was one of Arizona's famous sons, a character actor in 1950's Westerns and singer with the cowboy quartet *Sons of the Tumbleweeds.*

"Mm hmm. Which reminds me, you are coming to the gay rodeo on Friday, right? To see me do the Wild Drag Race?"

"Sure. Of course. You know I love your drag shows."

"This is no simple drag show—this is dangerous drag. People have been killed doing the Wild Drag event, you know."

"They have?"

"Well, there have at least been a few broken heels. So we're in teams of three—me and two hunky cowboys who—"

"Two hunky gay cowboys."

"Of course. And these cowboys somehow get me, in full feather as it were—"

"Which outfit?"

"I haven't decided yet."

"How about Patsy Cline? They could play "Crazy" right after they announce you."

"*Anyway,* they get me onto the back of a pissed-off steer. You ever seen a steer up close?"

"I will, when I come see you at the rodeo. And sorry to interrupt—"

"Like this?"

"But can we go back to Slim Littlewood just for a minute? Why did John Robert want his ranch? Does he have a thing for cowboys?"

"Honey, everyone has a thing for cowboys. But supposedly, Harmony Ranch was perfect because it has a theater room."

"With a screen and surround sound?"

"With a real—albeit small—theater stage."

"Ah, like Andrew Lloyd Webber." The creative genius who penned famous musicals like *The Phantom of the Opera* and *Evita* had a theater at his Hampshire country house where he could work on shows and stage them for backers in the privacy of his own home.

"Exactly. And..." Timothy leaned so close I could smell his hair gel. "The desert air seems to have done the trick. Word is John Robert is starting work on a new version of *Camelot,* set in the Kennedy era. Can't you just see it? The love triangle will revolve around John and Jackie and Marilyn, and..."

Timothy went on, but "Camelot" kept ringing in my ears. Camelot. Camelot. What was it about Camelot? Let's see, there was King Arthur, and the Knights of the Round Table, and jousting...

Jousting. My mind flashed on a face under a hooded cape, a familiar profile watching Riley and the little boy. Yes, it was him. John Robert had been at the Ren faire, right before the joust that killed Angus. And he'd been there in disguise.

"Hang on," I said to Timothy. The horse at John Robert's ranch, his appearance at the Ren faire...there had to be a connection. I pulled out my phone and dialed my agent, who actually picked up on a Sunday. "You have to get me an audition for *Camelot.*"

"I haven't heard anything about this," said Vicki. "They're filming *Camelot* in Arizona? With all the cactus and shit?" She barked a laugh. "Oh, you mean *Spamalot.*"

"No, no cactus in that either," I said. "And I mean *Camelot.* John Robert Turner just announced he's putting it together. He's workshopping it at his ranch here."

"Is he the Turner from Turner and Toe? You know I don't do theater." I didn't know how it worked in other cities, but in Phoenix, agents got actors film, commercial, and print work. Actors didn't need an agent for theater work—we just auditioned.

"I know, but I need to meet this director." And once I met him, I could figure out how to ask the questions I needed to ask. It'd be even better if I got cast.

"Didn't you say 'just announced'? Don't plays take awhile before they're produced?"

Exactly. There was no way I'd be able to audition for a Broadway, or even off-, or off-off-Broadway play. I wasn't even union yet—but... "It's well-known that Turner and Toe use actors at the beginning stages of their playwriting." At least that's what I thought Timothy had said when my brain was singing "Camelot." I met his eyes and he nodded.

"Like human props?" asked Vicki.

"Singing, talking, improvising human props."

"And you want me to get you an audition with one of these guys?"

I sighed. Vicki was a great agent, which meant she was all about business. I could see why she thought a human prop gig was not worth my (or her) time. "This is all about future work," I said. "Imagine how great it'll look on my resume." This was only partly true. Many film /commercial directors didn't care much about theater.

"I don't know." I could hear the frown in Vicki's voice. "I don't have any connection with Broadway theater. I don't even know who I'd—"

"I'll take you to lunch at the Arizona Biltmore." Vicki loved a good meal, especially on someone else's dime. I wasn't sure I had enough dimes for such a fancy lunch, but I'd scrape them up somehow.

"You got me. I'll look into it. Call around, see if I can submit you."

"Great."

"This is *Camelot*, right? What part should I submit you for? Guinevere?"

"Well, John Robert has decided to set the show in the Kennedy White House."

"Gotcha. But...I don't see you as Jackie."

I didn't either. No one had ever called me elegant. "Put me up for the part of Marilyn."

"Marilyn?" Vicki sputtered. Probably drinking coffee while we talked. "You're kidding, right?"

No one had ever called me a bombshell, either. "No, really. I do a great Marilyn impersonation." I hadn't yet, but felt sure I could.

Vicki had stopped sputtering and was laughing out loud. "Sure you do. Prove it to me, and I'll see what I can do about wrangling you an audition."

I hung up. "All right, Timothy. Let's go make me into Marilyn."

Chapter 14

"Oh, and maybe you can help me with my belly dancer disguise, too?" I asked Timothy as we stepped out of Genny's into the bright sunshine.

"Marilyn Monroe *and* a belly dancer? Why a belly dancer?"

"I need to go undercover at the Ren faire, and want to make sure no one knows it's me. This way I can use veils to cover up."

"Cover up? Well, part of you."

I really didn't think anyone would recognize me based on my belly button, even though it was an outie.

Timothy pursed his lips, then looked at me over his sunglasses. "I do love a challenge. Let's go."

I followed Timothy to his place just a few miles away in Central Phoenix. I parked and brought my duffle bag and the costumes from Bert Easley's into Timothy's apartment. He was already in the little kitchen. I set my stuff down on the living room couch and poked my head inside to see what he was doing (the rest of me would barely have fit. It was a really little kitchen). "Bloody Marys," he said happily. "With fresh squeezed lemon juice. Want some lemons to take home?"

Lemons, oranges, and grapefruit were the zucchini of Arizona. Lots of people had citrus trees and the fruit all ripened at the same time. Some would even put brown bags marked with "Free grapefruit" on the sidewalks in front of their houses. "Sure," I said anyway. I was never one to turn down free food. "And make my drink a virgin. I need to go out to the faire for a few hours."

"Got it." Timothy poured two drinks. "Grab your stuff and meet me in my boudoir."

When I got to Timothy's bedroom, he was already fiddling with a tackle box full of makeup. A platinum blonde wig perched atop a Styrofoam head on the bedside table. I showed him what I had for the belly dance costume.

"Good, good." He gnawed on his bottom lip. "What accent are you using?"

"Accent?"

"Didn't you just tell me you don't want anyone to recognize you? And that you're going to have to be you, Marilyn, and a belly dancer? Yes, accent."

"Um..." I was known for my dancing, not my grasp of accents. I had played Nancy in *Oliver at Sea!*, though. "I do a pretty good Cockney."

Timothy burst out laughing. "That's your best one?" Timothy had played Fagin in that particular production. "Omigod, okay, whatever. A Cockney belly dancer. Good thing everyone at Ren faires are eccentric or this would never fly."

It might still not. "Do I *have* to do an accent?"

"Didn't you just tell me that you're also going to be interviewing people as yourself?"

"Yeah. Oi don't know what Oi was finking." Hey, my Cockney accent sounded pretty good.

Timothy sighed. "It'll have to do. Now, are you really sure about becoming Marilyn? You may be invoking a few demons here."

"What do you mean?" I sat on the edge of his bed.

"Well, she didn't exactly have the happiest life. Some impersonators say they feel her spirit when they channel her."

"Bah," I said. "I'm not channeling, I'm acting." Still, a little shiver ran down my back as I reached out to touch the wig. It was a good one. Real hair. "Where'd you get this wig?"

"I used to do Marilyn."

"Really? You did Marilyn?" Timothy was the hairiest man I'd ever met. And it was black hair.

"A girl's gotta try," he said, tossing me a wig cap. "But now I stick to Amy Winehouse and Liza and of course, Cher." Timothy did an amazing version of "Gypsies, Tramps, and Thieves" which he said was autobiographical. His autobiography, not Cher's. "You'll need to get blue contacts, of course."

"Oh, do I have to—"

Timothy cut me off. "You're triple undercover, remember? Can't have anyone recognizing you by your green eyes."

While he was puttering with his makeup kit, I called the place where I bought the brown contacts. Yes, they had my prescription on file and dark blue costume contacts in stock. I could pick them up on my way to the faire. I hung up.

"Let's do this," Timothy said, tilting my face back and forth and up and down. "Ooh," he said. "I never realized how much you look like her."

"I do?"

"Have you ever seen those photos of her before she became famous, when she was fresh-scrubbed Norma Jean? Even her hair—her real hair—was the same color as yours. As your *real* hair."

"Dirt brown?" That was what Vicki had called it right before she told me to dye it blonde.

"This is going to be fabulous, just you wait." Timothy practically crackled with glee. "A little bit of shading, some eyebrow work...ooh." He actually rubbed his hands together, like a mad scientist about to begin a particularly exciting experiment. "Oh, wait..." He fiddled with his phone, then set it on the bedside table by the mannequin head. "Ambience," he said. Marilyn's voice filled the room, singing about kisses and diamonds and men. "Let us begin."

Timothy told me what he was doing step-by-step: foundation first, then shading with brown powder to make the contours of my face look more like Marilyn's, then blush, dark brown arched eyebrows, black eyeliner, red lips. "With a slightly darker lip liner of course." Like most drag queens I knew, Timothy was a big fan of lip liner. He rocked back on his heels and studied me, pursing his lips. "A little more bottom lip I think..." He leaned in and drew a larger line beneath my lip, then nodded with satisfaction. "Now for the pièce de résistance." He took the wig off the mannequin and pinned it onto my head. "And now..." Timothy handed me a mirror.

I took the mirror, then almost dropped it. Looking back at me was a blonde bombshell—no, *the* blonde bombshell. It was almost like looking at a movie screen.

"Timothy," I said. "You are a magician."

"*C'est moi*," he said. "And you, my dear, are Marilyn."

Chapter 15

We took a couple of pictures of me, bare-shouldered since I didn't have any fifties' style clothes with me, and sent them to my agent. Then I wiped off Marilyn's red lips, added some sparkly purple eyeshadow Timothy gave me, and dusted my face with bronzer. I put in my brown contacts, dressed quickly in one of the belly dancer outfits, and topped off the costume with the long dark wig and two more veils, one over my hair and another that covered the bottom half of my face.

I examined myself in front of Timothy's bathroom mirror. I was swathed in sheer fabric and synthetic hair, with only my midriff and eyes showing. Bangles and gold coins circled my hips and jingled when I moved—could be a nice distraction. I smiled at myself underneath the veil that covered my mouth. This could work.

"Nice," said Timothy as I dashed out the door. "Break a leg."

On the way to the contacts place, I called Doug to tell him that his undercover PI was on her way. "You really think you can pull this off? That no one will recognize you?" he asked.

"Of course," I said. "I'm an actor."

He made a noise that might have been a stifled laugh. I chose not to take it personally. "You could be a mermaid," Doug said. "It's a new show, so it could make sense to have a new person—"

"No." I'd been afraid of water ever since Cody's accident. A recent-ish scuffle in a swimming pool had helped vanquish that—mostly. I'd been able to picnic near water, wade in Saguaro Lake, and even take a cruise, but still...*water*. My chest got tight just thinking about it. Of course I didn't say that. No one wants a scaredy-cat PI. "I think it'd be tough to investigate while stuck in a tank of water wearing a tail," I said instead. "I've decided to be a belly dancer. I really want to make sure no one knows it's me. I'm pretty covered up this way. Can you help me join a troupe?"

"Sure. Whatever. I just want this taken care of quickly. You heard about Angus's death?"

"Yeah. In fact, is there any way for you to get me more information for me about the specific cause of death? Maybe from your insurance guy?" Insurance companies often hired their own investigators.

"I'll see what I can do."

"And I heard they found Riley's horse."

"Yes. Thank God."

Huh. Interesting that he didn't bring up this vital piece of information until I did. I added a question mark to my mental "Doug" file. I felt like there was something else hiding in that file too. Something Doug had said?

He went on to tell me that Thunder was in good shape. John Robert Turner had discovered the animal drinking out of his swimming pool. "He said he was in the middle of working, so he asked his gardener to take care of it, and to ask around if anyone was missing a horse. The guy did take good care of Thunder, but Turner doesn't think he put out the word."

"That sounds suspicious."

"Maybe," said Doug. "Or maybe the guy just wanted to keep the horse."

Maybe. I'd do my own checking on that. "I'll see you in about half an hour."

A pause.

"Is everything okay?" I asked.

"Yes." Doug's voice was tight and tired at the same time, like a frayed rope. "I just thought you would be here earlier today. May I ask what you've been doing?"

Sheesh, could you say micro-manager? "What any good PI would have been doing," I said. "Following leads."

* * *

Finally I was on the highway, headed toward the faire. "Oi fink you sound jolly good," I said, trying out my accent. Ack. Timothy was right. I'd have to keep my mouth shut as much as possible and study the accent at home. And did people still say "jolly good?" I'd have to look up British-isms, too.

Oh no. I suddenly realized that this wasn't just using an accent and pretending to be a British belly dancer. This was improv. And I sucked at improv. Maybe I should reconsider, just go in and ask questions as myself.

No. From what I knew of Ren faire folks, I was pretty sure they'd be nice and polite and completely close ranks if they needed to protect one of their own.

One of their own. Of course. It had to be one of them. There was a slim chance that a tourist might be able to joust—maybe he'd been to jousting camp or something—but he wouldn't have known the Phoenix Renaissance Faire as well as the mysterious jouster. A tourist wouldn't have known where to jump Riley, or if Riley's armor would fit him, or maybe most importantly, how to make his escape. I called Uncle Bob on speakerphone. "Oi haf good news."

"Ivy?" he said. "You sound funny. Are you getting sick?"

"What? No, that's my Cockney accent. For my undercover British belly dancer."

"Oh," said Uncle Bob. "Well. So, you have good news."

"Yeah." I told him what I'd realized about the jouster. "So we have way fewer suspects now. Just the Rennies. And John Robert."

"The guy who found the horse?"

"Yeah." I told Uncle Bob about seeing him right before the joust.

"In disguise, you said?"

"Well, in a Renaissance costume."

"Didn't you tell me that lots of people dress up to come to the faire?"

"Yeah..."

"Still, good work," said my really nice uncle.

"All righty, then," I said. "Toodle-oo." Yikes. I really needed to work on my British persona.

I pulled into the faire's employee parking lot at two forty-five. Twenty minutes later, Doug and I stood in front of Jasmine, the owner of Gimme Shimmie Belly Dancers, who couldn't keep her bells from jingling with irritation. "You're joking, right?" she half-whispered/half-hissed at Doug. "You know that isn't how this works. You can't just tell me to hire someone. This is a troupe, a company. A company that I own."

"A company that is employed by *my* company." Sheesh, this guy needed some practice in the art of negotiation. And in just being nice. "All I'm asking for is an unpaid position for my niece Prudence here." I'd picked the name from the Beatles song. "Like an internship," said Doug.

"It'd mean the world to me," I said. "Oi came awl the way from Liverpool just for this."

"You came from England to perform in a Ren faire in Arizona?"

She had a point. "Uncle Doug says it's brilliant. And Oi've always wanted to see America—cowboys and Indians and such."

Jasmine frowned at me. "That second veil, that one across your face? It's overkill. Can't you—?"

Doug came to my rescue. "I think she should keep it on." Then in a lower voice, "British teeth, you know."

"Oi! Oi am affronted for meself and for me countrymen," I said with as much dignity as I could, given my ridiculous accent.

Jasmine crossed her arms. "I don't have time to teach her the routines."

"She's a quick learner," said Doug. "And she's danced professionally."

She narrowed her eyes at me. "Belly dance?"

I nodded. "Graduated from the Prestigious Northern England School of Belly Dance. Otherwise known as Wigglebum Uni."

Jasmine laughed unexpectedly. She looked me up and down.

“She does have a nice figure,” she said to Doug, as if I wasn’t there. “I’ll figure out a way to use her.”

Chapter 16

As soon as Doug left, Jasmine said, "Come hither, wench." I was momentarily struck dumb, not so much by her serious manner, but by the straight-faced way she said the words. "Cat got your tongue?" she asked.

"Oh, yeah..." I remembered my Cockney accent in just time. "But Oi'm roight as rain now."

Jasmine sighed. "Do you not know how to speak?"

"Oi fought Oi just did," I said, thickening up the accent in hopes she'd give a break to a stranger in a strange land.

"No," Jasmine said. "You did not and you do not." She looked at me a minute, hands on her well-padded hips and exasperation on her fantastically made-up face (with all the sequins and gemstones stuck to her, she looked like she'd been bedazzled). Then a light glittered in her eyes and she walked over to a small sign hanging from a gold cord on the front of the stage: *Gimme Shimmie Belly Dancers. Shows at 1:30 and 4:30.* Jasmine picked up the sign and handed it to me. "Tie this around your waist."

"All roighty, then. Wait, around me waist?"

Jasmine grimaced again at the sound of my voice. Was my accent that bad? "So that it sits on your bum. Use the talents you learned at Wigglebum to lure audience members our way."

"You're not serious?" I said. "Oi mean, asking me to use me bum to bring in audience members, isn't that sexual ha—"

"Have you never attended a faire before?" Jasmine didn't wait for my answer. "Bawdiness is our meat and potatoes."

"Even wif all the kiddos about?"

"Bawdy, not dirty. There is a difference and you must learn it."

She stood back and sighed again. "There are many things you must learn." She rolled her shoulders to release the tension there. "I want you to stroll the faire and see what you can do to raise an audience."

"Wif a sign on me bum." I sighed back at her. "Yes, mum."

"During the show, you can stand at the entrance to our stage and wave people in. After the last show, go to the Enchanted Forest and find William the Wondrous. He's a wizard who's been around forever. Ask him to teach you faire etiquette, especially the language."

"What about learning the dance routines?"

"We'll see how you fare first."

"All right." I gave in. "Oi'll get you an audience. Oi can wiggle me bum wif the best of 'em." I turned to go.

Jasmine grabbed me by the shoulder. "One more thing: Don't speak. Not a word. Until I tell you differently, you are the mute belly dancer."

What began as an exercise in humiliation turned out to be a great thing, at least as far as investigating went. Since I didn't have to talk, I didn't have to concentrate on my not-so-great Cockney accent and could pay more attention to what was around me. Since I had a sign on my ass, people didn't look at my face—less chance I'd be recognized. Since I didn't have to learn any dance routines, I could stroll the fairegrounds and snoop.

So for an hour and a half, I strolled and wiggled and listened. I heard excitement ("Look, a fairy!"), whining ("Dad said I could have *two* turkey legs") and bad jokes ("What happened when Bluebeard fell overboard in the Red Sea? He got marooned"), but I didn't hear a peep about Angus—Angus, who was a major player at the faire, who was one of the most famous characters there, and who'd been traveling the circuit for years. Huh.

I kept an eye out for Riley and/or Bianca, but didn't see either of them. It was probably just as well since I really wanted to scope out the faire, get a feel for the place and the people. And what people! There were fire-eaters and bawdy jugglers and singing nuns. And mermaids, hidden away in the Undersea Grotto. I really wanted to see a mermaid (who wouldn't?) so I snuck into the grotto, bypassing the big line in front of it by muttering, "Employee coming through" (since I was sure I was already breaking a rule by jumping the line, I threw the 'no talking' rule to the wind too).

I stepped into the cavernous space. The transition from bright sunlight to watery blue-green light made me blink. A crowd almost as large as the one outside snaked through the cordoned-off waiting area. A smaller group waited to one side in front of an empty throne covered in plaster shells, with leaping dolphins for arms and a starfish at its crown. A sign propped up in front of it read, "Your photo with a mermaid!"

The focal point of the grotto was an enormous tank of water, like one you might see at an aquarium, maybe twenty feet tall and almost as wide. I could hear splashing coming from the tank, but the heads in front of me blocked my view. I slipped past all of the waiting people. I felt bad for being rude, but I had to peek and leave before Jasmine discovered where I was, and I didn't want to leave without seeing a...

Oh...A beautiful woman lounged on a narrow shelf at the top of the tank, her head propped on one arm out of the water, the rest of her submerged. She smiled, waved at the crowd, and flipped her tail. *Her tail.* It was green and glittery and looked like it was truly made of scales. Fairytales were coming true right in front of me.

The mermaid pushed herself off the ledge and dove down into the tank, her long blonde hair streaming behind her. She stopped at the bottom of the tank, peering out through the glass at her audience while her hair floated around her like a cloud.

"But how does she breathe?" asked a little boy beside me, and an invisible fist slammed into my solar plexus. The weight of water pressed against me, and it was cold and dark and freezing...

I sat down where I was, right there on the concrete floor, my back to the tank. I tried to breathe.

"Are you okay?'" The little boy next to me sat down on the ground beside me. He patted my knee. "It's okay," he said. "I'm afraid of water too."

I took a deep breath. "Thank you," I said to him. I got up, brushed the dust off my skirt, and excused myself.

I went outside and sat on a bench near the road. I felt shaky, not just because of the incident, but because I'd really thought I was over my fear of water. What was different about this time? I made myself picture the scene again, the tank, the mermaid underwater...that was it. Since the swimming pool incident I thought had cured me, I'd approached water from the *top*. I'd seen the top of a lake shimmer in the sun, felt the spray of a waterfall from atop a bridge, and cruised on a ship on top of the ocean. *Under* the water felt like a whole different world, a world that lured you and trapped you and wouldn't let you go.

Not all fairytales had happy endings.

Chapter 17

If I'd been by myself, I could've gotten lost in the past, pulled down by the weight of Cody's accident. But it was pretty tough to lose yourself in thought at the Ren faire. Too many interesting people doing interesting things. Like the Vermin Folke, who stuffed fabric rats with tomatoes, threw them into the crowd yelling "Rat!" and then smashed the stuffed things with big clubs, spilling their tomato guts all over the dirt road. It was disgusting—and fabulous, especially because it pulled me out of my stupor and into the world. Where I had some investigating to do.

I spent some time watching the employees, then sidled up to the friendliest, chattiest one I'd seen, a plump, middle-aged woman who ran one of the costume places. "Bloody brilliant place, this," I said, fingering a beribboned wreath.

"Oh you're from England!" she said.

Finally my accent came in handy.

"I just love England."

Oh no...

"I visit whenever I can."

I really should have thought this through.

"Where are you from?"

"Liverpool." I'd chosen it because was the hometown of the Beatles. I knew nothing else about it. Yep, really should have thought this through.

"Oh." The woman's face fell. "I haven't been there. I mostly like to tour the gardens and the National Trust houses. Do you..."

I leaned in close, a signal (and a gossip lure, I hoped) that I wanted to talk about something private. "Oi'm new here—"

"Oh, you work here."

"Yes 'm.'" I turned around and showed her the sign on my butt. "Oi saw on the news that somebody got killed here the other day, but nobody's talking' about it. Is it a big secret or somefin?"

Now the woman leaned in to me. "Not exactly..." Her gaze drifted above my head, as if she was considering whether to tell me something. "It's just that...well, no one is that surprised. Or upset."

"Really? No one?" I hardly knew him and I was upset.

"Not exactly...Do you know the song 'Billy Boy'? Sometimes called 'Charming Billy'? It's based on an English folk song called 'Lord Randall.'"

"Me education was a bit spotty. Was the dead bloke's name Billy? Or the guy who killed him?"

"No," she said quickly. "The man who was killed was Angus." She began to sing in a low voice: "Oh where have you been Billy boy, Billy boy? Oh where have you been, Charming Billy?"

I actually did recognize the tune.

"It's about a man who wants a woman who's too young for him." Was this a clue? Was Angus a pedophile? "The original song is much darker, a murder ballad, about a man who's poisoned by his fiancé."

"So this fella Angus was killed by his fiancé?"

"No, he didn't have one...I'm going at this all sideways. Angus was not a good man—he could be a bully at times—but he was not without charm. Someone called him 'Charming Bully,' and the name stuck." She shook her head sadly. "And no one really misses Charming Bully."

That was all I got from my first short round of sleuthing—that Angus was a charming bully. No one else spoke about him or the joust or the accident. It was weird. Had the Rennies already closed ranks, or were they just consummate professionals living in the here and now—or rather, the here and then?

After the belly dance show, I took off my sign and was about to do a bit more eavesdropping when I heard, "Prudence!" I turned around to see my ersatz boss, Jasmine. "Better catch William before his show ends."

Oops. "On me way," I said, then sang, "Oi'm off to see the wizard." Jasmine half-closed her eyes in a look of pain. "Omigod," I said. "What's wrong? Are you o—"

"Silent," she said. "You're like a belly dancing mime. Silent."

Chapter 18

"I'm off to see the wizard," I hummed to myself as I walked through the faire. Couldn't help it, such a catchy tune, and I was sure humming didn't count as talking. But oops, I must have taken a wrong turn. This place was bigger, and the paths twistier than I'd thought. I'd take home a map and really study it tonight. Along with Liverpool. And Marilyn and...

Since I was trying to think and walk at the same time (never a good idea with me), I almost ran into a tall tree, well, a tall person on stilts dressed as a tree. "Hey, where's the Enchanted Forest?" Seemed like he should know. The Green Man slowly turned around and pointed behind him with a gnarled limb/arm. I nodded my thanks and took off at a trot.

Ah, there it was. A wooden fence encircled a small enclosure, interrupted by an arched gateway made of bent tree limbs, with the words "The Enchanted Forest" fashioned out of twigs. I stepped through. On the other side was...magic.

You have to understand something about desert dwellers. We love our open blue skies and golden vistas, but we are starved for green. And here it was—every shade of green imaginable. I stopped under an emerald elm next to a jade shrubbery with lime green moss underfoot, and marveled. The set designer had created a magical forest in the desert, where tiny fairies peeked out from leafy green canopies, leprechauns sat under giant toadstools, and elves peeped from hollows in trees. Audience members of all ages sat on log-style seating, eyes glued on the wizard onstage. The stage itself was way cool, meant to look like the opening of a cave with a ceiling of glittering quartz that caught the light. But it was William the Wondrous who really entranced the audience. They leaned forward in their seats, straining to hear his every word. William had the requisite long white beard (which looked real) and wore a deep blue velvet robe embroidered with sparkling stars and planets. He wasn't tall, but he had presence, magnified by a sonorous voice that he used to its full potential. "As King Arthur once said," he intoned in the solemn tones of a monk, "Might for right. Can I hear you say it?"

"Might for right!" chanted the audience.

William took a piece of black paper from a robe pocket and held it high. "Darkness..." He crumpled the paper into a ball. "Will never be victorious..." He held the paper ball in front of him. "If we use might for right. Might for right!" He raised the clenched fist that held the paper ball. His voice boomed and echoed, even without a mike. "And light will overcome the night!" The wizard opened his hand and a fireball shot from it. The audience gasped and burst into applause.

"Always remember, friends," William knelt down in front of a row of enraptured kiddies. "Darkness cannot overwhelm the light." He stood. "Thank you all for coming. Go forth and use your might for right!"

Faire visitors immediately lined up to talk to William. Some wanted photos, some wanted him to sign their magic wands, and one little girl about six years old solemnly asked if he could make her a wizard, too.

"Indeed I can," he said. "I'm going to give you the incredible power of kindness." He tapped her gently on the top of the head with the carved wooden staff he carried. "Now, whenever you see an opportunity to be kind, you will take it and spread magic wherever you go." The little girl turned big eyes to her parents, who were a bit wide-eyed and misty themselves.

Finally, when everyone else was gone, I curtseyed to the wizard (just seemed appropriate), then making sure no one was around, I whispered, "Jasmine sent me. Oi'm new to the faire, and she said you could show me the ropes, as it were. And Oi'm whisperin' because Jasmine doesn't want me to talk."

"Jasmine—a good dancer but a hard taskmaster." William smiled, his eyes crinkling in friendly wizard fashion. "Follow me."

I thought maybe we'd go to a dressing room behind the stage, but instead William led me down one of the faire's dusty roads. "Is this your first faire?"

I nodded, conscious of the people around me and my order to stay silent.

"Where are you from?"

Wow, how to mime "England" or...? Ah. I pointed to a spot above my midriff, to the right.

"Ah, it's charades, is it?" William smiled. "Don't have the language down yet, I assume. Some of the people here are sticklers for authenticity." We passed a man who was half pirate, half squid. "Others not so much."

We'd reached a tent-like structure open to the street, with a gilded banner overhead that read, "William the Wondrous." Inside, oriental carpets covered the tent floor, lanterns with flickering (fake) candles hung from the ceiling, and jewel-toned floor pillows lined the edges of the space. As cool as all that was, my eyes were immediately drawn to the focal point of the space: a large chair elaborately carved with leaves and flowers and fairies and elves. Swaths of indigo velvet draped across the arms, falling in blue puddles to the floor. William sat in the throne and waved in the direction of some pillows. "Bring one close, so we can talk. And yes, you can talk in here, though I think I would like to play that first round of charades you proposed. So you are from..." He placed a hand on his abdomen about where I had touched mine. "Belly Button? No, that's in Arizona"—thanks to Uncle Bob's love of trivia I knew there was such a place, up near Snowflake. Yep, that's a real town, too. "No, your accent is...Ah, you must mean Liverpool, England."

"Brilliant." I sat down on a pillow facing him.

"I am a wizard, you know." Up close, I could see William wasn't as old as I'd first thought. His white beard and hair gave the impression of age, but his stockinged calves were muscular, and the only lines on his face were a few crow's feet. I suspected he was in his fifties, probably around the same age as Uncle Bob.

"Before Oi forget," I said. "Jasmine said somefin about learnin' the difference between dirty and bawdy?"

"An important distinction. 'Dirty' is outright crude, while bawdy—at least by our definition here—is double entendres. Jokes that rely on wordplay. Think Mae West."

"Got it. 'Oi used to be Snow White, but Oi drifted,'" I quoted. I loved Mae West.

"Exactly." William reached down along the right side of his chair into the folds of the blue velvet there—must be a hidden pouch. "Now, as far as faire language goes..." He took out a piece of parchment-looking paper and a fountain pen. His pen scratched against the paper. "Here are a few websites. Not a period research method, I know, but we travel light here. No room for a library. These sites will give you vocabulary lists, but the best way to learn is to listen. That's the reason some people like Jasmine ask newcomers to stay mute. When people can't talk, they generally listen better, instead of thinking about their next comment."

Huh. Sounded like good advice for a PI, too. I'd have to try to be quiet more often. "Try" was the operative word. I was not naturally quiet.

"One of the most important things you need to know is how to address royalty."

"Royalty?" I couldn't imagine Prince Harry or Princess Kate or—

"*Our* royalty," he said. "Each faire has a queen and a court. Ours is Queen Elizabeth, whom you address as 'your majesty.' If you see her, you stop where you are and curtsey until she passes." I must have looked incredulous because he said, "Not learning the proper forms of address is considered a snub, both when you're in character and out."

"Oi wanted to ask you about that," I said. "When do people stop being"—I made little air quotes—"on?"

"For some, maybe many of us, these characters become part of who we are. It's not about learning a certain role. We choose our personas and we live with them. All the faire's a stage. Some of us spend as much time being knights or fairies or wizards as we do being regular folk. So the answer about when—or if—people slip out of character varies."

"You don't all travel with the faires, do ya?" I knew part of this answer, but wanted to hear how a Rennie would see it.

"Imagine our faire as a tree, all of us serving different functions. Some are leaves, roots, bark, but we're all part of a whole. The people who work at the kitchens are no less important than the queen herself, though she might beg to differ." I had the feeling William had given this speech more than a few times. I wondered what had happened to make community and wholeness so important to him—and I wondered why he hadn't answered the question I asked. "And don't worry, I am about to answer your question." Maybe he was a mind-reading wizard. "But you'll soon find that there are social stratas within the faire. I want to make sure you understand you are no less important than anyone else. To look at my tree analogy in another way: If you cut a tree and look inside, what do you see?"

I pulled up an image of the last log I'd seen. It wasn't easy. Not a lot of logs in Phoenix. "Um, rings?"

"Exactly. The locals form the outermost ring, and next are the workers in the kitchens and restaurants and booths. Vendors—the merchants and artisans—are closer to the center of the tree. But closest to the center is...?" He waited for my answer.

"Royalty?"

"No." He smiled, giving the impression he'd hoped for that answer so he could explain. "The closest to the center are the big acts, the people who travel from faire to faire, who make this life their lives."

"Loike you?"

"Like me," he admitted. "But also the magicians, the musicians, the jousters—"

Ah, here we were..."Ooh, I love the jousters. In fact, Oi'd love ta...Oi mean, d'ya fink Oi could be one? Are there female jousters, like?" I hoped he'd say no so I could eliminate half my suspects.

"There are female jousters," William said slowly, "but..." he looked at me, well, at my body to be more specific. "Maybe. You're a dancer, so you have some strength, but it takes a lot of upper body and core strength, and you need to be an excellent rider."

I felt my face fall. His answer did eliminate some suspects, but only weak females who couldn't ride. A help, but not a huge help.

William must've thought I was disappointed in my future as a jouster. "I think you'd be happier as a dancer, or maybe something else, anyway. Jousters—like any group of people given elite status—can be brutally competitive." Hmm, was Angus's death a jousting rivalry taken too far? I made a mental note to dig into the other jousters' backgrounds.

William rose. "I think you'll fit in nicely here." Dang, guess we were done for the day. I'd hoped to get more.

I got up off my pillow. "Look up that vocabulary, stay silent for the first week, and remember to listen." He stepped forward, hands outstretched toward me, but the hem of his robe caught on his chair, snagged in the teeth of a face carved in the bottom of one of the chair's feet—a grinning malevolent face at odds with the other magical creatures that adorned the chair. William extricated his robe with an expert tug, then followed my gaze to the unsettling face. "It's a goblin," he said. "A reminder that evil exists among the good, waiting. An important reminder."

Chapter 19

I got in my truck and grabbed my cellphone from below the seat where I'd stashed it (Doug had warned me that Jasmine would not allow me to have it at the faire). The little light was blinking: a text message. Part of me hoped it was from Matt, and part of me didn't, in case it meant bad news. But it wasn't him. It was Vicki. "Call me ASAP," she wrote. I called her right there and then, still sitting in the dusty employee parking lot.

"Your timing couldn't have been better," Vicki said when she picked up. "I talked to a friend at a New York agency today. You're right on both counts. That guy does want to hire actors to help him with his new play, and yeah, you actually can—do—look like Marilyn. A lot. I got you an audition for tomorrow morning."

"Tomorrow?"

"Yeah. I've emailed you a side." A side was actor-speak for the scene being read at an audition.

"Brilliant."

"You have a cold or something?"

Oops. I ditched my Cockney accent and switched to a breathy Marilyn-esque voice. "Don't worry. I can do this." I threw in a Marilyn quote I'd always liked. "It takes a smart brunette to play a dumb blonde."

Silence. "Vicki?" I said in my normal voice. "Everything okay?"

"Yeah. It's just...you really sounded like her right then."

Maybe it was just Cockney accents I sucked at.

"So this audition is a little unusual," Vicki continued. "In fact, if I didn't know who this guy was I wouldn't send you out."

"Why not?"

"He wants to keep this secret, so you can't tell anyone you're auditioning, or that you're working with him if you get the part."

"Okay..."

"And he's not using any of the casting agents in town. He's holding the auditions himself. At his ranch, somewhere out in the desert. You comfortable with all that?"

"I am." An audition at the ranch where Riley's horse showed up. "In fact, it couldn't be better."

It was after eight by the time I got home. I flopped down on the couch, then dragged myself off it after a few minutes. Sure, it'd been an incredibly full day *and* I'd been up early for me, but I still had a lot to do. I made myself a big bowl of mac and cheese and ate while studying the Phoenix Renaissance Faire map. I wrote some notes about Angus being a charming bully, and/or a possible pedophile, and reminded myself to ask around about jousting rivalries. I rehearsed the scene for tomorrow's audition, found some clothes that would work, and watched a few more videos of Marilyn, just to get her speech patterns right. Then I did a bunch of research on Liverpool, and waited for Matt to call. Finally, close to eleven o'clock, he did.

"Sorry to call so late," Matt said. "But I didn't really have a chance before and I knew you'd be up."

"No worries. So...how is everything?"

Matt filled me in briefly: It was too early to tell for sure, but his mom's prognosis looked good. "Ends up she was pretty lucky to have had the stroke at church in town instead of out on the farm because they got her to the hospital right away."

"How are you doing?"

He sighed. I bet he was taking off his glasses and rubbing his eyes, like he did when he was tired. "I don't know. I've been at the hospital all day. It's like being in the Twilight Zone."

"Yeah." My memory of the hospital after Cody's accident was both fuzzy and clear, like being in a thick fog where I'd suddenly bump into something too close: my mother's red swollen eyes; my father hands curled into fists; Cody's sweet, sweet, unresponsive face. Even now, it took effort to pull myself back to reality.

"So, this may sound weird," said Matt, "but I've been talking and thinking about my mom all day, and I really just want...can we talk about your day? Wait, no. I don't want to hear about murder, either."

"Okay...um...I have other stuff to talk about...Did you know that Liverpool has two excellent football teams?"

"I actually did know that." The relief in Matt's voice was palpable.

"Or that people who live there are called Liverpudlians or Scousers?"

"Scousers?"

"I guess Scouse is a kind of stew. *And* Liverpool is home to the Spaceport, an interactive space museum which—wait for it—houses a huge collection of *Star Wars* memorabilia."

"When do we leave?"

I loved my geeky boyfriend.

"Anything else good and non-murdery happening there?"

"I've got an audition tomorrow morning." I explained about John Robert and the play. Sort of.

"You're going undercover as Marilyn Monroe?" asked Matt. "Seems like the jig would be up, seeing as how she's...dead."

"I'm not saying it right 'cause I'm tired." I yawned. "And I carbo-loaded and everything."

"What?"

"I had a bunch of work to do when I got home, so I ate a bunch of carbs to give me energy."

"I don't think that's how it works."

"You're telling me." I yawned again. "All I can say is, if you ever have trouble sleeping, eat an entire box of mac and cheese. It'll do the trick."

"I'll remember that. Good night, Ivy."

"Good night."

Chapter 20

Cockadoodledoo!

Cockadoodledoo!

Cockadoodledoo!

Arghh. I grabbed my cellphone from my nightstand. Really needed to change that ringtone. *Cockadoodledoo!* Only seven o'clock. No one who knew me would call this early in the morning unless it was an emerg—

My eyes flew open. No, not Matt—phew. A local number, but not one I recognized. I turned off my phone and went back to sleep.

I got up an hour later, took a shower, made some coffee, and put on the Marilyn outfit I'd come up with: a pencil skirt, a form-fitting vintage sweater, high-heeled pumps, and a girdle I'd worn for a production of *Picnic*. I made up my face the way Timothy showed me, put in my new blue contacts, and pinned on my wig. It was amazing: I didn't quite have Marilyn's hourglass figure (though the girdle helped with that), but I really did look like her.

I snagged a banana for the road, grabbed the audition scenes and directions to Harmony Ranch that Vicki had emailed me last night, and jumped into my truck. But something was bugging me, and it wasn't just that I was up before my usual time. Let's see...Angus...no...John Robert...no...Matt...

Yes. What was it? I replayed our conversation from last night. We'd talked about the auction and Liverpool and his mom...That call this morning. Maybe it was Matt calling from a different phone. At a red light I checked my cell. A voicemail pending.

"Ivy? Oh shit. Man, I wish you were picking up. I don't know who else to call about this..."

Not Matt. But who? The connection was crackly.

"Could you, uh, I don't know, find me a lawyer or something? They're holding me at the Fourth Avenue Jail. And...uh, shit I wish I could talk to you. Just...yeah, a lawyer. And thanks."

Riley. It was Riley.

I called Uncle Bob from the road. "So what do I do? I tried calling the jail, but inmates can't receive incoming calls."

"Yeah. Tell you what; I'll see if he has a lawyer yet. If not, I'll get someone down there."

"Thanks. Oh, before I forget: someone said something yesterday that made me wonder if Angus liked young girls. Wouldn't that have shown up on his criminal record?"

"Probably, but I'll check the Sexual Offender Database. Are you coming in this morning?"

"Not 'til this afternoon." I told Uncle Bob where I was going.

"I don't like the sound of this," he said. "Out in the middle of nowhere with a guy who might be connected to a murder, and you're not supposed to tell anyone where you are?'

"If you promise not to call *Backstage,* I'll give you the address."

"Call who?"

"Yeah, I think it's safe to tell you." I gave him the particulars. Harmony Ranch was twenty miles northeast of the Ren faire. The closest town was Gold Canyon, fifteen miles away. John Robert must really like his solitude. I promised to keep my pepper spray in my purse and my cell phone on, then hung up and merged onto the highway.

But something still felt off, like a bed sheet that had come untucked during the night. It was about Matt. I tried again to remember our conversation. It went well, didn't it? We even had that little joke about *Star Wars,* then I got sleepy and we said goodnight, just like usual.

No wait, it wasn't like usual. Matt didn't say he loved me.

Chapter 21

Matt always said, "I love you" at the end of our conversations. Always.

Get a grip, Ivy. The man just spent all day with his mom in the hospital.

Right. I turned on the radio to crowd out my ridiculous thoughts and drove. When I finally reached the road to John Robert's ranch, I was glad he'd given Vicki really specific directions ("the turn-off is just past the skeleton of a saguaro cactus") since my GPS didn't recognize the road as, well, anything. Not even a road. I bumped down the washboard dirt track until I spotted the ranch. Then I pulled off to the side of the road (there was no shoulder), partly screened by a big patch of creosote.

The house wasn't fenced. There was a gate across the drive, but it would only stop people who wanted to drive up to the ranch. Sure, there was a ditch alongside the road and some big rocks, but anyone who wanted to walk, drive a truck with good clearance, or most importantly, ride a horse could get to the house. It was as if John Robert expected everyone to be polite and obey the rules.

Matt didn't say I love you.

For heaven's sake, Ivy. Focus, would you? You have to be Marilyn, get through an audition, and do some sleuthing all at the same time.

The voice in my head was right. I needed to stop thinking about what was probably nothing and gather my wits about me. I'd text Matt really quick and call it good. "Hope you have a better day. Love you." Then in a formidable show of restraint, I turned off my phone, put it in my bag, drove up to the driveway gate, and buzzed in like I'd been asked to do. "Hello?" a male voice crackled through a speaker mounted on a gatepost. It was John Robert. I'd listened to a few interviews with him late last night.

"It's Marilyn," I breathed. I'd been told to do that, too, to act like Marilyn during the audition. Something about John Robert's creative process.

"Fabulous," he said. "We're having mimosas on the lanai."

Being an ace detective, I noticed two things about that sentence (three if you counted the fact that there would be mimosas). One, as a playwright, John Robert must have an ear for dialogue, so if he was still saying "lanai" he hadn't mixed with the locals much. Arizonans didn't say lanai. Patio or deck or even terrace, but not lanai. Secondly, he said, "we." Were there going to be a bunch of wannabe Marilyns trying to outdo each other over morning cocktails?

Hey, that could actually work in my favor. After all, this was really an investigation, not an audition. I was damn lucky to be here at all—I didn't have a snowball's chance in hell of getting the role. This way I could relax, let the other Marilyns upstage me, and snoop while they were doing so.

The gate swung open and I drove up to John Robert's hideaway. The ranch house was beautiful in an Old Arizona way—a low-slung adobe building laid out in a U-formation, with shaded porches that ran the length of the buildings (an architectural trick that was as much about keeping the sun from beating on the walls as it was about sitting outside). Not many plants, just a few well-placed mesquite and acacia trees, plus some prickly pear cactus. I couldn't see behind the house, but caught just the edge of a split-rail fence in the near distance—a corral, maybe? I parked, checked my look in my rearview mirror, swapped out my sneakers for high heels, and walked to the front door. I was just about to push the doorbell when the door opened.

"It's...you," I said in my Marilyn voice. I hadn't expected John Robert to answer the door himself.

"And oh." He clasped his pudgy hands together in front of his chest, like a little boy getting an unexpected gift. "It's you, Marilyn. He ushered me in with a sweeping gesture. "Please, please, come in."

"Why thank you." I made sure to do the starlet walk, one foot in front of the other in a near-straight line. It gave me a sultry sway.

"Good, good." John Robert watched me with eager eyes. Well, maybe. I might be mistaking eagerness for the fact that his eyebrows naturally slanted up toward the middle of his forehead. He looked like an amused teddy bear. "We're just out this way."

That "we" again. It was a little odd. Though actors in community theaters often auditioned in front of the competition, professionals usually did not. Oh well. So much of John Robert's process wasn't typical—this was probably just one of his things. I followed the playwright over Saltillo-tiled floors, surveying the house's interior as I did: dark and cool like the old adobe houses were, with hand-hewn tables, expertly worn leather chairs, and Navajo rugs hanging on the walls. Nothing to suggest that one of the leading lights of Broadway lived here. No photos, posters, or Tony Awards (Turner and Toe had won several). Nothing personal at all, like the whole house had been done by a decorator. And no sign of a horse, of course. I made a mental note to bring up the horse conversation. It would be tricky, as it wasn't public information. Hell, even John Robert's Arizona residency was pretty secret.

Huh. Pretty secret. Was that an oxymoron? I'd have to ask Uncle Bob later. Right now I needed to smile at John Robert as he held open the French doors to the patio.

I stepped outside. The morning sun was bright (plus my eyes were still half-shut, this being morning and all), so at first all I saw was a lawn so green I wondered for a moment if it was Astroturf, like the "lawn" surrounding the tiny pool at my apartment complex. But no, the grass must be natural, because real flowers—bright pink petunias and deep blue lobelia—filled the flowerbeds edging the lawn and the turquoise pool. "Oh...Isn't it delicious?!" I said, quoting the famous floating white skirt scene from *The Seven Year*

Itch. “All these flowers.” I flashed a delighted Marilyn smile. “I must get the name of your gardener.” Might as well jump right in.

John Robert’s face clouded. “Juan? You don’t want him. I had to let him go.”

“Oh, they can be so frustrating, can’t they? My gardener is forever leaving the grass clippings on the lawn.” Of course my apartment complex had no gardener. Our Astroturf didn’t need much care.

“I’m afraid he disobeyed me. About something...big.”

“I’m so sorry.” I put a light hand on his arm and looked into his eyes. “What was it?” Might as well come right out and ask.

“It’s a long story.” I gave a little Marilyn pout. “About a horse,” he added to appease me. Wow, that pout thing actually worked.

“Oh, you’re joking with me,” I said. “My uncle used to say that. You know, ‘I have to go see a man about a horse.’” I laughed, hoping they used that saying in New York too.

They must have, because John Robert blushed. “No, a real horse.”

I pointedly looked at the nearby corral and the two horses inside it. “Oh! I love horses. Can I meet him?” Maybe I could get a closer look at the corral.

“He’s not here anymore. Long story,” John Robert said again. Someone cleared her throat behind us. I turned, and my mouth fell open of its own accord.

Chapter 22

Jackie Kennedy sat behind us in the shade of a green-striped awning, slim legs crossed in a ladylike manner, leaning back in her chair like she was relaxing on the lawn at Hyannis Port. I blinked. Jackie was dead. I knew she was dead. And even if she weren't, she certainly wasn't this young, but...I blinked again and made myself shut my mouth.

John Robert clapped his hands together in another happy little boy gesture. "Marilyn, meet Jackie."

The woman rose and held out a white-gloved hand to me—gracious, but with touch of formality, maybe even disdain, as if she were the real first lady meeting her real rival. "Charmed," I said.

I was. The actress was impeccably dressed in a powder blue Chanel-type sheath with matching jacket. She had Jackie's large, wide-set brown eyes and generous mouth, played up with makeup to look even more Jackie-esque, but even more impressive was the way she carried herself: like a queen, but one who might be friendly to the right people.

The French doors opened behind me. "Fancy a drink?"

I turned to face the voice behind me. I had to shut my mouth again.

The man grinned boyishly and held out a fuchsia cocktail. "I'm Jack. And this is a prickly pear mimosa."

"Thank you," I said, dropping my chin and looking at him at him through my lashes. It was both a Marilyn gesture and a good way to stare without seeming to do so. The man wasn't as much of a lookalike as the Jackie-actress was, but he'd certainly pass muster. He had Kennedy's squarish jaw, the easy smile, the dark side-parted hair that flopped charmingly onto his forehead, but his eyes were a brighter blue—almost like the lobelias in back of him—bigger than the former president's and not as deep-set. In other words, he was even more handsome than JFK.

I took the mimosa from him, and took a big sip, partly to steady my nerves. When John Robert said "we," he must have meant the four of us. There were no other Marilyns, no cover for sleuthing. Just the opposite in fact: John Robert and the two other actors were studying everything about me from my heels on up. I took as deep a breath as my 1950's-era girdle would let me, and sat in the chair John Robert indicated.

"So," said John Robert, "as you know, I am writing a new version of *Camelot*, using the Kennedy White House as the backdrop. So many reasons why: The Kennedy's loved the musical, their brief shining reign was the Camelot of modern America, and as in *Camelot*, there was a love triangle."

Given JFK's many supposed indiscretions, I was pretty sure there was more than a triangle, but I kept quiet, partly because I was channeling Marilyn, partly because I was auditioning for a famous playwright, and partly because I'd never heard anyone say "love octagon" or the like.

"You are here because I like to see my ideas on their feet, to hear how the lines sound, how the scenes work—or don't. Working with actors helps me to visualize the outcome more clearly. Speaking of which, I want the actors I work with to be in character at all times—always in costume and always answering to their character's names."

All the time? I didn't know there were Method playwrights. I used the under-the-eyelashes trick again to look at the other two actors to see what they thought of the idea, but their faces gave nothing away.

"I already found my JFK and Jackie." John Robert motioned to the actors, who were now seated side by side, Jackie leaning slightly into JFK. "But I'm looking for a Marilyn who can not only act, but..." He smiled. "Well, we'll get to that after the formal audition." My agent had emailed me the audition, a scene from the musical *Camelot*. "Jack will read with you. Are you ready?" asked John Robert

"As ready as I'll ever be." I laughed Marilyn's tinkling laugh, put down my mimosa, and stood up, my copy of the scene in hand.

JFK and I read the scene, which took place before the famous song, "If Ever I Would Leave You." Jack was a marvelous Lancelot, full of longing and unrequited love and simmering sex. Acting opposite him was a dream. That was one of the things about getting better as an actor—the higher I moved up the ranks of professionalism, the more often I worked with great actors, which in turn made me a better actor. It was a glorious loop.

"Nice. Very nice," said John Robert. "Marilyn, I'd like you to do one more thing for me. You'll find a new costume in the powder room, just to the left of the front door, where you came in. Please put it on and come back out here."

This time I used Marilyn's nervous, unsure laugh. "Okay. I'll be back in a jiffy."

I walked slowly back through the house, surveying the house again as I went. Still nothing that stood out as unusual. I opened the door to the powder room.

Oh no.

My costume hung there, winking at me in the light. I slowly undressed, carefully folding my Marilyn sweater and skirt and then stepping into the dress left for me. The silk lining felt cool against my skin, but the myriad sequins and beads weighed a ton: Marilyn's chain mail. I sucked in my stomach as I zipped the dress up the back. It was tight, but that was appropriate. I read somewhere that Marilyn had to be sewn into this dress.

I checked my look in the mirror. Good. Maybe great. But yikes, acting was hard enough. Recreating an iconic real-life scene was enough to make me throw in the girdle (truth be told I was ready to throw in the girdle). But I thought about Riley and Angus, and yes, maybe a little about auditioning in front of a Broadway playwright, and bucked up. The dress's tight skirt hobbled me, so it took me a while to walk back to the waiting group. I flung open the French doors (might as well make a dramatic entrance) and stepped through onto the patio.

A soft intake of breath from JFK. Jackie cleared her throat and re-crossed her legs. John Robert was so excited he was nearly dancing sitting down. "Well," he said, actually twiddling his fingers. "I'm sure you know what I want you to do."

"Of course." I'd watched the short YouTube video several times last night. I flashed a smile at John Robert, shaded my eyes like I was looking past stage lights, and settled my gaze on JFK. I took in and let out a deep breath, and began. "Happy...birthday...to you," I sang to him. "Happy birthday...to you." I took audible breaths like Marilyn. I'd thought it was a studied affectation on her part, but I was beginning to think it was the girdle. "Happy birthday, Mr. President...Happy birthday...to you."

When I finished, Jackie clapped with gloved hands, JFK smiled broadly, and John Robert jumped out of his chair. "Yes!" He said. "You've got it. Not just the part, though you've got that, you also have, I mean you have...oh, I'm so excited I'm stumbling all over myself. What I'm trying to say is that you have it." He smiled at me happily as if I should know what he was talking about.

"Charisma," said Jackie. "He means you have charisma."

I did?

"And you have sex appeal," said JFK.

I what?

"That's right. That's it. You're in," said John Robert.

I was?

"So let's talk about your availability this coming year."

Chapter 23

"Broadway?" I croaked.

"Well, not at first of course," John Robert said. "Once we get it hammered out here, we'll workshop it at La Jolla Playhouse." Omigod, La Jolla Playhouse. I'd get to work at one of the West Coast's premiere theaters. "From there we'll decide if the show will move on to off-Broadway or if it's ready for Broadway." Broadway.

Broadway.

"I can't promise you'll play Marilyn on Broadway—the backers will want to have their say about casting—but I'll do what I can."

John Robert would do what he could. John Robert Turner, of Turner and Toe. *The* Turner and Toe.

"So," John Robert extended a hand to me, "I'll be in touch with your agent. I can't wait to have you join us."

I felt as if I was in a play myself. This couldn't be real. I was just Ivy Meadows.

I maintained my composure until I was back in my pickup. Then I rolled up the windows and whooped with joy. Omigod, omigod, omigod. This was it—my career-defining moment. I sat in my warm truck cab and closed my eyes, savoring the moment. For a moment.

Cockadoodledoo!

I glanced at the phone—the number from this morning. From jail. I boxed up my actor enthusiasm for the time being. "Riley?"

"Hey, Ivy. Yeah, it's me. Sorry I called so early this morning. I was pretty freaked out and didn't think, and I knew you were a PI and all—"

"Don't worry about that. What happened?"

"Hey, before I forget, thank your uncle for getting me a lawyer, okay? He's cool. Your uncle, I mean. Well, I guess the lawyer's cool too, for a dude that wears three-piece suits in Arizona. Hey, your uncle called you by another name."

"My real name is Olive Ziegwart."

"I like Olive," said Riley. "Makes me think of pizza."

"Riley, why are you in jail?"

"Well, the cops asked if they could search our fifth-wheel and I said okay, but I kinda forgot the weed."

"Weed?"

"Just a little, you know, for a bowl at night. Medicinal, really. Jousting's tough on the ol' bod."

"Medicinal. That should be okay."

"Well, it's not like I have a card or anything. Still, I mean, when do they ever arrest anyone for a little bit of weed?"

I was thinking the same thing, but instead said, "Why did you call me?"

"I figured you're a detective, so you'd know what do. And you did."

Riley was a good actor but a bad liar. That wasn't the reason he called me. I figured he might be too embarrassed to call his folks, wherever they lived, but... "Why not Bianca? I'm sure she'd know what to do and she's bound to be worried."

Riley's voice got quiet. "She's uh, not speaking to me."

"Why not?'

"I..." he said something so softly even he couldn't have heard it.

"Riley," I said. "What did you do?" As I said the words, they echoed in my head—the same thing Bianca had said after the joust.

"We had a fight and I sort of shoved her."

"You *what*?" Riley was a big macho guy, but he'd always had a sense of chivalry, even before becoming a knight. "Why?"

"I didn't hurt her." His voice took on a defensive whine. "She was off balance anyway, so she fell down, but just on the ground. She didn't get hurt or anything."

"Why?" I asked again.

"I didn't mean to. It was a reaction. Anyone would have done the same thing if...if they found out...she was hooking up with Angus."

This was bad. It gave Riley a motive. "Are you sure? About Bianca and Angus?"

"Yeah. That's why she had his helmet that day." Bitterness crept into his voice. "Everybody knew about it except me. They'd been getting together for months now, since the Louisiana Renaissance Festival. I don't get it. Everybody knew he was an asshole. And she was going to leave me for him."

"How long have you two been together?"

"I moved in almost a year ago. She's got a real sweet fifth-wheel...Oh no." Riley groaned. "I'm going to have to move out. And I hate living in a tent."

Bianca and Angus. That was why she was at the hospital that night.

I asked Riley for her phone number before we hung up, and then texted her about meeting up. I was just about to put my phone away when I noticed its light blinking. A text from Matt. "You too," it said.

"You too" what? I scrolled back to my text: "Hope you have a better day. Love you."

You too. Did he mean he loved me too? Or that he hoped I'd have a better day? Was my day bad yesterday? I couldn't remember. It seemed so far away.

My mood sank momentarily, but popped back up like a rubber ducky in the tub. Broadway! Broadway!

The glow I felt must have showed on the outside too, because when I walked into the office, Uncle Bob looked up and said, "What? Did we catch the bad guy?"

"Um, no. In fact, the only info I got was the first name of the gardener."

Uncle Bob still looked at me, waiting for more.

"But I think I'll get a chance to go out to the ranch again." I didn't want to say anything about getting the role until I'd heard from Vicki. I'd had deals go south before. Best not to say anything until the paperwork was in order.

Uncle Bob nodded and waited.

"Oh, and I talked to Riley. He says thanks for getting him a lawyer."

"Okay. If you don't want to tell me, you don't want to tell me. *Me*, you know, the guy who's there for you no matter what. Who makes you coffee and buys you donuts..."

"Donuts? Are there donuts?"

Uncle Bob pointed with his chin toward a Dunkin' Donuts box partly hidden behind the coffeemaker. I grabbed a maple bar, my favorite, and waved at him in thanks. I really would miss the guy when I moved on with the show.

Another momentary mood dip, like a wave bowled over my rubber ducky. Then his sunny yellow face popped back up and sang, "Broadway!" I grabbed another donut (two donuts are always better than one), poured myself a cup of coffee and sat down at my "desk," a wooden TV tray by the window that overlooked the jail across the street.

"So John Robert..." Uncle Bob said. "You think you'll see him again?"

I nodded.

"Good. Keep an eye on him. I'd say he was just a Ren faire fan if it weren't for the horse. Riley say anything interesting?"

I chewed and thought. "Sort of. Remember how I said that after the joust Riley seemed more worried about his armor and his horse than Angus?"

"Yeah."

"Same thing today. He said Bianca broke up with him, but seemed more concerned about losing his lodging than losing his girlfriend."

"Displacement, maybe?"

Ah. Guess I wasn't the only one with a bag of emotional tools.

"Easier to talk about losing your housing than losing the love of your life?"

"Yeah."

"But...he also said that during the breakup fight he shoved Bianca."

"Really? Seems unlike him from what you've told me. Have you talked to Bianca?

"Not yet. I left her a message. But...I guess what bugs me is...could Riley have done it? Killed Angus, or at least set him up to be killed? Now we know he had a motive, and shoving Bianca is evidence of a temper."

"One problem: He wouldn't have hit himself over the head."

I thought of the practical jokes Riley had played on the cast of *Macbeth*: fake reviews, plastic cockroaches in coffee cups, and the Mentos-Coke fountain where he'd sprayed half the cast.

"I don't know," I said. "I think he might."

Chapter 24

I spent the rest of the afternoon in Uncle Bob's office investigating everyone involved in Angus's "accident." I first called the jousters and squires on Doug's list and got voicemail every single time. I texted all of them, too, saying it was vitally important I speak with all suspicious persons ASAP, hoping the message would unnerve them enough to call me back. Then I dug into their backgrounds. A bust. One had a citation for public drunkenness, but that was the only black mark among the lot.

I moved on to Riley. A load of debt, but no criminal charges. I texted Bianca again, then Googled her and ran her through our databases. Bianca Henry, age twenty-six, was squeaky clean, had even been given Volunteer of the Year for a wildlife rehabilitation center a few years back. Nothing. Nothing except...

Broadway! I tried to corral my wayward mind, but it kept breaking into show tunes. I checked my phone for the umpteenth time. Nothing from Vicki yet. That stopped the music in my head, for a little while at least. John Robert had seemed sincere. The delay was probably just contract stuff.

Every time my phone crowed, I grabbed it before the second *Cockadoodledoo*, hoping it was Vicki. And it rang a lot, because every single jouster and squire called me back. Guess my vaguely menacing message worked. But none of them gave me any new information. No one had seen anything. No one had heard anything. No one really seemed to like—or miss—Angus.

I didn't hear from Vicki all day. My mood soured: No news wasn't always good news. And my detective day had been lackluster, to say the least. I was grumpily answering the last of the agency's emails when Uncle Bob stood up, brushed the crumbs off his pants (he liked to eat at his desk), and grabbed his car keys from his desk drawer. "You seeing Cody tonight?" he asked.

Matt and I had a standing double date on Monday nights with Cody and Sarah—a nice way for the guys to stay in touch since Matt stopped working at Cody's group home. Because of our tight budgets, we usually watched a video and ate pasta at my apartment. Tonight it was just going be Cody and me, so I was going to splurge on dinner out. "Yeah. I think I might take him to MacAlpine's." The soda fountain had been around since 1929 and had the best ice cream sodas in town. "Want to join us?"

"Nah, I got some stuff I gotta take care of. But have a good time."

"You too."

There it was—the other reason for my bad mood. *You too*. It echoed in my head. What had Matt meant? Did he love me?

My phone rang. Matt. Well, I guessed I was going to find out. "Hi," I said, curtailing my neediness for the time being. "How was it today? How is everyone?"

"Well...you first."

That seemed like a bad sign. "Um..." Should I tell him about the audition? No, not yet. Right now I had nothing to tell. "Well...this case is complicated—so many suspects. And Riley was arrested." I filled Matt in on the story. He didn't say much, as if he wasn't really listening. "And how are things out there? You okay to talk about it?"

Matt launched into full social worker/caretaker mode, talking about treatments and insurance and estimated outcomes—a sure sign he was nervous. But his anxiety didn't seem to be about his mom. They thought she'd have a near-full recovery. "She'll probably have a little weakness on her left side, maybe some difficulty with speech," Matt said. "She'll be in a rehab center for a few months, though. That's what we're dealing with right now."

Funny how you can tell, even over the phone, when a silence is comfortable or tense. This was the latter. "Um...How long do you have family medical leave?" Maybe he was worried about work. I hoped it was work.

"Twelve weeks."

"Good. I guess. I mean, I don't want to be away from you that long, but..."

"Yeah. Speaking of that..."

Oh no. Matt was back home. Where he was needed. Where his old girlfriend lived and was probably helping out with his mom and being indispensable and—shit, was that was he'd been thinking about—moving back to Nebraska? I couldn't breathe.

"I love you, Ivy," Matt said.

Matt loved me. It felt better than Broadway.

"I love you, too." I did—I felt it as I said it. I could almost breathe again. "Almost" because I could tell that "I love you" wasn't the end of Matt's thought.

"And I want to live with you."

Oh. Now I could breathe. "That's silly," I said. "My apartment is way too small for two people." Somewhere in the back of my mind, I registered the fact that I'd taken a tool out of my emotional rescue kit.

"I'm talking about living together, not moving into your tiny apartment."

"So we'd move into yours?" Yep, the deflection tool, at my service.

"C'mon, Ivy." Matt sighed into the phone. "It took me a lot to be able to ask you this."

Ah, *this* was what had been on his mind.

"You just said you love me," he continued. "I know it's a big step, but it's also a natural next step, right?"

"...I don't know." I did know that I loved Matt. I did know that he loved me. But my "love is better than Broadway" feeling had turned into a sort of stage fright. It made my stomach hurt. Maybe I should've eaten more than peanut butter crackers for lunch. Hey, I just used the deflection tool on myself. I was a mess.

"You okay?" he asked gently. "What's the problem?"

Problem? I was the problem. Relationships with me were the problem. After Cody's accident, I kept everyone at arm's length. Didn't want to be responsible for anyone else getting hurt so I built a nice tall wall. For years the only person I allowed close at all was Uncle Bob, mostly because he forced his way into my fenced heart, the lovable old coot. "Uncle Bob wouldn't like it," I said by way of an answer.

"You're kidding, right?" Matt called me on my bald-faced lie. "Uncle Bob loves me. Your parents not so much, but your parents don't really like anyone."

"My dad likes you." I chewed the inside of my mouth. "But yeah, Mom would go ballistic."

Not only did my mom disapprove of everything I did, she especially disliked Matt. He'd worked at Cody's group home—that's how we met—and was the first person who insisted we all treat my brother like an adult.

Another silence. Tense again.

"Ivy, this should be a good question, a happy discussion."

"I know. I'm...just not sure."

"Okay. That's honest. But I'm not forgetting about this. I want to live with you. I want to wake up next to you."

"I look awful pre-coffee."

"I want to hang out together after work and spend weekends together."

"We already do."

"I want to be there when you've had a bad day."

"You really don't."

"I really do. Just think about it, okay?"

This time we both said, "I love you" before we hung up. I stood there in the office, staring out the window at the jail across the street. Matt loved me. And I loved him. So why was I so freaked out by the idea of moving in with him? He'd be easy to live with. He even did dishes (sometimes). I had just decided to really think about it (instead of deflecting, denying, or distracting myself—my typical responses) when my phone buzzed. A text from Vicki. "You got the job! First rehearsal same place, crazy early—from 7-11 a.m. Emailing contract now."

Broadway, my mind sang again, but in a sad, out-of-tune voice. My career was taking off. And Matt loved me. Why did I feel so miserable?

Because I had some choices to make. Hard choices about important things. I'd loved acting since I was little. Matt was the love of my life. And it looked like I was going have to choose.

Chapter 25

I sat across from my brother in one of MacAlpine's dark wooden booths and flipped through the songs on the mini jukebox affixed to the wall. The songs were mostly classics, heavy on Elvis.

"Do you want to play a song?" asked Cody. "I have a quarter."

"Maybe." I turned the knob on the jukebox again: "Jailhouse Rock," "Love Me Tender," "It's Now or Never." Sheesh. My life was an Elvis album.

"Are you gonna finish that?" Cody pointed at my half-empty "Some Like It Hot" ice cream soda (fireball soda and vanilla ice cream). His banana split was already gone.

"I don't think so." I slid it toward him.

"Thanks." He scooted the soda within range and grabbed a new straw from a cup on the table. I looked at the jukebox again: "Heartbreak Hotel." Would it break Matt's heart if I moved on with my acting career? Would it break my heart if I didn't take this chance? The tension of the past few weeks rushed back, curdling the ice cream in my stomach.

A straw wrapper hit me on the side of the head. "Bulls eye!" Cody grinned, the offending straw-weapon still between his lips. Then the smile in his eyes faltered. "What's wrong?"

I loved Matt. I did. But why did he love me? Would it last? Could it? What if I screwed up again someday? How would he be able to forgive me when my parents never could? "I've just got a lot on my mind."

"About the jouster?"

"That's part of it." I remembered Cody crying in the parking lot, Sarah comforting him. "Where's Sarah tonight?"

"I told you."

"I forgot."

"She's with her mom. They're shopping for a bridal shower. Her sister's getting married. We get to go to the wedding."

"That'll be nice..." Then out of the blue my mouth asked, "Are you and Sarah in love?"

"Duh. Of course," he said easily, so easily I felt a twinge of envy, then a twinge of guilt because I envied my brother's happiness.

"How do you know?"

Cody looked at me wide-eyed and incredulous, as if it were the dumbest question ever. "I just do."

I persisted. "How do you know she loves you?"

"She tells me."

"What do you love about her?"

His eyebrows drew together in consternation. "Um...everything. Except when she gets mad at me for something."

"But *how* do you know you love her?" I knew I was asking my brain-injured brother to answer an incredibly difficult, if not impossible question, but I couldn't help myself. "How does she make you feel?"

The tension slipped off Cody's face like a cool rain. He smiled into his soda. "Better."

"Better about...?"

"Better about everything. But that's not what I meant."

I waited.

Cody looked up then, at a place somewhere past my ear, still smiling. "She makes me feel better. Like *I'm* better. Like I'm a better person."

Chapter 26

Did Matt make me a better person? Yes. The question was, did I do the same for him?

After a turbulent night filled with dreams about Matt and Elvis, I dragged myself out of bed. I drank an entire French Press pot full of coffee while putting on my Marilyn wig and makeup. I didn't know why John Robert wanted to rehearse so ridiculously early, but I was glad. Today was student day at the Ren faire, and I needed to be shaking my ass by noon.

By the time I finished making myself look like Marilyn, I was beginning to get excited again. I was going to rehearse with a famous playwright and fabulous actors. And I didn't have to make any decisions today. The contract John Robert sent to Vicki (and that I signed) was for the Arizona part of the play-creation process. There'd be another contract once the show moved to La Jolla. I bet John Robert wasn't worried about getting those signatures right now since no actor would turn down an opportunity to move on with a Broadway show. That would be idiotic. Right?

I made myself stop thinking about it. I had work to do. I took my belly dancer ensemble out to my pickup truck, got in, and headed east to Harmony Ranch. I had just passed the Mesa city limits when...

Cockadoodledoo! The jail phone number. Riley had asked yesterday if he could call me while he was in jail, just to keep in touch with "someone on the outside." Of course I said yes, not just because he was my friend but because whatever Riley said might help me in the investigation. Which he didn't know about. The situation felt a little dishonest, but I reminded myself that solving the crime was good for Riley too. At least I hoped it would be.

"Good morning!" Riley said when I picked up. "How you doin'?"

"You are way too chipper for being in jail. In the morning."

"We had pancakes."

"Ah." My stomach grumbled. I hoped I still had a granola bar in the glove compartment.

"Hey, is this too early to call? There wasn't anybody in line for the phone."

It was 6:40—*way* too early to call. Normally. "It was good timing today. I'm on my way to a rehearsal, and I have to go to"—oops, almost said the Ren faire—"work afterward."

"A morning rehearsal? Crazy," said the man who was in jail.

"So I only have a few minutes," I said, "but about Bianca...um..." I didn't want to tell Riley that she hadn't returned my texts. Break-up or no break-up, it seemed like you'd get back to the PI on a case involving your ex-boyfriend—your *two* ex-boyfriends.

Except I hadn't mentioned I was a PI. For all Bianca knew I was just Riley's friend who might berate her for two-timing him. No wonder she didn't get back to me.

"Yeah?" said Riley. "What about her?"

"Um...How did you two get together?" It was a punt, but a good question too.

Riley said they'd met over a year, ago, sort of circled around each other. "Then one night, we were all around sitting around the fire..."

"Sounds romantic." It did, firelight against a deep blue backdrop of stars...

"And I took her hand..."

I could almost see it, the knight kneeling down in front of the fair maiden...

"And then she let me take something else." Riley hooted with laughter, breaking the spell. I bet the jail had never seen such a cheerful prisoner.

"And you've been together ever since?"

"Moved into her fifth wheel that night. It's sweet, with an inside bathroom and everything. We had a real nice thing going until a couple of months ago. I didn't know what was wrong, but it was Angus. I shoulda known. All the girls liked him."

I understood. I remembered the way Angus looked at me, spoke to me—like I was the only person at the entire faire.

"Women were always throwing themselves at him. Once a tourist even sent him her panties in the mail."

That took me out of my gallant knight reverie and brought me back into PI mode. I resisted thinking about whether those panties were clean and instead thought about suspects. Could another one of Angus's women be behind the killing?

"I don't know why women liked him so much. He always said it was his animal magnetism." Riley sighed, all of his pancake cheer used up. "Maybe it was. Why else would Bianca leave me for him?"

Chapter 27

"You're late," John Robert said when I buzzed him at the gate. It was ten after seven.

"I'm so sorry," I began. "I underestimated morning rush hour."

"How very Marilyn of you!" He sounded delighted. I'd forgotten Marilyn had a reputation for tardiness. "You can let yourself in. We're out on the lanai."

I parked and switched out my sandals for pumps (I hated driving in heels). I checked my look in the rearview mirror. Today I wore capris and a buttoned-up elbow-sleeve cardigan. I really needed to find time to go thrift store shopping for a few more Marilyn-ish outfits. I walked through the house, and back to the lanai/patio. Jackie and JFK stood around a small table that held pastries, champagne, and a carafe of orange juice. I smiled hello at them.

"John Robert said to help ourselves," said JFK. "He'll be out in a minute."

"Fabulous." I grabbed a cheese Danish (there was no granola bar in my glove compartment) and poured myself a glass of orange juice.

"No champagne?" asked Jackie. "Don't tell me you're a working girl."

"I guess it depends on your definition of working girl," I said in my real voice. "I make most of my living as an actor," I sort-of-lied (my PI job often saved my financial butt). "You?"

"Right now I work at being Jackie Kennedy." She smoothed the white gloves she always wore. "But I do have other talents."

I looked behind me to make sure John Robert wasn't in sight.

"What's your real name?" I whispered.

Jackie smiled. "Bouvier."

"I'm not such a stickler," JFK said. "My name's Hayden Sanders."

"Ivy Meadows," I said.

"Ivy Meadows?" Jackie said. "What's *your* real name?"

"Touché," I said, sidestepping the question. I didn't want them to know I was really Olive Ziegwart. It'd be too easy for them to find out that I worked at Duda Detective Agency.

"Oh, just look at the three of you! I can hardly stand it." John Robert's grin stretched across his teddy bear face. "Grab your refreshments and follow me inside to the theater."

We all grabbed our drinks and followed our leader. As we made our way through the house, I said in Marilyn's voice, "I saw the most darling sign on the highway on my way here today. Knights on horses and princesses in gowns, oh..." I gave a little shiver of delight. "I'm positively dying to go. Have any of you been to the Renaissance faire?"

They all shook their heads. So much for asking outright. But I saw John Roberts that day before the joust. Was he lying or was I mistaken?

We reached a pair of carved wooden doors. John Robert stopped in front of them, then ceremoniously threw them open.

Wow. The faire faded, crowded out by the theater. The space wasn't big—the stage had no wings or backstage to speak of and the house (the audience section of the theater) probably held just fifty people—but its high adobe walls lent it an air of spaciousness, the rustic wooden beams crisscrossing the ceiling added charm, and the punched-tin Mexican star-lights threw magical-looking shadows across the walls and floors.

"Isn't it magnificent?" said John Robert. "Take a seat, and we'll get started." When we'd all settled in, he spread his hands in welcome. "I can't tell you how happy I am to have you all here. Bringing the Kennedy story to the stage has been a dream of mine for years. In fact, you could say I was born to it..." He paused dramatically.

Marilyn would be the one to suck up to a director, so I said, "How so?"

"My name!" he chortled. "I was named for the Kennedy boys, John and Robert. By the way, as to avoid confusion, I'll be John Robert, and you," he pointed at Hayden, "will be JFK or Jack. No wait, not Jack. Too close to Jackie. Just JFK."

"Sounds good," said Hayden/JFK.

"So I'd like to welcome you to the first rehearsal for our new musical..." John Robert spread his arms wide to the sky. "*Kennelot*!"

Silence.

He dropped his arms. "*Kennelot!* Get it?"

"Um," I said, "Doesn't that sound a little like kennel? As in dog kennel?'

"No, no, no. Don't you see? It's a combination of Kennedy and Camelot."

I was pretty sure we all got it.

"Now let's talk about your characters. Of course, I want you all to research Jackie, JFK, and Marilyn respectively. Let's talk about them as they relate to *Camelot*. We'll get back to the songs tomorrow. The only ones I really have worked out so far are "Kennelot" and "I Love You, the Hell with Silence."

"That's a reworking of 'I Loved You Once in Silence'? The song Guinevere sings to Lancelot?" Hayden asked.

"Exactly. But now you're going to sing it to Marilyn."

"But did he really love Marilyn? I mean, me?" I really hoped John Robert was serious about feedback, because I couldn't seem to keep my mouth shut. "Wasn't it more about sex?"

"Honey, how old are you? Do you really not know that men confuse sex with love?"

"If you're talking to Marilyn, no, I don't think I ever did figure it out. If you're talking to Iv—"

"No, no, no. Stay Marilyn."

"It does seem rather a generalization," said Jackie. "And it's not just men who confuse the two. Though I do think women are more likely to confuse love and romance."

"Which brings us right back to *Camelot*," John Robert said. "Since that's precisely what Guinevere does."

"So I'm Guinevere?" I asked. "And JFK is Lancelot?"

"Exactly," said John Robert. "Now..."

"Wait, I thought I was Arthur," said JFK. "Wouldn't that make Jackie Arthur?"

"Well...oh." John Robert's face fell. "That's a problem. Yes." His tongue played with his front teeth while he was thinking. "So...Marilyn, you're the one who destroys Camelot."

"I'm pretty sure it was Lee Harvey Oswald."

"In the *play*, you're the one who destroys Camelot. So you're Lancelot."

"And I'm Guinevere?" said JFK. "I really need to be a man."

"You are a man, darling," said Jackie. "That's why you're president."

"Okay, maybe I need to rethink that song. I've also been wondering about the round table...Who do you think should be invited to the table?"

"The Cabinet?" said Hayden.

"Too boring." John Robert shook his head. "Maybe it's full of JFK's women?"

"Mistresses aren't very knight-like," I said.

"Maybe it's the Kennedy women," said Jackie. "You know: me, Ethel, and Joan?"

"Ooh, we could do 'The First Ladies Who Lunch,'" John Robert said. "Maybe even use the tune from the song in *Company*. Do you think Sondheim would approve?"

I doubted it.

Chapter 28

I got into my pickup after rehearsal, my mood dragging. Did all Broadway musicals start off this shaky? Did any? It was tough to imagine anything we'd done today making it to any stage.

But it didn't matter right then. What did matter was changing into my belly dancer disguise and getting to the faire on time. I started up my truck and took off down the road. A few miles later, I saw a 7-Eleven. That'd do. I pulled into the parking lot, took off my wig and fluffed my hair (good thing it was going to be covered by another wig), grabbed my duffle, and went into the mini-mart. I purchased a surprisingly decent cup of coffee from the pony-tailed Native guy behind the counter, then went to the restroom. Thankfully, the bathroom was a family-style one-stall room, with plenty of space to change into my costume. I did so, then changed my blue contacts to brown, put on more eye makeup and brushed on some bronzer. My dark brown wig was a bit tangled from being squashed in my duffle, but it gave me a wild Bohemian look that seemed perfect for a belly dancer, especially when topped with my veiled headdress. I fastened another veil across the bottom half of my face. Perfect. The only bit of me visible was my now-brown eyes and my midriff.

I unhooked the face veil (it might look suspicious to drive with it on) and tried to slip out of the quick mart without being seen. No such luck.

"Ren faire, huh?" called the guy behind the counter. "Love it out there."

Ren faire. *Camelot.* Ren faire. *Camelot.* The two ideas ran through my head as I drove to the faire. John Robert had been at the Ren faire, and he wanted to reimagine *Camelo*t. Which came first, the Ren faire chicken or the Camelot egg? Did it matter? I couldn't see how, and yet it was a question I wanted answered.

I also wanted to know more about Riley and Bianca, specifically about their fight. Once I reached the employee lot for the faireground, I parked, pulled out my phone and began to punch in Bianca's number. Then I stopped. Could I tell her I was a PI on the job? Probably, since I could also investigate her while I was undercover. But what if she did talk to Riley and mentioned it? I didn't want him to know—he'd be more open with me if he didn't. In the end I called and left a message on Bianca's voicemail saying I was helping Riley with some of the legal stuff (I *had* gotten him a lawyer) and asking her to call me when she could. Then I stashed my phone under my seat, locked up my truck, walked to the Gimme Shimmie pavilion, and grabbed my ass-sign.

"Here you are." Jasmine was bedazzled again, a rainbow of colors sparkling in the sunshine. "Listen, we didn't get a chance to talk after your day on Sunday."

"We didn't talk because Oi'm a mime."

"Hey, a talking mime," said a teenaged passerby. I bit my thumb at him, a Shakespearean-type gesture that meant "up yours."

"Nice," said Jasmine, sounding like she meant it. "And yes, before you ask, you still need to stay mute today. Also, I wanted to say that you did a great job on Sunday. We had a few dozen people more than normal. So, we're going to keep you as an audience grabber, rather than a dancer. At least for right now. Sorry."

I made the disappointed face she expected, but inside I was celebrating. I'd already realized it'd be tough to fit dance lessons and/or learning new routines into my already full schedule. Plus, walking around the faire was much better for snooping purposes. Even the mime bit had worked out well—William the Wondrous was right about being quiet and listening.

"Hope you're not too upset," she said. "See you at the show."

I circled the faire, past a mud-wrestling pit and a giant blow-up dragon slide and the Enchanted Forest, smiling and jiggling my sign and reminding myself that I was wiggling my ass to catch a murderer, sort of like a worm on a hook. Then I got a bite.

"Oi!" I spun around to see who'd grabbed my sign. The pimply teenager I'd seen at the gate. Dang. It was kind of like catching a carp when you were hoping for trout.

"See, a talking mime!" he said to his buddies

"Sure, she talks," said a tall skinny guy. "But how do we know she's a mime?"

"Do something mime-y," the first guy said to me.

I bit my thumb at him again—until I saw the twenty he was waving. What the hell. I quickly mimed pulling a rope hand over fist (like a lot of actors, I'd studied movement theater). When I got to the end of the rope, I grabbed the cash and pretended to kick the lead teen in the rear. His friends roared. Ha. The kid reached to take back his twenty so I tucked the bill inside my belly dancer bra. Ha again.

A trumpet sounded. "Her royal majesty, Elizabeth!" An entourage of people dressed in velvet and brocade walked down the road at a regal (i.e. incredibly slow) pace. Probably too hot to move fast; those clothes were designed for England, not Arizona. "Curtsey, wench!" said the stout man who'd announced the queen. He looked a bit like Henry the Eighth after he'd gone to seed. "Do you not recognize your queen?"

I smiled and curtseyed.

"Ah, I'd heard tell of a new subject," said her royal majesty. "A belly dancer, I see. Perhaps you would dance for me?"

Ack. I didn't think I could fake a belly dance. I shook my head, cringing. I'd seen a set of stocks in one section of the faire.

"You dare defy her majesty?" said the King Henry-looking guy. "Answer for yourself."

I stood up from my curtsey, and zipped my lips, then shrugged my shoulders. A lady-in-waiting whispered in the queen's ear. "Ah," said the queen. "You are the mime."

Wow, misinformation sure got around fast, but hey, maybe I could use it to learn something.

I nodded happily, then held out my hand in an invitation, a "shall we play?" gesture.

"I do love mimes," said the queen. "Perhaps she'll build a box."

So I did, but then I grabbed invisible bars on the front of the box.

"Oh," said the lady in waiting. "I think she's in jail."

As she said "jail," I watched their faces, but nothing. Surely news of Riley's arrest would be all over the faire by now. Maybe I hadn't been clear enough. I galloped like a pony, and pawed at the ground.

"A horse," cried the duke or whatever he was. "My kingdom for a horse!" Everyone laughed obligingly, but still no forthcoming information.

I mimed putting a helmet on my head.

"She wants a new veil."

"No, she's going to become a nun."

I picked up an invisible lance and tucked it under my arm.

"What's she carrying?"

"A book?"

I shook my head. Now to put it all together. I put on my "helmet," picked up my "lance," and galloped.

"By George, I think she's jousting."

Yes! I gave Henry a big thumbs up, then staggered back and fell on the ground.

The group of royalty was silent for a moment.

"Is she dead?" said the lady-in-waiting.

"Is she Angus?"

"Is this supposed to be funny?"

I'd begun to nod in answer to the first two question, but unfortunately I was still nodding when Henry asked the last question.

"Not a laughing matter," said the queen. "In terribly bad

taste."

I shook my head and traced mime tears down my face, but I was too late. The entourage walked away, heads held high. "Too bad," said the queen. "I was thinking she might make a good jester."

Chapter 29

What had I been thinking? That one of them would give themselves away? That one of them would confess, or—

"Were you wanting to know about the killing of Sir Angus?" The scratchy soft voice behind me was familiar. I turned around. The fortuneteller. "I warned you," she said.

She had. I'd forgotten. "But how did—" I clapped a hand over my mouth.

"The crone knows." The woman smiled.

Dang, dang, dang. She'd warned *Ivy,* not this brown-eyed belly dancer-mime. Now she knew we were the same person. How did she recognize me? Would she tell people? Did everyone already know who I was?

The fortuneteller turned away, holding an arm above her shoulder and crooking a finger, beckoning me to follow.

I followed. What choice did I have?

When we got to her caravan, the woman waited at the steps to the entrance. "Tell your fortune?" she said to me. I nodded.

"Fifty dollars."

Fifty! Surely she didn't charge...oh. Fifty dollars might be high for a reading, but it was cheap for an information bribe.

I pulled the twenty the teenager had given me out of my bra. "I can get you the rest later." The woman nodded and went up the steps and into the caravan. I followed.

Inside, the wooden caravan was painted floor to ceiling in scarlet, with gilt trim around the small windows. Maybe in Romania or someplace like that it'd be cool and gypsy-ish, but here in Arizona it felt hot and stiflingly close, like being inside a vein.

The crone sat on one side of a small table draped in red (of course). I sat opposite her.

"When you bring the rest of the money, you ensure my silence."

I nodded. "Um, how did you recognize—"

"The crone knows," she said again. It was beginning to get on my nerves.

"What can you tell me about Charming Bully?" I asked.

"You do not mean the song."

"No." Besides, the song was called Charming Billy, but I didn't think I should correct her right then. "Was Angus a pedophile?"

"What? No. Oh, I see, from the song."

"It's about a man who wants woman who's too young for him, right? Maybe Bianca is younger than I think?" I watched to see if mentioning Bianca in conjunction with Angus would surprise the fortuneteller. It didn't.

"Not so young. Mid-twenties. No, it is only the name of the song that suits—suited—Angus."

"Do you have anything else to tell me?" I really hoped I wasn't paying fifty dollars just for her to keep quiet, though it was sort of a bargain when I thought about it that way.

"Yes," she said slowly. "The trouble is not over."

"How do you mean?"

The woman put her hands to her temples. Maybe she was a real psychic. An actor surely would have avoided such a stereotype. "I see...a storm. Trouble. Danger."

"Could you be more specific?"

She opened her eyes, motioned for me to be quiet, then held her hand over a deck of tarot cards that lay on the table. I'd had my cards read at a theater party once. The guy doing the reading had asked me to shuffle and cut the deck. This woman just plucked a card from the pile, and lay it on the table between us.

The card showed a man in a red robe, one arm raised high in the air holding something—a wand? A candle burning at both ends? He stood behind a table that held a cup, a sword, a staff, and a coaster-looking thing with a star on it. "The Magician," said the crone. "A practical card, usually associated with skillful communicators."

"That doesn't sound so bad."

"But he's reversed."

"So I'm not a skillful communicator? Oh. I'm a mime, duh. That fits."

The woman shook her head. "The magician in this position means trickery..." I *was* sort of tricking people by being undercover. "Untrustworthiness." That was going a bit far. I was just doing my job. "Greed..." *Hey.* "Manipulation and mis-utilization of skills toward a bad end." She looked deep into my eyes, in a mesmerizing gypsy sort of way. "For evil."

Oh. I was pretty sure the crone wasn't talking about me. She was warning me about someone else.

Chapter 30

It may sound funny, but I'd actually forgotten there was a dangerous killer around. I don't know if it was the fact that my brain was preoccupied with Matt's offer (which I was *not* going to think about at work) and my career (Broadway!) and the play (*Kennelot*? Really?) or the fact that the faire just seemed like an innocent place, full of merriment and bad jokes and people playing dress-up. No matter. Despite having been lulled into a false sense of wellbeing, I now felt awake and alert and ready to do some detecting. I decided to start with Bianca.

The falconry show stage was in the center of the faire. I got to the entrance about ten minutes before the show, but just as I was going in, I heard a voice: "Prudence!" Dang. Jasmine walked up to me, belly dancing bells jingling in exasperation. "What are you doing? No one will take notice of you there. They'll be watching the birds." She looked to the heavens. "Oh Lord, thou hast sent me a lubberwort."

"Oi! Don't be calling me an idiot." Jasmine arched an eyebrow, surprised I'd know the insult. "Oi studied Shakespeare, you know. Fellow countryman and all that." I huffed like I was offended and strolled back into the thick of the crowd. Twenty minutes later, I checked to make sure Jasmine was nowhere in sight, then ducked into the falconry show again. The stage area was an oval-shaped dirt plot surrounded by small hills lined with benches. At one end of the space was a large perch, at the other a two-story permanent structure built to resemble a castle. Several turrets with balconies rose above a wooden stage, which was set simply with a table and chair. The show was in progress.

Bianca wore the outfit I'd seen before, leggings and a leather bodice, but with the addition of a large leather glove, and a vulture. The enormous bird sat on her arm, flapping its wings a little. "Just to show you how quickly one of these birds can strip meat from a bone, we have a demonstration." Another young woman came out from the structure behind them, holding something behind her back. "Delia has a chicken drumstick. Once Igor reaches it, let's count together to see how long it takes him to clean it up." She turned herself and the vulture toward Delia, who threw the drumstick on the ground between them. Igor launched himself off Bianca's arm and was on the chicken in seconds. "One," counted Bianca. "Two," the crowd chanted with her. "Three," I said along with everyone else (I loved audience participation). Igor was done with the drumstick by the count of nine.

"Impressive, yes?" said Bianca. Let's give Igor a hand." The crowd applauded and the bird flew back to the "castle" where Delia was now waiting for him. Bianca walked toward the structure. "Now, you've seen owls, hawks, falcons, and vultures, but you haven't met the most magnificent bird in our troupe, the pinnacle of our show." She stepped onto the stage and held out her arms like a ringmaster. "Edgar!"

The audience turned to the turret where Igor had flown. The other birds must have been released from there. "Edgar!" Bianca said again, sitting down at the wooden table on the stage. The crowd scanned the sky, then a few began to laugh and point at the stage, where a (comparatively) small black bird hopped toward Bianca. "Edgar," she admonished. "Did you forget we were dining together?" He cocked his head at her, then flew up to the turret, where he took a small apple from Delia's outstretched hand. "Ravens like Edgar and their cousins the crows are the most intelligent of birds," said Bianca. "Thought to be as smart as great apes or even small children." Edgar flew back to Bianca and deposited the apple on the table.

"But Edgar, if you want to share," Bianca said. "I must cut it." He looked at her a moment. "With a knife." Edgar flew a short distance to the side of the stage, picked up a knife by its wooden handle, and brought it to Bianca. She cut him a piece of apple, then said, "That's all well and good, but I am a little hurt that you forgot my birthday." The raven shook its head from side to side, then flew back over the audience, where a man dressed in a tunic held out his hand. Something shiny dangled from it. Edgar grabbed the object and flew back to Bianca, where he placed it on the table. "A locket," she said, "How lovely." She bent her neck forward. Edgar picked up the locket by its chain, hopped onto her shoulder, and slipped the large silver chain over her neck. She raised her head and reached back to stroke his feathers. "I'm so sorry. It's just that last year you didn't remember so I thought you forgot my birthday again." The raven shook its head. "Nevermore."

Like the rest of the audience, I leaned forward, holding my breath, trying to hear, to understand. Was it the bird that...

"Nevermore," the raven said again. Yes, it was Edgar who spoke.

After the show, I lined up with the other fairegoers to see Bianca and Edgar. When it was my turn, I lowered my voice, and said, "Hi, did you get—" *Ack.* I'd nearly said, "my message," but I'd left the voicemail as Ivy, not as the belly dancing mime. I almost blew my own cover. "Oi mean, where did you get Edgar?"

"From a wildlife rehabilitation center, like most of the birds in my act."

"She said that at the beginning of her show," said a tourist behind me in line. "If people would just *listen...*"

I smiled and excused myself. There wasn't much I could ask her as my present persona. I wiggled my ass back to the woman in the costuming booth I'd talked with on Sunday. "That falconry show is brilliant," I said to her in a lull between customers. "Just bloody brilliant. Especially that bit with the raven. Nevermore, ha!"

The wrinkles on the woman's plump face all turned downward. "I heard you're supposed to be silent."

"But there's no one around," I said. "What's the harm in a little gossip?'

"Gossip?" The wrinkles all turned the right way up.

"Oi just wanted to ask about that bird woman. Oi mean, Oi fought she was pretty effin' amazing to begin wif, and then someone said it was her boyfriend just died. But Oi'd heard he was in jail. So..."

"Poor Bianca." The woman shook her head. "The lass has remarkably poor luck with men. One dead, one in jail."

"Cor blimey," I said, hoping people in England still said that. "They was right? She's got a dead boyfriend and a jailbird? A love triangle, eh?"

"Indeed."

She didn't say any more, so I gave her a tidbit, hoping to get one back. "One of me boyfriends was in jail once. Nicked a bicycle." Of course, my tidbit was a lie, but it was all toward a good cause. "What'd her guy do?"

"Well, the one in jail, they say he had something to do with the other's death, but I don't believe it."

"Why not?"

"Not smart enough. Now, if it'd been the other way around..." Her eyes grew hard. "That Angus was a bad man."

How had I misread Angus so badly? Was I really that susceptible to charm? "Angus, the Charming Bully?" I said to the woman. "You mean the bird lady's boyfriend was the jouster? Why was he bad?"

But the woman had set her mouth in a "not saying anything more" line.

"Was the other bloke—the jailbird—bad too?" She shook her head but didn't say anything more. I took a different tack. "Well, that woman's even more brilliant than Oi thought. Performin' like that after a love triangle death, when she must be broke up about it and all."

"Maybe not as much as you'd think." She leaned in: Ah, here was the juicy gossip. "I heard she found out they were both using her."

"That's a bad business. Using 'er how?"

"Don't know. But I also heard she broke up with one of them before everything went to hell." She frowned. "Or maybe both of them. I heard several different versions of the story. People talk a lot around here, you know, like a small town or a big family."

I wanted to ask more, but figured I'd pressed my PI luck enough for the moment— didn't want the woman wondering why I was so interested.

"Well, Oi'd better get back to shakin' me arse," I said. "Toodle-oo."

"Fare thee well."

I walked away, swinging the sign on my rear and thinking about what I'd learned: Yes, Bianca was with both Riley and Angus. Both of them somehow used her. She broke up with one or both of them. Riley hadn't said anything about Angus using Bianca. Did he know? Was he telling me the truth? Or was he using me too?

Chapter 31

I'd heard that nights in Ren faire camps were rowdy, lots of drumming and dancing and drinking. Just the sort of environment where people talked. And, it being off-hours, I figured I could talk, too (instead of being a mime), and find out more about Bianca and Angus and Riley and jousters and killers.

The faire closed at six thirty. I hung out for a few minutes until I saw some Rennies heading off in one direction, toward the edge of the faire. I headed that way too, through an opening in the ring of buildings that made up the faire. The desert opened wide before me, but a few feet away were tents, maybe a hundred of them. A little further away, a group of RVs huddled together. Portapotties ringed the area at a discreet distance and campfires glimmered here and there like small party beacons in the gathering dusk.

I found the jousters around one fire, accompanied by their squires and a gaggle of young women showing lots of cleavage—a large group, so I mingled easily. They mostly talked about the day's jousts, but then one young wench said, "Where's Squire Riley?"

"*Sir* Riley, you mean," said Sir Collier the Red (real name: Grant Collier). "He's a knight now."

"And he's in jail," said Riley's squire, name of John Hopper.

"He shouldn't be," said Collier. A murmur of agreement. I leaned in. "Everyone knows it was an accident."

Really? They were going with that? Even after they saw the murdering knight ride away?

"Dreadful thing, though," said the Blue Knight (aka Daniel Overton, actually British). Another murmur of agreement. "That poor horse."

I stayed long enough to hear that Thunder actually hadn't been injured or even gotten dehydrated, and was getting extra attention from Riley's squire. When the conversation turned to beer making, I moved on.

People weren't unfriendly—they offered drinks and places to sit beside the fires—but the cliques seemed well established. My hopes of starting up casual conversations slid away with the last of the daylight. Then I saw a familiar face.

William the Wondrous sat off by himself, at the edge of a pool of firelight. Still in full wizard gear, he smoked a pipe, his eyes unfocused. I squatted beside him. "Hiya. So can you blow rings and all? Maybe a smoke-dragon?"

He started. "What?"

I sat down in the dirt next to him, hoping my belly dancing costume was washable. "You look like Gandalf, sittin' and smokin' on the hillside in the Shire."

"I wish I were he, my dear lady. I wish I were."

"Everyfing all right?" I'd just met William the one time, but I liked his gentle spirit.

"Fine, fine." His eyes focused on me. "And how are you getting on at our faire?"

We chatted for a few minutes about Ren faires in general and our faire in particular, and then I said, "Oi've been finking about what we talked about before—me jousting, you know? Oi was wonderin' if maybe someone could give me a few pointers. Not the jousters here, you know, much too busy"—plus I'd already vetted them—"but maybe some who used to joust? Or is workin' up to bein' a jouster?"

"I'm sure they could."

"Do you fink you could give me a few names?"

William gave a low laugh. "Just look around you, my dear. Many of us—in fact I'd say most of us—who can ride have attempted jousting at one time or another."

"Really?" Please no.

"Given the opportunity to be a jouster—a brave knight in

shining armor thundering into an arena on horseback—who wouldn't want to give it a try? Of course, most aren't suited to the sport. It takes a special talent to be a good jouster."

Dang. Maybe another tack. "That guy who died, was he a good jouster?"

"Yes. And no." William's voice took on the sonorous tone he used during his performance. "Angus had talent, no question. But...he lived off of others, with no regard for community. It happens, that people enter our midst disguised as one of us, living at our expense, draining our life force like psychic vampires. They think we are naive, but we have learned to recognize them and kindly escort them from our midst. We have become warriors of sorts to protect what we have created here."

Whoa. Was William trying to tell me something? Or was there something besides tobacco in that pipe he was smoking? "But what happened wif Angus...that weren't no kindly escortin'."

William shook his head as if to clear it. "No. No, it wasn't." He rose from the camp chair he'd been sitting in. "It's been wonderful speaking with you, but I have another appointment."

I watched him walk off in the direction of the RVs. What did he mean about the community and Angus? Was he implying that his death was plotted by a big group? That seemed hard to pull off...plus, why not just kindly escort the psychic vampire from their midst? Why kill him?

I hung around the camp a few hours longer, hoping to hear more about Angus or Riley or Bianca or even just jousting, but I didn't. Everyone seemed firmly anchored in the pleasures of the evening. I gave up and joined them, dancing to the beat of drums, the bells on my hips jangling, firelight flashing in my eyes. It felt good, the heat and light and life of it all. It felt tribal and yet personal, like freedom and possibility and make-believe and a very present reality all mixed together. Heady stuff.

Then the wind came, suddenly, as if God had turned on a fan.

The drummers faltered, then, “Haboob!” someone yelled. “Take shelter!”

People began to run toward the tents and RVs, the wind battering their backs. Haboobs, those giant desert dust storms, can be dangerous if you’re driving—visibility can be down to a foot or so. If you’re out in the open like we were, they’re just really uncomfortable. Imagine your face as a car’s windshield, and dirt and twigs and bugs hitting your face at fifty miles an hour. We could still see, so the worst of the storm wasn’t upon us yet. I ran toward the parking lot, upstream against a scrambling mass of people. I bumped into one of them. “Sorry,” I said. Our eyes met. We both held the glance a moment too long. The man quickly melted into the crowd. I tried to follow him, but there were too many wenches and pirates, plus about a billion guys dressed like him in poet shirts and breeches. I lost him, but it didn’t matter. I’d seen the man’s eyes.

They belonged on Jackie’s face.

But it couldn’t be Jackie, could it? Maybe she had a twin broth—

The wall of dust was on us quicker than I thought possible, roaring above the sound of RV doors slamming and tents zipping. Shutting my eyes against the grit whipping against my face, I ran through the empty faire toward the parking lot and my truck. My eyes were open just a slit, which is why I didn’t see what was right in front of me.

Oof! I landed hard on the pebbly ground, the gravel stinging my knees through my flimsy costume. Whatever had tripped me was a few feet behind me. I opened my eyes enough to see what it was.

A body.

Chapter 32

"Help!" I yelled. My words were swallowed up in the howl of the haboob. "Help!"

The body—a man—lay face down in the dirt, sprawled as if he'd staggered and fallen there. I turned his face toward me. William. He was unconscious.

"Someone help!" I yelled again. My cell phone was in my truck. Should I run and get it? No, no time to get the cell phone. William needed help now. His breathing was ragged and irregular.

I pulled him over so he was on his back, and tried to shelter him from the blowing dirt stinging my face. Now what? CPR? Mouth to mouth? I'd never had first aid training. I didn't know what to do, but I had to do something. I straddled William's still form. My belly dancing skirt blew up over his face. I tucked it underneath me and yelled to the deserted faire one more time. "Help!" Then I put my fists underneath his clavicle and—

"What's wrong? Omigod, William." Bianca, her hair blowing across her face.

"Do you know first aid?"

"Yeah. And he's done this before. I know what to do."

I climbed off William. "Thank God. You take over. I'll get my phone. It's in my truck."

"Use mine." Bianca slid a hand into a near-hidden pocket in her thigh high boots and handed a phone to me.

I pushed the emergency call button. Nothing. I looked at the phone. "No signal."

"Go to the mews—where I keep the birds—to one of the second story balconies. You should get a signal there." Bianca took my place on top of William. "If the storm hasn't taken out the cell tower."

I raced to the mews, ran inside the unlocked door, and scrambled up a narrow staircase onto a landing with a door. I pushed open the door and ran onto a balcony, holding Bianca's phone in the air. A signal.

I called 911. After they promised to have someone out there right away, I ran back to Bianca. She sat in the dust next to William, crying. Oh no.

But as I got closer, I saw that William was breathing again.

"Thank God you found him in time," Bianca said through tears of relief. "Thank God."

"I don't really know what happened," I said to Matt on the phone. I'd showered when I got home, but was now trying to brush the dust out of my belly dancer wig. "Bianca told the EMTs he'd probably overdone a recreational drug. After William came to, he said something about hearing the mermaids sing." The dang wig had a ton of hairspray and the dust stuck to it like it was glued on. "But it seems awfully coincidental, him having this accident right after he told me about escorting psychic vampires away from the faire."

"I'm not even going to ask you what that means."

"Good. I think I'm too tired to explain." I gave up on the wig. Good thing the veil would cover most of it. "You must be tired too."

"I am." Matt caught me up on the day's events in Grand Island, which mostly consisted of talking with insurance people and visiting his mom and making meals for his dad. "Good thing he likes omelets and sandwiches. I make a mean baloney sandwich." He paused. "So..."

"I, um, didn't really have a chance to think about your...question today," I said. "Not with the Ren faire and rehearsal and all."

"Rehearsal?"

"Oh. Right. Vicki texted me after we talked yesterday. I got the Marilyn role."

"That's great!...Why don't you sound more excited?"

"Well..." It wasn't that my excitement had dimmed (Broadway!), but it was all muddled with the choice that was in front of me along with the confusing who-was-whom rehearsal. I decided to talk about the latter.

"Wow," Matt said after I gave him the rundown. "And you say this guy's supposed to be good?"

"A Broadway legend. With his partner, at least."

"Yeah. Sometimes the whole is greater than the sum of its parts." His voice got soft. "In fact—"

"Yeah." I cut him off. "Um..." I *had* to tell him about the play's planned future. Matt and I recently had a big fight when I neglected to tell him about a touring opportunity. This was bigger—I'd be gone more than a few months. "John Robert said the play will move to La Jolla Playhouse and then to off-off Broadway and then to Broadway." I said it all in a rush, the vocal equivalent to ripping off a Band-Aid.

"Omigod, that's great! Broadway!" Matt sounded genuinely happy for me. "I always knew you had the talent and now you got the luck. This is so great. Broadway!"

"Thanks." I fake-yawned. "I've got get to bed. I'm beat." I wanted to get off the phone while the conversation was still happy, before Matt realized the implications.

"Yeah, me too. Goodnight. I love you."

"I love you too." I meant it. I didn't know what I was going to do about us, but I meant it.

Chapter 33

I stood in front of my closet and stared, bleary-eyed after too little sleep. Nope, nothing that said fifties bombshell. Dang. I really needed to get some more Marilyn clothes. The outfit I'd worn to the audition hung over the back of a chair. I picked it up and sniffed it. It'd do, at least for the few hours I'd be rehearsing.

I did my makeup, put on my wig, and grabbed a banana and piece of toast on the way out the door. I was on the highway when my cell rang. I picked up on speakerphone. "Morning, Riley."

"Mornin'."

"I'm guessing you didn't have pancakes today."

"Scrambled eggs. I think they were powdered."

"I thought maybe you'd heard about William. Oh, duh. Sorry—of course you didn't hear."

"Yeah, I'm sort of cut off the grapevine in here. Like a raisin. What happened to William?"

Since Riley didn't know I was undercover at the faire, I told him the story as if I'd heard it secondhand.

"Man, I'm happy he's okay," Riley said. "It'd suck if anything happened to him. He's like everybody's cool uncle."

I understood. I had one of those.

"He really is like a wizard," Riley continued. "It's like he knows everything, and he's been around so long that he's really wise about stuff too. They said it was an accident?"

"Must've been an overdose. I guess he was talking about mermaids singing. It probably was accidental unless...Do you think he's the kind of guy who might hurt himself?"

"William? Can't see it."

"Would anyone want to hurt him?"

"No way, man. Like I said, he's the cool uncle. And William likes to...experiment, you know? Just natural stuff: mushrooms, peyote, once some datura—that shit is bad. They call it devil-weed, you know...You said it was Bianca who helped him?" He sighed heavily. "She's awesome. I screwed up royally, man."

"I saw her with the birds yesterday. She's great."

"She's crazy about them. Did you see Edgar? He's wicked smart."

"Yeah. And Bianca does seem pretty cool." But why did she think Riley was using her? And how to ask him? Maybe... "Seems like someone that, uh, focused could be hard to live with, though."

"Nah. We got along great. That's why this thing with Angus whupped me upside the head."

"You didn't fight?"

"Well, sometimes, about little things. Like when I'd eat all the Cheerios and forget to buy more. Or drink all the beer. Or use up all the toilet paper. That was a big one."

"No other fights?"

"Not until that last one."

"What happened there?"

"I was pretty pissed off about her and Angus and she said she didn't know why I'd care—don't know what *that* meant—and then she said something about me not being much different from Angus. That's when I shoved her." A thump. I could almost see Riley hitting his head against the wall. "Which does make me kind of the same. An asshole."

Chapter 34

There was so much I wanted to do. I wanted to call Bianca back—she'd never responded to my messages. I wanted to talk to Doug, to see if there was any news about William. And, I remembered when I walked on to John Robert's patio for another brainstorming/rehearsal session, I wanted to figure out exactly who it was I saw afterhours at the Ren faire last night.

After John Robert's delight over me being Marilynishly late yesterday, I figured I had a little wiggle time, so it was five minutes past eight when I arrived. Rehearsal was already in progress: Robert and JFK in the audience, Jackie onstage.

"Where are the simple joys of Hyannis Port?" Jackie sang. "Are those languid summer evenings gone for good?"

Now that I was looking, I could see Jackie's shoulders were broader than they first appeared and her hips were suspiciously slim.

"Shall I have to endure the public eye; To smile when I want to cry?"

Could she really be a man? The way she sang the song, so wistful and vulnerable, felt so feminine.

"Where are the trifle-y joys? The mother and the wife-ly joys?

Where are the simple joys of Hyannis Port?"

I clapped when Jackie finished, but she didn't look at me. Was it because she didn't want to meet my eyes?

"Good!" said John Robert. "Very good!" With the exception of trifle-y and wife-ly, the song was a marked improvement from yesterday's *Kennelot* ideas. I probably just needed to relax and trust John Robert's process. After all, it had already taken him to...Broadway! He turned to me. "Marilyn."

"I'm so sorry about being late," I said. "I've been on a calendar, but I've never been on time."

"Delightful," John Robert said. "You've been doing your homework."

I had. Marilyn had a surprising number of really good quotes.

"I have a song for you, too." John Robert handed me a few sheets of paper. "This one's sung to the tune of 'The Lusty Month of May.'"

I kinda figured that, seeing as how it was called "The Lusty Years of Men."

"It's about your marriages. I'm sort of setting the scene for the character, putting you into context, like I did for Jackie with "Simple Joys of Hyannis Port," said John Robert. "Sing it acapella for now. I just want to see it on its feet."

"Of course," I breathed ala Marilyn. "Tra la!" I sang. "It's James! Those lusty years of James! That lovely man who taught to me all the marriage games."

"Should that be 'sexy games'?" John Robert thought out loud.

"Tra la! Then Joe! Then Joe DiMaggio! Famous for home runs on the field and in our bed, you know."

"Maybe 'with gusto?'"

"Then Arthur! Arthur!" I stopped.

"Yes?" John Robert asked. "Do you need help with the tune? I know the name is two syllables instead of one."

"It's not that," I said. "I wonder if that won't confuse the audience. I mean, won't everyone to be thinking about Arthur the King versus Arthur Miller the playwright?"

"Why would they?"

"Because it's *Camelot?"*

"Drat." John Robert deflated like a sad balloon.

"Which of us will sing 'C'est Moi?'" I asked, hoping to cheer him up. "Me?"

"No." John Robert shook his head. "You're too unsure of yourself, Marilyn. Besides, the song's about purity."

"Hey." I pouted in mock offense.

"It has to be JFK," said Hayden.

"Didn't he say it was about purity?" I said to Hayden. "That puts you outta the game, fella."

"Which leaves me," said Jackie. "And I do speak fluent French."

"Exactly," said John Robert.

"So Jackie's Lancelot?" I asked.

John Robert deflated again for a moment, then brightened. "I did figure out what do with 'If Ever I would Leave You.' JFK could sing it to Marilyn. "

"That would be wonderful," I breathed.

"It'd be all about sex..."

Not so wonderful.

"We'd call it, 'If Ever I Could F—"

"*Forget* you," I said quickly.

"Forget?" said John Robert. "That's not what I was thinking."

I knew that.

He frowned. "I'm not sure 'forget' works. Too many syllables. But the other—it's too crude, right?"

We all nodded in relief.

"Okay. I get it. So...how about 'If Ever I Would Shtup You'? No? 'Bonk' maybe?"

Chapter 35

I took turns watching John Robert and Jackie, trying to put the Ren faire puzzle together. He had been at the faire in costume before the joust. She was a Rennie (and a man). Riley's horse ended up here at the ranch. There had to be a connection, but what?

Maybe Jackie could tell me.

When we had a break, I began a conversation with Hayden, watching for my chance. As soon as Jackie left the theater I excused myself and followed her. When she went into the powder room I crowded in behind her and shut the door. When she turned, I grabbed her hands and peeled the glove off one of them. "Man hands!" I said. "I knew it was you I saw yesterday."

"Give me my glove," Jackie hissed.

I held my cotton treasure aloft. "Only if you promise to tell me what's going on."

"If I tell..." Jackie's mask crumpled for just a second, revealing a vulnerable face beneath it.

Sometimes I hated being a PI.

"If I tell you," she said, her voice more under control. "Will you promise not to tell?"

"I promise," I lied. Yeah, hated it.

"We can't talk here. Follow me after rehearsal. My place isn't far. Now..." Jackie was a first lady again, straight-backed with a little ice to her elegance. "Please return my glove to me."

After rehearsal, I asked Jackie for her address and texted it to Uncle Bob. I had to be careful. She/he seemed like the harmless type, but at the very least, the harmless duplicitous type.

I followed her to a trailer park in Apache Junction. It was a nice one, a "mobile home community" with well-kept homes with window boxes full of petunias and little gravel yards full of lawn ornaments. Jackie parked in front of a vintage singlewide trailer. No room for more than one car. Jackie got out of hers, a baby blue 1960's Cadillac. "Guest parking is down the road."

She met me there and we walked the couple hundred feet back to her place. "Are you transgender?" I asked. "And what would you like me to call you?"

"I'm not transgender," Jackie replied. "I'm a female impersonator who identifies as male and gay. And you can call me Jackie or Benjamin—she or he—depending on the setting."

"So last night at the faire you were Benjamin." I was curious about the two personas, but more curious about something else. "What were you doing there?"

"I work there, just like you. At From Hoods to Snoods—the hat shop? I'm only there when the faire's in town—I don't travel. I have full-time work at a milliner's shop in Mesa." We passed a yard full of citrus trees in bloom, their scent sweet and strong.

"Really?" I was about to ask how any milliner in Arizona could hire full-time assistance (Phoenix is not big on fancy headwear) when Jackie said, "We mostly work with cowboy hats."

Ah.

"And where do you really work?" Jackie climbed the steps to the trailer.

I followed. "I'm an actor."

"I see." She unlocked and opened the door. "You're an actress-slash-belly dancer from Liverpool who just happens to have a Phoenix agent who got you an audition with John Robert."

"Um..." I said, then, "Wow." My "wow" was partly intended to distract Jackie from her question while I thought up a good answer, and partly because, wow.

I had just stepped into a trailer, but I felt like I turned a corner into the sixties. A long low silk sofa sat on a faux fur rug.

Sumptuous draperies in federal blue hid two of the walls. Another was lined with bookshelves. It was as if Holly Golightly had decided to have breakfast at the Kennedy White House.

The remaining wall was covered with material and acted as a soft bulletin board. Onto this wallboard was tacked dozens of photos of Jackie and Audrey Hepburn and Grace Kelly. I turned to look at Jackie, who lowered herself gracefully onto a velvet banquette window seat. "I long for the elegance of bygone times," she said. "I was born in the wrong era."

"And the wrong body?" I was still curious about the boy/girl thing.

"No. I don't want to be someone else all the time. I just like the feel of slipping into another persona." A slight smile played on her lips. "You should understand."

I did. Some people think actors are trying to hide from themselves, or don't have their own personalities, but for most of the people I knew, it was more about curiosity and empathy—given a character with this particular background, at this particular time in history, in this particular set of circumstances, how would they act?

And maybe there was a little of the "hiding from ourselves" thing too.

"Why go to all this trouble?" I asked. "Why not just do drag?"

Jackie arched a tweezed eyebrow. "Have you ever seen a queen do Jackie? Or Audrey? No. They like the bold, brassy types. Like Marilyn. Which you do fabulously, by the way."

"You're an amazing Jackie," I said. "And I'm not just returning the compliment. You've got her looks down, plus her voice, her walk..."

She shrugged modestly, but a shy pleased smile played on her lips.

"Does John Robert know you're—?"

"No."

"So you didn't know him before this play?"

"No." Her lips pursed in puzzlement.

"From the faire, maybe?"

"No." Still puzzled, a bit tense.

"I heard that that jouster's horse was found at John Robert's ranch."

"Oh." Her shoulders relaxed. "Everyone says that was just a coincidence."

Jackie seemed like she was telling the truth, but then again, she was a wonderful actor. Maybe if I cracked her façade a little... "And you're sure that John Robert doesn't know you. Benjamin, I mean."

"I said no." Jackie stood up and took off her jacket. For the first time I noticed muscled arms and broad shoulders usually disguised under sleeves. "And he can't."

"You do know that he—or someone else—will figure it out one day."

"Once John Robert really truly believes in me, believes in what I can do as an actor, I'll tell him. Then we can figure out how to spin it for PR."

"Huh. That could actually work."

"I'd say you have the bigger problem."

"Me?"

Jackie hung her jacket over the back of the window seat, sat down, and looked at me thoughtfully. "It's obvious why I'd want to be Jackie, just like it's obvious why you'd want to be Marilyn. It's the British belly dancer that's the problem. A lot of us at the faire have been suspicious of you from the beginning."

Dang. And here I thought I'd...

"It's not your acting or your disguise, though," Jackie continued. "They are lovely." Lovely? She must have seen the doubt in my eyes. "Truly. Lovely costume, fun accent. But your story isn't right. First of all, people in Liverpool don't have Cockney accents."

Arghh. I actually knew that. If I wanted to be Cockney, I should have chosen London as my hometown. Dang Beatles.

"And as you know, faire acts are their own businesses. Doug foisting you on Jasmine is like some shopping mall administrator making Forever 21 hire his teenage daughter. It just doesn't happen. Whatever you're doing for the faire—and I have my own suspicions about that—Doug should have given you a better cover. You could have been a strolling wench. There are so many of them—no one would ever think twice about you."

"The belly dancer disguise was my idea—all those scarves, you know—but yeah, Doug should have known better."

Doug. He'd made this big gaffe, he'd suggested the really bad mermaid idea, and...that thing that had been bugging me circled my head again, buzzing like a mosquito. I grabbed at the thought and actually caught it. Yes. Doug had talked about Angus in the past tense when he was still alive. Could he be involved with Angus's death? "What do you know about Doug?" I asked.

Jackie told me what she knew: that Doug was Mr. Corporate, never dressed for the faire, never treated anyone as anything more than an employee. "So?" I said. "Sounds like a lot of bosses I've known."

"Ren faires are different. We don't work there for the money—some of the local talent make no money at all, just tickets. People work and live the Ren faire life for the creativity, for the community and camaraderie. The Phoenix Ren faire has become so big and so money-focused we're worried—the community is worried—that it's losing its heart." Jackie glanced at a clock on the wall and stood up. "I've got to turn into Benjamin-pumpkin and get to the hat shop." She stepped toward me. It wasn't a threatening move, but it did remind me that she was actually a man, and from the look of those arms, a strong one. "I'll keep your cover if you keep mine," she said. "I'll even tell the people who are wondering that you really are from Liverpool." She smiled. "Most people don't know a Cockney accent from a Cornish one. Do we have a deal?"

Hmm. I had a lot to lose if my cover was blown—basically my entire investigation, and possibly my chance to be on Broadway. What did I have to lose by keeping Jackie's secret?

Chapter 36

I drove back to town, thinking about corporate profits and community and heart. It wasn't until I hit the Phoenix city limits that I realized I had learned all about Doug, the faire, and my undercover problems, but very little about Benjamin/Jackie. Dang. Luckily I had his first name, address, and license plate number, plus the fact he worked in a milliner's shop in Mesa. That info should be enough for a background check. If not, I could look through the list of employees for a Benjamin. He didn't seem like a killer, but I still hadn't figured out the John Robert-Ren faire connection, and Benjamin being in both places seemed awfully coincidental.

Since the faire was closed on Wednesdays, I was on my way to the office. I called Uncle Bob to see if he wanted anything from Filiberto's ("Just a shrimp taco. No, two shrimp tacos. And some horchata."), picked up lunch for the both of us, and got into the office a little after one. After wolfing down my carnitas burrito, I called Doug. "This is Ivy," I said when he picked up. "Any word on William?"

"He's going to be fine. They just kept him overnight. He needs to rest for a couple of days, but should be good to go on Friday. God, what an idiot."

"What do you think happened?"

"God only knows. Some drug thing."

"Are you going to fire him?"

"If I fired everyone who got high around here, I'd have to get a whole new crew."

"Really?" I hadn't noticed a lot of drug use when I hung out after-hours.

"Besides, William's one of our biggest draws. People love his wizard show."

Ah. Corporate profits.

"Are your insurance guys going to inspect the accident?"

"No. It wasn't a big deal cost-wise." Plus he didn't want William's drug use on record, I bet.

"If they do, or if you hear anything more about it, would you let me know?"

"Why? You think it's connected to the Angus thing?"

"Maybe."

When I hung up, my uncle said, "Why do you think this OD might be connected to our investigation?"

"I was talking to him beforehand, and he said something that made me think the jousting accident may have been a group effort."

"Was he high when you were talking to him?"

I remembered William's distracted air as he puffed on his pipe. "Probably. So yeah, I'll take everything he said with a grain of salt...And there's another thing..." I hated blowing Jackie's cover, but it was part of my job, and the guy I was telling was the most trustworthy man in the world. So I told Uncle Bob about Jackie, and about seeing her as Benjamin at the faire before William's OD. "I don't know how or if that connects, but it seems strange."

"Did she—he—know John Robert before?"

"Going to find out about that right now."

Or not. I found out zippo about Benjamin, except for his last name, which was Maxson. No debts, no offenses, not even a traffic ticket as far as I could tell. Ah. There was another way to find information.

I called the horse's mouth. "Want to go thrift shopping?"

"Now?" Timothy asked. It was four o'clock. Timothy worked temp jobs between gigs. Right now he worked evenings as a banquet server.

"Come on, seize the day. I need you help me pick out a few Marilyn outfits."

"Why? You can't possibly need any for the *Camelot* gig, because if you got the job you would have called your friend—your good friend—who helped you get it."

Dang. "I'm sorry, there's just been so much going on..."

"And a text takes *so* long."

"But I am coming to see you in the gay rodeo on Friday and—"

"I'm thinking of wearing Cher's "Half Breed" costume."

"The one that shows a lot of skin?"

"I've been working out."

"Didn't you tell me this was dangerous drag?"

"Oh. Drat." Timothy sounded a little depressed. "Back to the drawing board."

"Remember how I was saying 'and' before we started talking about Cher?"

"Right."

"*And* I saw a gorgeous silk tie at Re-dud that I was thinking of buying for you."

"...What color?"

"Peacock blue."

"See you at Re-dud in fifteen."

Timothy met me in the parking lot, all atwitter. "So, remember when I told you about BWBG?"

"Um..."

Timothy rolled his eyes. "BWBG—Boys Will Be Girls?" He opened the door to Re-Dud and held it for me. "That new company where we'll do classic musicals and plays—like ones by Rodgers and Hammerstein and Tennessee Williams—and men will play all the roles? How can you not remember this?" It was a good question. "Omigod, it's going to be fabulous. Can't you just see me as Blanche Dubois?" I could. "So, it looks like it's really going to work. We're still deciding on a season but the first show is slated for September. And really, honey, sometimes you need to be a better listener."

Ouch. But he was right. "I'm sorry."

"You're forgiven as long as you tell me all about *Camelot*."

"You mean *Kennelot*."

"No, really? Ooh, this is going be good..."

After swearing him to secrecy, I told Timothy all about the play while perusing racks of clothes.

"I wish I was a fly on that wall. And at the Ren faire, so I could listen to the Cockney belly dancer."

"Well, you could come out and see for yourself, but you couldn't listen. I told Timothy all about my new mime gig, and then worked the conversation around to: "So I met this guy at the hat shoppe out there..."

Timothy held a yellow polka-dotted top up to my face. "Oh. No. Not your color."

"He also works at a milliner's shop in Mesa."

"I think you should leave the hats to Jackie. Marilyn didn't really do hats."

"No, I'm...I just want to know more about this guy, Benjamin. He's gay and a female impersonator, so..."

"So you came to the right place," said Timothy. "Except no one comes to mind. Let me think on it. And..." He thrust a black ballet-neck top at me. "Go try this on."

I was in the dressing room and had just wiggled my way into a tight pair of pedal pushers when my phone rang. Matt.

I picked up on speakerphone "Hi. I didn't expect you to call so early. I'm out shopping."

"Dad and I are going over to the neighbors' for dinner and cards. Not sure what time we'll get home so I thought I'd call now. You're shopping?" Matt knew I wasn't a shopper. I rarely had any disposable income.

"Costume shopping."

"Knock, knock," said a voice outside my curtained cubicle. "Are you decent?"

"Yes, but—"

Timothy pushed aside the curtain. "Oh honey. Just say no to plaid."

"I'm out shopping with Timothy. And," I said to Timothy, "these pants aren't plaid, they're gingham. I'm sure I've seen photos of Marilyn wearing gingham."

"That was farm girl Marilyn, not bombshell Marilyn. *No.* Is that Matt on the phone?"

"Yep," said Matt. "Hi Timothy."

"Tell Ivy to listen to the man who got her the part. I am Henry Higgins, she is just Eliza."

"Just?" I said. "Eliza is pretty dang cool *and* she can sing, which is more than—"

"You saw the Marilyn photos, right?" Timothy continued. I'd sent pics to Matt at the same time I'd sent them to my agent. "That was all my doing. Plus I helped her out with her belly dancer persona."

"Belly dancer?" Matt said, laughter just beneath his voice.

"Sorry, I could've sworn I told you. I'm undercover as a belly dancer at the Ren faire. I'll send some photos. And I already had my costume, Mr. Wants-To-Take-Credit-For-Everything."

"But I'm the one who told you you needed an accent. I'm the one who told her," Timothy said into my phone.

"And look how well that turned out. They want me mute."

"Pshaw," Timothy stepped outside my cubicle. "And tata for now. I'm going to find you some more clothes, Eliza." He let the curtain drop with a swish.

"They want you mute?" Matt asked.

"Yeah. I have to mime everything."

"A belly dancing mime?" Full laughter now. I loved Matt's laugh: It was a deep rumbling sound that bubbled up from inside and burst onto the scene like a happy Saint Bernard. It surprised people when they first heard it, coming from a slim bespectacled guy, but the sheer joy of it soon made them join in. Like I did right then. Even though we were sort of laughing about me.

"A mime belly dancer. Different thing altogether."

"Right." I could picture him on the other end of the line, taking off his glasses and wiping his streaming eyes. "Are you going to pull an imaginary rope? Or build a box?"

"Already checked off my list."

"Is your accent really that bad? Say something for me."

"Oi don't fink me accent's that awful."

Matt laughed again.

"Oi! Cut it out or I won't do Marilyn for you."

Matt's laughter cut off. "You can do her voice, too? It was incredible how much you looked like her in that picture."

"Of course, I can do Marilyn," I breathed into the phone in her voice. "I'm an actress, silly."

"Dad!" Matt yelled. "You've got to hear this."

"Oh. No," I said quickly. I'd never even talked to Matt's dad before. "I don't think—"

"Hello?" said a male voice. Was this really the way Matt wanted to introduce me to his dad? Okay... "Hello sir," I said in my best Marilyn accent. "I'm so very pleased to meet you. I'm Marilyn Monroe."

A booming laugh. Now I knew where Matt got it. "By God she does sound like her," his dad said loudly, then back into the phone, "You sure look like her too. Matt's hooked himself a good one." A rustle, then "Thanks." Matt's voice again, softer. "First laugh he's had in days." He dropped his voice. "I know I said Mom's prognosis was good, but...she's not going to be the same. Things are going to be different around here. She—and Dad—are going to need some help. So thanks. For being Marilyn. And for being Ivy. I needed that laugh too."

"Glad I could do something." I was, even if it was just to entertain them for a minute. I was also glad Matt hadn't brought up the living together question, although I knew it was probably because of the shopping-with-Timothy/dad-in-the-room situation. "Let's just hope he doesn't expect me to really look like Marilyn Monroe."

"Maybe you should keep the wig just in case. Or maybe just for dress-up."

"You mean like Halloween?"

"No..."

"Oh." Warmth crept up my neck and then...downward. "I do

love you, you know," I said.

"I know."

We hung up soon afterward. I waited for Timothy in my little curtained cubicle. Its closeness felt comforting, like a hug with no strings attached. But even there, my dilemma crept under the curtain and raised its head. I did love Matt. And I loved acting. But one meant settling down and the other a life on the road. Not even slightly compatible. What was I going to do?

Chapter 37

I left Re-Dud with a new pencil skirt, two pairs of capris, several tops and a bit more information. "I called my friend Frederick when you were trying on clothes," Timothy said. "I remember him talking about a Benjamin a few times. I asked if the Benjamin he knew worked in a hat shop. He does. And he works at the Ren fair."

"Did you get anything else?"

"Frederick said he never could understand the attraction to the Ren faire. Too macho for him, and maybe too macho for Benjamin. He got beat up a few times."

"A few times?"

"Spread over several years. And before you ask, I don't think Frederick was exaggerating about the beatings. He said that one time someone broke Benjamin's ribs."

I thought about this as I made my dinner of red beans and rice. Or I tried to. Mostly what I thought about was Matt. And an acting career. And Matt. And an acting career. Then I thought: Candy.

My best friend Candy had made this same decision a couple of years ago. I'd introduced her to Matt (before I'd recognized his charms) and they dated for eight months until she broke up with him in order to pursue a film career in LA. And though her career did take off eventually, the dark side of the entertainment industry had nearly killed her: She was now in an eating disorder rehab facility in Taos. And she could take calls between six thirty and eight thirty.

"Hey, girlfriend," Candy said when she picked up. "It's good to hear from you."

It was good to hear her voice too. She sounded better, more like herself. And I realized I couldn't ask her about her decision, not now when she was still regaining her sense of self. Turns out I didn't have to.

After about ten minutes of chat, Candy said, "So you've told me about belly dancers and murder and Marilyn Monroe, but you can't fool an old friend. There's something else on your mind. Talk to me."

Maybe if I put it in general terms..."Do you think actors can have successful relationships?"

Candy hooted with laughter. It was nice to hear. Sort of. "Darlin', you know you are askin' the wrong person."

"No," I said. "I suspect you've thought about it a lot."

"Well. Well, maybe you're right." She sighed. "In my experience, an actor with a successful relationship is about as common as a man who does dishes. Our lifestyles are just different from other folks. We keep weird hours. Our schedules change all the time–I can't tell you how many dates I've broken. We work hard, and often for nothing–"

"No, we don't."

"Hon, do you get paid to go to auditions? No. And you're probably giving up work in order to go."

"...Yeah."

"Anybody who gets involved with an actor has got to be pretty damn grounded, enough that they can see you having faux sex with someone and be all right with it."

"What if I–or you–just decided no sex scenes?"

"That's a possibility. But then you–or I–have got to be willing to give up roles that could make us money or get us ahead in the industry."

"You don't have to make those kind of decisions as often in the theater."

"No, you don't. In the theater, your partner just has to understand that you may be out of town and on the road for months at a time."

"Right." I'm sure I sounded depressed but I couldn't help it.

"Listen," Candy said. "I'm just talking about myself and what I've seen. There are people who make it work. You ever think about Dolly Parton's husband?"

"Uh, no."

"He and Dolly have been married for dog's years. She jets all over the world while he stays home. They seem happy."

"Huh."

"I assume we're really talking about you and Matt?"

"Yeah."

"Have you talked to him about it?"

Chapter 38

Of course I hadn't. *Baaawk, bawk, bawk.* My brain made chicken noises at me as I hung up with Candy. I would bring up the acting-relationship dilemma, I told my noisy mind. I'd talk to Matt about it all tomorrow. My mind must not have believed me because it clucked at me all night.

The next morning I got into the Marilyn wig and makeup (extra concealer under my tired eyes), dressed in one of my new outfits—capris and a button-up shirt tied at my waist over a cropped tank—and got on the road on time for a change. Traffic was a little lighter too, so I was just getting off the highway when Riley called. He didn't sound pancake-happy, but not scrambled-eggs-sad, either. "Hey," I said after we'd exchanged pleasantries. "Do you know a guy named Benjamin? He works at the hat shop at the faire."

"Kinda quiet gay guy?"

"That's him."

"Not really. He lives here in town somewhere, doesn't travel with the faire. I mostly know him 'cause of what happened with him and Angus."

Well, that was easy. "Which was?"

"One of Benjamin's friends came to the faire wearing a kilt. Angus was pissed."

"Because he was wearing a kilt?"

"'Cause he was wearing a kilt and eye shadow. Angus said something about the pride of Scotland and pushed the guy into a cactus. Benjamin slapped him across the face." Riley laughed. "You shoulda seen it. Angus was so mad. I think he woulda knocked his block off if Doug hadn't come up right then."

Doug again. Interesting. "What happened then?"

"I dunno." He laughed. "Angus's face got so red I thought it'd explode." Huh. This didn't help—it seemed like Angus would have been the one looking for revenge. Riley's laugh stopped with a gulp. "Oh shit. Is it bad to laugh about a dead guy?"

"Not sure. Wouldn't do it in court, though."

"Court. Shit. Court."

"Sorry, didn't mean to go there."

A pause, then, "Is William okay?"

"Yeah. I think he'll be back at work this weekend."

"Cool."

William. His name knocked against my skull reminding of something...yes. Female jousters. Could Bianca have posed as Riley? "Can I borrow your suit of armor?" I'd come up with this idea a while ago but kept forgetting to put it into action.

"Why?"

I had my excuse ready. "A friend's doing an indie film."

"About knights?"

"Sort of." Arghh. You'd think that the Cockney-belly dancer-from-Liverpool-debacle would have taught me to think through my stories. "Yeah...It's about suits of armor...that come alive."

"Haunted suits of armor? Cool."

Phew. "So I can borrow it?" And find out if your girlfriend could have worn it and killed Angus and framed you?

"Sure. Just ask Bianca. It's in our trailer."

Dang. "Is there any other way to get it?"

"Not really. You can try the trailer, but I'm pretty sure she keeps it locked, especially after all the bad stuff going on. I'll leave her a message. She'll let you have it. She'll probably let you have all my stuff." Riley sighed loud enough to remind me he was still there. In jail.

"Riley?" I said. "You holding up okay?'

"I guess so. I was just thinking about Bianca. It's gonna suck, seeing her at the faire, but not you know, *seeing* her. But hey," —

this guy just couldn't stay in a bad mood—"I also want to thank you. For trying to help me, you know, by figuring stuff out."

"Sure." I crossed my fingers when I said it, partly because I felt weird about not letting Riley know that the Ren faire hired me, and partly because I really hoped that whatever I figured out about the case would help Riley—because it could just as easily go the other way.

Chapter 39

I stepped through the French doors onto John Robert's flagstone patio. I loved that he liked to begin our mornings outdoors. I also loved the fact that he provided food. I grabbed a slice of banana bread and poured myself a glass of orange juice, careful not to spill any on my new/used Marilyn top.

Jackie and JFK were already there and chatting, about swimming, it seemed. "But a cold dip is so much more invigorating." Hayden said this in his JFK voice, so it sounded like "in-vi-gah-rating."

"I like a bit more warmth. Better for the muscles, I'd think," Jackie said. "Hello, Marilyn."

"Where's John Robert?" I asked between mouthfuls of banana bread.

"He'll be out in a bit," JFK said. "Said he's scrapping the ideas of the last few days, and has something completely different for us."

"Oh, thank the Lord..." Uh oh. I sensed a presence behind me. Plus Jackie's eyes got big. "...for thrift shops. And thank *you* for the compliment," I said to Jackie. "It *is* a new top." I put my hands on my hips, modeling my midriff-baring blouse.

"Did Marilyn have an outie?" asked John Robert, who, yes, had come up behind us.

"Not sure," I said. "Maybe she did and she had it fixed."

"Can they do that?" asked JFK.

"Darling, Hollywood plus enough money can do anything," Jackie replied.

"So," said John Robert, "before we go inside to the theater today, I'd like to talk to you about my new idea." We all sat down in the lawn chairs grouped together on the patio. "Though I liked some of the ideas we've batted around these past few days, I felt like it just wasn't coming together, so I'm going to open up the story by using *The Once and Future King* rather than just the musical. *Camelot* was based on the book too, you know."

"I'm sorry." I gave a tinkling Marilyn laugh, hoping it would soften my question. "I don't understand. How does this open up the story?"

"Since the book covers more of King Arthur's life, we'll have more time to play. I'm going to add a bit at the beginning with the sword in the stone. It needs to be something that highlights JFK's service in World War Two. I've always wanted to use that great hero quote of his."

"What quote?" I asked, just because he was dying to tell.

"When asked how he became a war hero, Kennedy said..." He looked at JFK, who smiled. "It was involuntary," they said together. "They sunk my boat." Jackie clapped politely.

"One problem," John Robert said. "What exactly is JFK's sword in the stone?...Oh! Since so much of the play is going to be about the love triangle and sex, maybe it's his di—"

"How about a missile?" I said quickly, "Since it takes place during the war and all."

"Brilliant!" Said John Robert. "That gives us some nice foreshadowing for the joust at the end of Act One."

"It does?"

"Sure. Didn't I tell you? That's going to be the Cuban missile crisis. It's where we'll add the rallying cry for the whole play: 'Might for right,'" he said, "'Might for right!'"

Chapter 40

After rehearsal, John Robert walked us all to the front door, just as he'd done the last few days, when something caught my eye. "Do you mind if I powder my nose?" I asked.

"Of course not," he said. "It's a long drive back to town."

I slipped into the bathroom, then listened to see if John Robert was walking Jackie and JFK out to their cars like he usually did. The front door shut. I peeked my head out of the bathroom. Yes, they were all out front. I ran to the console table near the door and quickly sorted through the papers there: mail, magazines, and...a map. Of the Phoenix Renaissance Faire.

The map's corner had been sticking out from under the latest copy of *The New Yorker*. I replaced it just as John Robert came back inside. "I'm off," I said, air-kissing him on both cheeks. "'Til tomorrow!" He held the front door open for me and I left, waving to show him that he didn't need to see me to my car. He smiled and shut the door.

Those maps were only distributed at the faire. John Robert had said he never attended. Why did he lie?

I pondered the question as I drove to Mother Cluckers (since it wasn't a faireday I had time for lunch). John Robert didn't want anyone to know he'd been to the faire because...why?

Before sitting down at the restaurant, I slipped into the restroom to fix my wig hair and wipe off my Marilyn makeup. I'd worn today's outfit specifically so I wouldn't have to change—it worked as well for everyday clothes as it did for a costume.

John Robert didn't want anyone to know he'd been to the faire because...he was embarrassed about being a Rennie? Why would he be?

I continued to ponder the problem over my two-piece broasted chicken special. John Robert didn't want anyone to know he'd been to the faire because...because he was really a jouster in disguise and a killer who'd murdered another jouster with no ties to the theater. Yeah right. It was about as likely that he'd worked in the oil fields with Angus.

After finishing lunch, I gave up pondering and went out to the fairegrounds. I'd texted Bianca to let her know I was coming. She replied that she would be at the mews.

The faire was closed, so there was no traffic, no line to get in. I parked close to the entrance, walked through the quiet fair to the mews and opened the unlocked door. Bianca was there feeding an owl, Edgar perched on her shoulder. I stepped inside. "So you got Riley's message?"

She didn't say anything to me, just nodded and handed over the keys to the fifth-wheel. She kept her back to me.

"So you must have gotten mine, too."

Bianca nodded again, but didn't turn around. "I didn't have anything to say about the situation."

"But you're open to helping Riley?

She shrugged. It wasn't a no. I'd give her a little time to get used to the idea, and then talk to her when I returned the keys. "How will I find the trailer?"

"It's on the southwestern edge of Tin Can Alley, the RV section of the camp. There's a big eagle painted on the side. You can't miss it." She turned her attention back to the birds.

I thought about Bianca's reticent attitude as I trotted back to my truck. Was it belligerence? Nervousness? Or was she just concentrating on her birds?

I drove to Tin Can Alley, figuring Riley's armor might be awfully heavy to haul all the way to the jousting arena. The trailer was easy to find. I unlocked its flimsy door, stepped inside the gloomy interior, and immediately backed out. You know those little boxes they use as solar ovens? Must have been inspired by a metal trailer in the desert sun. I left the door open for the little air circulation it'd provide, and went back inside. All the windows were closed. Did Bianca keep it closed up for safety's sake? Seemed like roasting to death was more likely than being murdered in her bed.

Maybe not, I reminded myself. There was a killer loose, and he—or she—was connected to the two most important men in Bianca's life. I'd probably keep my place shut up too.

I flipped on a light switch. Oh shit. I backed away from the figure on the bench seat. His armor shone dully in the overhead light, his eyes black holes.

Because it was Riley's suit of armor. Sheesh, Ivy. I walked over to the invisible knight, maybe a little slower than usual, reached out my hand toward his face, and raised the visor. Empty. Phew. I knew it would be, and yet I was relieved. The way the suit of armor was seated was creepily lifelike, as if it was waiting for a tankard of ale or someone's head on a pike.

I examined the armor. Still a bit black around the seams from being burnt, and a very slight dent on the back of the helmet where the killer had hit Riley. I rapped a fist on the helmet. Made of pretty sturdy stuff.

Next I looked around the interior of the fifth wheel. The place was neat—it'd have to be when you had two people living in an eight by thirty-two foot space—and had few places to hide things. No wonder the police had found Riley's weed. I searched through the drawers and cupboards and found dirty underwear (Riley's), books on birds (Bianca's), and a photo face-down in a cupboard: Riley and Bianca in Ren faire finery, smiling at each other rather than the camera. Nothing of real interest.

I wrangled Riley's suit of armor out of the trailer and into the bed of my pickup. It took longer than I thought it would—the armor was unwieldy as well as heavy, but as I put it into the back of my pickup I realized something wasn't right. I closed my eyes, the better to see that fatal joust. That was it—the jouster wasn't wearing the full suit of armor. He—or she—wore chain mail, plus Riley's helmet and gauntlets and shin guards or whatever they were called.

I went back into the trailer. Ah, there was Riley's chain mail. The suit-of-armor-knight must have been sitting on it. I lugged the incredibly heavy stuff outside and placed it alongside the armor in my pickup.

I hopped into my truck and started it, soaked through with sweat already. I parked as close as I could to the jousting arena, got out of my truck, and picked up the chain mail. Yikes. So that's what chain mail felt like after sitting in direct sun. I'd made a tourist's mistake—forgetting that the weatherman measured the ninety-degree day in the shade. It was at least a hundred in the sun. I touched the metal-plated armor. Yep, even hotter, probably due to the shiny surface.

Huh. I sat there baking in the sun along with Riley's armor. How could I cool it down? I could put in the cab and run the AC, but that might take more power than my little truck had. Too recently, I'd watched the engine light creep into the red zone while I was stuck waiting for a train. The faire was closed, and even so, most of it was outdoors and not air-conditioned.

Except for the administrative offices, which weren't too far away. I grabbed the helmet, and dropped it. *Ow*. Too hot to carry. And it wouldn't get cooler sitting here...Ah. I rifled through my duffle bag. There it was—my magic roll of duck tape (aka duct tape to those who don't know the waterproof tape's WWII origins). I wound it around both hands—triple strength—and picked up the chain mail. Still hot, but not so much I couldn't carry it. I carefully carried it and Riley's chain mail to Doug's office. When I opened the door, Doug and his assistants looked up without interest. Guess they were used to people carrying weird stuff. "How about a few minutes in front of your air conditioner?" I said.

Chapter 41

I made a second trip to the admin office with the helmet and gauntlets and shin-thingies. Once everything was nice and cool, I wrangled it outside to a semi-shady bench. Setting the sheet-metal-armor stuff down, I took off my button-up shirt and slipped Riley's chainmail on over my tank top. The cool silvery fluidity of it made me feel like I'd become a magical fish. A really heavy magical fish. I was pretty strong, but still, the weight of the thing made lifting my arms quite the workout. I eyed the rest of the armor I'd brought, which looked less like a fish and more like the can the tuna came in. Oh, well, in for a penny in for pound, as they said in England. As I *hoped* they said in England. Really did need to look up some current British slang.

I put on the rest of the garb so I was wearing exactly what the killer did during the joust, and started walking to the jousting arena—right into a signpost. Couldn't see much at all out of the eye slits in the helmet. It was sort of like wearing a Halloween mask that covered my whole head, except it didn't move with me as easily. I had to turn my head to have even the tiniest bit of peripheral vision.

And walking felt like slogging through shoulder-high mud. Could Bianca have worn this and pulled off the joust? She'd have to be awfully strong.

I walked (clanked) past a few vendors who were restocking their wares, raising a hand in greeting. They raised theirs, too, even though it was clear they didn't know who I was. The armor was a perfect disguise. Maybe I should have disguised myself as a knight instead of a belly dancer. Wouldn't have to go to the gym.

Nah. Too hot. Besides I never went to the gym anyway.

By the time I reached the jousting grounds, I'd been wearing the armor for about twenty minutes, and realized that whoever had worn it and jousted was a lot stronger than me. I dragged myself to the arena and pointed my helmeted head (the better to see, my dear) toward the staging area.

Dang, the helmet was hot, like someone had miniaturized Bianca's trailer and stuck it on my head. I felt like I was inside an EZ Bake oven.

Sweat poured into my eyes, obscuring my vision even more. The helmet was claustrophobia-inducing, but it also curiously focused my attention. When you can only see a sliver of the world, that sliver takes on new importance. Before, the arena floor had looked like a wide expanse of plain old Arizona dirt, but now, tilting my head downward, I noticed hoof prints, a scrap of lace, a turkey leg bone. I was lost in those details when suddenly, I was inside the mind of the murderer, watching Angus ride toward me, his black horse flying, his lance pointed at me, coming closer and closer until all I could see was the slash of black across his eyes.

Yikes. As an actor, I put myself in other people's shoes on a daily basis. That ability to really understand someone had also helped me in my PI work. But I'd never had it happen when I wasn't trying to get into character. It was kind of creepy. I pushed the discomfort away and walked across the arena to the staging area. It took me forever.

Finally. The gate opened easily and I walked in. A tall wooden fence enclosed the space. There were two entrances: the gate I'd just used to enter the arena, and another gate that led to one of the faire's dirt streets. I stood in the exact spot where we'd found Riley. Yes. If Riley was facing the arena, his back would be to the street entrance. It was possible, even probable, that he wouldn't see anyone coming in, especially given the restricted vision he'd have had when helmeted. It would have been hard to hear anyone too. There was the crowd noise, the announcements and cues to concentrate on, and the peculiar Darth Vader-like sound of breath inside a helmet. Wait, was that my breath, or—

Bang! I felt the sound as much as heard it, and then...blackness.

Chapter 42

Tap tap tap.

The sound was close by and loud, ringing metallically in my ears. Someone rapping on a metal desk? Drumming on a tin can?

Tap tap tap.

I opened my eyes. I couldn't see, and my head felt thick. I was lying down. I experimentally moved a leg. Heavy.

Tap tap tap. I lifted a hand with some effort and touched my head, which was encased in...ah. I pulled Riley's helmet off. A flutter and a little cloud of dust, then a beady eye staring at me. Edgar. Probably ascertaining if I was dead and therefore okay to eat.

"Not dead, Edgar," I said, sitting up slowly. "But thanks for checking."

"Edgar! There you are." Bianca ran up to us, long legs covering the ground easily. She pulled up short in front of me. "Ivy? Why are you wearing that? I mean, I thought you just wanted to see Riley's armor."

"I wanted to see what he could see that day. Or not see, as it turns out." I rubbed my head. "Someone hit me on the head too."

"Are you okay?" Bianca knelt down in the dirt next to me.

"I think so."

Bianca and I had both been through Riley's hit-on-the-head scenario, so we thought we knew what to look for, and decided I wasn't concussed. "It looks more like dehydration to me. Maybe you fainted." Maybe I did. I'd lost about a gallon of water in sweat. "Come back to the mews with me," Bianca said. "I've got water there, and it's cool and dark. You can sit for a while until you feel better."

Maybe getting hit on the head was worth it. Maybe now Bianca would talk to me. We walked slowly back to the mews, where she sat Edgar on a perch and me on a stool, and gave us both some water. I shucked off Riley's armor and chilled for a while, watching Bianca with the birds. She fed and watered them, then cleaned their cages, sometimes lifting the heavy cages to get at the dropping-filled newspaper underneath. Definitely stronger than me.

After about a half hour, I stood up, not too fast, and fished Bianca's keys out of a pocket. I gave them to her, then sat down again. "I'm going to hang out awhile longer, if that's okay. Don't want to get woozy on the freeway."

"Sure."

"Do you want me to take Riley's armor back to your fifth-wheel?"

"No. I'll take it when I go back tonight." Bianca seemed nervous, fussing with the birds, looking in their cages while she talked to me.

"That's a really nice place you've got."

The flash of a scowl from Bianca—almost a micro-expression—quickly replaced by a placid look. Huh. She clucked at Igor, smiling at him like he was a little baby sparrow instead of an enormous bird with sharp claws and a beak made for tearing meat.

I got up and walked slowly among the cages. There was an owl, a falcon, Igor the vulture, Edgar's empty cage (identified by a wooden sign with "Edgar Allen Crow - the Raven" in Olde English lettering), and a large cage near the back with a white sheet draped over it. I started to lift a corner.

"Don't!" Bianca snapped. "Sorry," she said quieter. "It's just...she's sleeping. She's been sick."

"I heard you help out with some wildlife rehabilitation place." I nodded at the sheet-draped cage. "Is she part of that?"

"No." Bianca's voice caught. "I don't do that anymore."

"Why not? It sounds cool. And you obviously love birds."

Bianca turned away quickly and ducked her head, busying

herself with Edgar's cage. I almost missed the slight shake of her shoulders. "What's wrong?" I went to her and put a hand on her shoulder. "Are you okay?

She snuffled, and turned toward me, wiping her eyes. "It's nothing," she said. "Just...Angus."

"I'm so sorry," I said. "I'm such an idiot. Of course you're still grieving."

"So you know about me and him."

"Riley told me."

"Stupid Riley. I can't believe he thought to mention it. He doesn't care, not about me. Just about..."

C'mon, c'mon, tell me what Riley was doing, how he was using you...

"Oh, never mind."

C'mon... "You think he only cares about...?"

"It doesn't matter. We're over."

Dang. So close. "Were you going to leave him for Angus?'

Bianca bit her lip. "I was, but..." She shrugged.

Wow, she was hard to pin down. "Were you in love with Angus?"

"Angus was an assho—a charming bully."

Guess that really was his nickname. My gossip source had also said Bianca had discovered that Angus was using her. But what did that mean?

Bianca reached up to get a cobweb off the top of a cage. The loose sleeve of her white shirt slipped down, exposing a bit of her upper arm, tinted the purple and yellow of a healing bruise.

"Did you have a fight with Angus?"

Bianca quickly dropped her arm and flipped her long hair over her arm. "We were always fighting and making up. One of the things that made our relationship exciting."

"Really?" I hated fighting with anyone. Especially Matt.

"It's actually how he wooed me. He stormed into the mews once, sent the birds squawking and flapping. He was yelling, 'I am slain by a fair cruel maid!'"

I recognized the line from a song in *Twelfth Night*. Seemed Angus used Shakespeare to get the ladies. I felt my face flush. I'd been won over so easily.

"I laughed at him, and he said, 'O, what a deal of scorn looks beautiful in the contempt and anger of your lip!'"

Another *Twelfth Night* quote. Angus was mixing up the characters, but the lines were still pretty darn effective.

"I told him I had no time for flirting, and he said, 'Flirting? This is beyond flirting. I can't stop thinking of you. I burn for you. I can't sleep at night."

He should have stuck to Shakespeare.

Bianca's eyes were unfocused, dreamy. "You don't know how incredibly exciting it is to have a man say those things to you, to say he's coming to you because he's powerless to do anything else. It was...well, let's just say that's not how it was with Riley. So I gave in to Angus. The sex was amazing. The sense of danger added to the thrill too."

"Danger?"

"Of getting caught, of course. Plus, Angus was...volatile. You felt like he might go too far at any given moment." Bianca subconsciously pulled at the sleeve that hid her bruises. Then her eyes focused on me and her face closed down like a shade was drawn across it. "I don't want talk about it."

Sheesh, first she tried to tell me about fantastic sex, which was really too much information, and then she wouldn't tell me about Angus "going too far," which was just the information I wanted. I tried a different approach. "You said that's not how it was with Riley. How was it with him?"

A slight smile, again subconscious. "Riley's like a big happy kid. He just loved hanging out with me, eating Oreos inside the trailer when it rained, sitting around the fire with me by his side, everyone drinking and singing songs."

"But?"

"But he never really committed to me. He'd tell me how cool other women were, but never that I was cool. He'd drop my hand when they were around. When he talked to them, he always said, 'I', never 'we.' You know, like 'I'm going on a road trip,' or 'I live in a trailer on site,' that sort of thing."

"Ah."

"But the straw that broke the camel's back was when I overheard someone say, 'I hear you're with Bianca. She's like, amazing.' And Riley said, 'Yeah. She's got a sweet fifth-wheel.'"

Chapter 43

"Just one last thing," I said. "Tell me about the fight you had with Riley."

"Why?" she said. "Why are you so interested? And why did you borrow his armor?"

I was relieved she'd asked the question—after all, she had to be thinking about it. "You can't tell Riley."

"I won't."

I was pretty sure she wouldn't. After all, she wasn't speaking to him, and even if they did make up, it sounded like it would be awhile. "I'm not just Riley's friend. I'm also a private investigator. The Ren faire hired me to look into Angus's death. Riley doesn't know." I figured it was safe to tell her. If she lied to me because I was investigating, I could always use my undercover belly dancer-mime persona to find out the truth. Too bad I couldn't do the same with Riley. I hated keeping him in the dark. "I borrowed his armor today so I could replay the scene."

"Looks like you replayed it more than you intended."

"About that: Was anyone around when you and Edgar found me?" Yep, that was the first time I thought to ask that question. My mind was still awfully foggy.

"I didn't see anyone. You, Edgar?" She looked at the bird as if he might really reply. I was beginning to wonder myself.

Bianca could have hit me herself, of course. "I don't think whoever did it meant to hurt me." I watched her carefully. "I think they would have hit me harder." No reaction. "Probably just trying to scare me." Not a flicker. Okay, a new tack: "Do you have any idea who might have wanted to kill Angus?"

"I know *so* many people who wanted to kill him," she said. "But no one who tried to do it."

"Did you break up with him?"

"How do you break up with a guy you're not exactly with?"

Having sex with a guy counted as "with" in my book, but maybe not everyone's.

"But you did break up with Riley?"

"We broke up. Not sure who started it."

"Was Riley ever violent before your last fight?"

"No...What do you mean, 'before our last fight'?"

"Riley said he shoved you. Hard enough to make you fall down."

"Riley said that? Really? He reached out for me and I stepped back. Tripped over a rock."

"So he's not violent?

"No. He's just an idiot."

Though I felt good enough to drive, my head still hurt, so after getting a milkshake at the Whataburger drive-through I went home so I could lie down for a bit. "A bit" was all I got. My head throbbed, as much with questions as with pain. Who hit me? Bianca didn't react, but she was an actor as well as a falconer, so she could've fooled me. Jackie could have done it, followed me there from rehearsal. John Robert too. It could have been any of the Rennies hanging around. It could have been...

Doug. He knew I had the armor. But why would he try to scare me off his own investigation? I got up, booted up my laptop, and got back to work. About fifteen minutes later, I found something interesting. Doug had been upper level management for a large corporation before going to work for the Ren faire. His new job had to be quite a step down, both in pay and prestige. Why would he do that? He didn't seem to be in love with faire life, so...

I called his former place of employment, Alber Enterprises. "Hello, this is Irene from What a Temp! I'm calling to—"

"What a Temp? I've never heard of you."

Arghh. I should have come up with a better name. Dang head. Dang Whataburger. Hey. "Actually," I lowered my voice, "I'm from Whataburger. One of your former employees has applied for a management position here."

"Really?"

"That's why I said 'What a Temp.' People can be funny about burger work."

"Burger work? You're trying to tell me that one of our employees is applying for burger work at Whataburger?"

"We have very good benefits," I said in a haughty tone. "All the fries you can eat."

"Rosie?" she said, "Is this you? Very funny."

Dang. Really messed this one up. That'd teach me to try to be clever after being hit on the head. "Seriously, it's Irene with Whataburger. I just want to know if you can tell me why Doug Agravaine left your employment."

"*Doug*'s applying at Whataburger?"

"Free fries."

"Huh. Well, I can tell you he was terminated."

"Oh. Can you tell me why? Maybe we don't want him at Whataburger."

"All I will say is that if he winds up there, it would serve him right."

"Good thing you didn't use In-N-Out Burger," Uncle Bob said when I called him just after five. "I can just hear *that* conversation. Hey, I'm on my way somewhere. Can we talk a little later?"

"Sure." I was hoping that was an invitation to sit in his backyard and drink beer. "Your house?"

"No, uh, well..."

This was mysterious. Uncle Bob rarely vacillated. "Where are you going?" I asked.

"The gym," he mumbled.

I had never heard my uncle use that particular word. "Gym? What gym? I'll meet you there."

"The LA Fitness off Camelback on Thirty-second. Say seven fifteen?"

"See you then."

I arrived a little early—not typical for me, but I wanted to do a little spying, see if I could catch a glimpse of Uncle Bob lifting weights or riding a bike or whatever. I told the guy at the reception desk I was just looking for someone. He looked me up and down, smirked, and waved me in. Must have decided I didn't look like someone who would sneak in to use a gym. I couldn't decide whether to be offended or not.

I went first to the big room with all the bikes and stair climbers. No Uncle Bob. I walked past all the disgustingly disciplined people in the weights area. No Uncle Bob there, either, unless he'd grown some really big muscles. I made my way through the women's locker room to the pool, where the chlorine tang nearly knocked me off my feet. Several people were swimming laps in the roped-off aisles. None of them were my uncle.

Huh. I walked slowly toward the gym's entrance, past the classrooms. Was this just a convenient place to meet? No. There were plenty of restaurants and bars nearby. So where was my uncle? A blast of Latin music about knocked me off my feet as a door opened and a woman scooted out of one of the classrooms. An amplified voice said, "All right, Zum-bers. That's it for today. See you—" The door closed again, but only for a moment. A wave of women in brightly colored workout gear swept into the hallway. I hugged the wall to let them pass by: women chattering about their kids, women wiping their faces, women fluffing their hair—and my uncle, red-faced and smiling.

"Uncle Bob?"

He gave me a sheepish grin.

I looked back at the open door. He'd come from there, right? "Were you in a Zumba class?"

He nodded, probably because he was still breathing so hard he couldn't speak.

"Oh." A light came on in my head, and I got close enough to smell a sort of soapy sweat mixed with the Old Spice deodorant he always wore. "You're investigating someone, right?"

He smiled and gulped air. "I'll explain." Big breaths. "After a shower."

Chapter 44

At seven fifteen on the dot, Uncle Bob met me in the gym's lobby, his hair still damp and his skin still glowing. "You wanna grab something here?" He nodded at the juice bar.

"Um, no. Not unless you need to for...work, you know." Maybe whoever he was investigating liked smoothies.

He shook his head. "Okay, let's go to Tee Pee."

Fifteen minutes later, I stepped inside Tee Pee Mexican Food, and headed toward the bar. This was more like it: a semi-dark space with Christmas lights on all year and a bar with a "D Backs" license plate mounted above the margarita blender. Comfy but not hip, sort of like Uncle Bob.

He beat me there by a couple of minutes, so he was already talking to the bartender: "And a Diet Coke."

Good thing I didn't a have drink yet 'cause I would've done a spit take. Who was this and what had he done with my uncle? I ordered a Negro Modelo and a Tee Pee special and sat down at a nearby booth with my uncle. "Bobby, you got some 'splainin' to do."

"Nice." Uncle Bob was big fan of *Lucy*. "So, how'd it go today?"

"Bobby..." I shook my head at him.

He laughed. "All right, all right. I'm just trying to lose a little weight, you know."

I didn't know. My uncle had always seemed perfectly happy being, um, portly. "Really? And Zumba? Seems like you'd prefer..." I was stuck. The Uncle Bob I knew preferred hand-to-mouth exercise, preferably with a beer or a chicken leg in that hand.

"I know." He chuckled. "But after Bette and I took those salsa lessons..."

Now I did do a spit take.

"I discovered I really liked Latin music. Once I joined the gym…" I would have choked again if I hadn't already seen him there. "I was planning to swim, but on my way to the locker rooms, I heard the music." He grinned so wide I could see a glint of gold in the back of his mouth. "So, Zumba. I've already lost eight pounds."

The waiter dropped off a taco salad and my Tee Pee special. As you can tell from the name of the restaurant, it wasn't the most authentic Mexican food in town, but I loved the way they covered everything in cheese. My meal must have been three billion calories. "But you were just eating broasted chicken and drinking tequila a few days ago." I dug into my enchilada.

"That was a slip-up." Uncle Bob looked at his salad, a little sadly.

"Okay. Losing weight's good," I mumbled around a mouthful of melted cheese. "But why?"

"Well, last time I saw Bette"—since Uncle Bob's girlfriend lived in Colorado, they only saw each other a couple times a month—"she said something about hoping we'd be together for a long time. Or maybe I said that." Even in the dim light of the bar I could see his cheeks flush. "Anyway, I realized that if I want to be around for a while, I'd better clean up my act a little." I must have looked stricken, either at the thought of my uncle dieting or the idea that he wouldn't be around forever, I wasn't sure, but something must've shown on my face because Uncle Bob reached over the table and patted my hand. Then he grabbed my taco. "But I'm not goin' crazy with this health kick. Moderation, you know." He took an enormous bite of taco and gave it back to me. "So, what did you learn today?"

"Not as much as I'd hoped." I told him about Riley and Angus and Bianca.

"Did you say you met Bianca's muse?"

"No, I met her at the mews. It's what they call a place where you keep birds."

"Mews…" mused Uncle Bob. He loved new words. "You really

think Bianca could've pulled off the joust?"

"I do." I also still wondered if she could have hit me on the head, but I didn't tell Uncle Bob about that particular incident. I felt dumb enough without having to hear him say it too.

"So she's a good rider?"

Arghh. I knew I forgot to check on something.

Cockadoodledoo!

"Where are we?" asked my uncle. "Old MacDonalds's farm?"

Saved by the rooster. I picked up. "Doug? Yeah, thanks for calling me back. I'm just checking everyone's background. Just typical procedure. I'm sure you understand why. So...may I ask why you left Alber Enterprises?" Uncle Bob raised an eyebrow at me. "So you weren't terminated?" My uncle sat back in his chair. "I see. Thank you for being honest. Yes, we'll both be at the faire tomorrow." I hung up and answered the question in my uncle's eyes. "Insurance fraud. He resigned before they could fire him."

"Really? Did he serve jail time?"

"Nothing on his record, but he was accused."

"Big difference between accused and guilty, Olive. You should know that."

"I know. But I do think there's something...hinky about him."

"Hinky. Love that word. Don't know why. Hinky."

"But...insurance fraud. Could that fit into this scenario?"

"Didn't you tell me he wasn't going to have his insurance guys investigate the incident with the wizard?"

"Yeah."

"That seems like the opposite of insurance fraud."

"Maybe you can stop in and see him tomorrow when you're at the faire, see if you think he's..."

"Hinky." He grinned. "But about tomorrow, do you really think you need me actually there, or—"

"Yes." Uncle Bob always picked up information I didn't.

He sighed. "It's going to be like backstage at the theater, isn't it?"

My uncle was not a big fan of loud people running around in

their underwear and breaking into show tunes. "No, it won't. All these people will be clothed." I thought about the guy in the fur diaper. Maybe he took Fridays off. "I think you should probably wear a costume yourself."

"I thought the same thing. If I really need to go, that is."

"You do. Do you want me to rent a costume for you?"

"Nah." Uncle Bob sighed dramatically. Sheesh, and he thought actors were bad. "I suspected you'd want me there, so I already figured it out. All of this clean living I'm doing now..." he took a big slurp of his Diet Coke. "I'm gonna be a monk."

"I think you'll like this ringtone much better." Uncle Bob reached across the basket of chips to hand me back my phone. "Not nearly as annoying. Sorta soothing, even." His hand grabbed a tortilla chip on the way back to his side of the table, but just one. "So, see you tomorrow morning? You wanna drive together?"

"I can't. I have rehearsal beforehand."

"I forgot. It's weird, you rehearsing in the morning. You know, you haven't said much about that lately. Other than the fact that Jackie's a man."

"And she—he—had a fight with Angus."

"The plot thickens. Anything more on the composer?"

"Nothing more on him, but..." I used the ripping-off-the-Band-Aid trick again: "John Robert said the play will move to La Jolla Playhouse and then on to New York and hopefully to Broadway."

"Wow." Uncle Bob pushed back his chair. "Wow." His jowls jiggled as he shook his head and his eyes...shone? Were those tears? "I am so proud of you."

I reached a hand across the table and put it on top of his big paw. "Even though it means I'll have to leave?"

"You'll come visit your old uncle, I know. And I've always wanted to go to a Broadway show. Especially one starring my niece." His smile dimmed. "But what about Matt?"

"I don't know." I took my hand back and picked up my beer.

"The timing couldn't be worse. He just asked me to move in with him."

"He did?" Uncle Bob's eyes got that shine again. "So? One choice doesn't necessarily preclude the other, you know. Have you ever heard about Dolly Parton's husband?"

"Yeah. As a matter of fact I have. Thanks."

"Sorry." Uncle Bob held up his hands in surrender. "I didn't mean to make you sore."

"It's just..." I picked at the label on my beer bottle. "I don't know what I want."

"Do you love Matt?" This was awfully straightforward for my uncle. For anyone in my family, really.

"Yeah."

"Do you think it's fear of commitment?" said my new straight-talking uncle.

"What?" I said. "No. It's having to choose between Matt and a Broadway career."

"You know, I don't think that's it. I think that part could be worked out. I think you're afraid."

"Afraid of commitment."

"Afraid to be loved." Uncle Bob's eyes went from misty to hard, like they wanted to cut something. "Sometimes I just want to shake them. Your parents. They have no idea how much they screwed you up."

Uncle Bob's defense of me was comforting, but... "Am I that screwed up?"

His eyes got gentle again. "Listen, I've known you since you were little. After Cody's accident you went from being a sunny outgoing kid into a little snail curled up in a shell. The only time you poked your head out was when you were onstage. And even then, that was as a character, not as yourself. It's just been this past few years I've seen the real Olive take some steps out into the world. I think part of that was about getting to know your brother better as a person instead of a symbol of what went wrong. And the other thing—person—who's drawn you out is Matt."

I didn't know what to say. Uncle Bob reached over and patted my hand. "It's okay to be afraid of things, Olive. Even love. It's scary stuff. You might get hurt, or hurt somebody else. You have to decide for yourself if it's worth it."

Chapter 45

I wasn't feeling great when I got home. Could have been the hit on the head, the realization that yes, I was pretty messed up, or the three pounds of cheese I ate. But an hour later, I felt better. Mostly because I was talking to Matt. His mom's prognosis was looking good—maybe a month or two in a rehab facility, then she could come home. "I'm trying to find some help for Dad," he said. "Someone to come and help him clean and cook, do the laundry, that sort of thing. I'm helping him figure out the books for the farm, the household bills. All of that."

"It's a lot. You holding up okay?"

"I don't know. It's tough being back home. Here I'm not Matt Jenkins, I'm Robert and Mary Sue's son. I love my folks and friends here, but I swear I revert to my sixteen-year-old self every time I open my mouth."

"I do that most times I open my mouth."

He laughed. It was a beautiful sound. "Tell me about your day. Catch any crooks?"

"No, but..." I hadn't planned on telling Matt about getting hit on the head, partly because I didn't want him to worry about me and my PI job, and partly because the whole idea seemed stupid in hindsight. But I was tired of being that little snail in its shell, so I told him all about it.

He was quiet for a moment afterward, then said, "You sure you're okay now?"

"As clever as ever. Hey, that rhymes. See, I can rhyme, so I must be okay. I think that's one of the tests they do."

"The famous Ziegwart Rhyming and Comprehension Test,"

Matt said. "One of the top cognitive measurement tools."

"Hey," I said, poking my snail head out a little further. "I've been thinking about your question."

"Yeah?"

"But I have a few questions for you first."

"Okay. Shoot."

"Does it bother you when I have to kiss other actors onstage?"

"Well, it is sort of weird, but I understand it's not you doing the kissing. It's your character. Right?"

He sounded like he needed a little reassurance. "Right. Same thing with me being onstage in my underwear? It's weird but you're okay with it?"

"Yes."

"How about nudity?"

"Um...I don't know about that."

"Me neither. Not sure I could even do a nude role, but I had to ask."

"Fair enough."

"You know, I'll probably never make a lot of money, which means our apartment—*if* we had one—wouldn't be deluxe."

"I was raised in a hundred-year-old farmhouse without air conditioning," Matt said. "I can live without deluxe. And maybe you will make money. "

"It's pretty unlikely. You need to know that up front. Even Broadway actors don't make the kind of money you'd think. Except for the lucky few who make it big in film, we're a poor lot. We only make money when we're working, and there are only so many roles a year that I would be right for, and those roles will dwindle as I get older."

"...Okay."

"If I'm here in Phoenix, I can pick up work from Uncle Bob. But things could be tighter if I have to move—and I'll probably need to move. Especially if I go on with this play."

"Oh...Of course. To New York?"

"To San Diego first, then maybe New York. I have to go where the play goes." This didn't sound great, even to me. "It's not exactly a stable life."

"...It doesn't matter. This is your dream come true. We can work something out."

But could we? How could he move with me to all these places? I didn't even know how long I'd be in each city (runs got extended or cut short all the time). My head suddenly hurt a lot. I didn't think it was the blow that caused it.

"Listen," I said, "I've got go to bed. I'm beat."

"Okay, but please don't worry. We can work something out. I love you."

"I love you too."

Maybe we could work something out.

Chapter 46

Lord, my head hurt. Way worse this morning than it did yesterday. I swigged down an Advil with my coffee and hoped it would kick in by the time I got to rehearsal.

The traffic on the Superstition Highway didn't help my headache. Or the thought of being late to rehearsal again. How long did it take Advil to work anyways? I was still wondering that when Riley called. "You sound rough," he said. "You okay?" Yes, my friend who was in jail and no longer had a girlfriend or a place to live asked if I was okay. It put things into perspective.

"Just a headache."

"That sucks. Hey, you know how hard is it is to get an aspirin in jail? It's like they're made outta gold or something."

"Are *you* okay?"

"Yeah. It's just...I didn't think I'd be here this long. The first few days I just thought of it like camp"—Riley's camp experience must have been wild—"so it wasn't so bad. But it's not like camp. I mean, the food's crappy like it is there—except for the pancakes—but," he lowered his voice, "some of the guys are pretty scary, you know? And people around here keep telling me it's way worse in prison. I'm not going to prison though, right?"

This was awkward. I was hired by the Ren faire, not Riley. Sure, we were talking every day. I'd told myself it wasn't for moral support, but to find out what he knew. But I'd been treating him like a friend. I needed to start treating him like a suspect. So I didn't say anything.

Riley waited, then gave a big defeated sigh. "Yeah. Well...Hey, how'd filming go?"

Filming...filming...Ah. “Great. The armor worked out great. By the way, did you talk to anyone outside the jail yesterday—besides your lawyer, I mean? Tell anyone about loaning me the armor?”

“No.”

“Does everyone know you’re in jail?” Maybe somebody thought I was Riley.

“My mom doesn’t.”

“What?”

“I don’t want to tell her unless I have to. She hates that I smoke weed.”

“Does everyone at the Ren faire know?”

“Yeah, nobody there cares if you smoke. In fact, one of the guys—”

“Do they know you’re *in jail*?”

“Oh. Yeah. Word gets around pretty fast.”

Then my attacker knew it wasn’t Riley wearing that armor. I was the target. But why? Was someone trying to steer me away from Riley? “Is there anyone at the faire who’d be likely to defend you?”

“Like on a witness stand?”

“No, sorry, my head is a little fuzzy. Like someone who might try to convince me that you weren’t purposely involved with Angus’s death.”

“I dunno. Everybody there likes me pretty well, and...yeah. They probably would. Defend me.”

A little jolt of excitement cleared my head for a moment. “Who? And why?”

“I dunno. See, they’d do it, but it wouldn’t be about me. It’d be about the clan, the tribe, you know. All for one and one for all.”

“Were the Three Musketeers in the Renaissance?”

“I dunno. But you get what I’m saying, right?”

I did. Hitting me on the head was a warning: to back off and leave the faire alone.

But I was made of sterner stuff. Plus now that my head was a little clearer, I remembered the question I really wanted to ask

Riley. I decided to go at it sideways. "I saw Bianca with the birds again yesterday," I said. "She really loves them."

"Yeah."

"So does she love all animals? Hey," I said as if a thought had just occurred to me, "can you have cats and dogs at the fair? Or just birds and horses?" I put the emphasis on "horses."

"It's too hard to keep a pet when you're traveling. You'd have to keep him locked up in your trailer or tent and it can get hot or cold. But a lot of people have animals in their acts."

"Like your horse. You ever ride him off hours? With Bianca?"

"Sure. Angus would usually let her borrow his horse. Oh man..." Riley groaned. "I never even thought of that before. Should've known something was up."

Dang, had I let him know my suspicions?

"Her and Angus, man. Can't believe I didn't see it."

Phew. I hadn't shown my hand. And I had my answer.

Bianca knew how to ride.

So did John Robert.

And Hayden.

It wasn't my fine deductive skills that enabled me to suss out this information. It was Jackie, who met me at the front door at the ranch house. "The boys are out riding." She led me through the house as if she owned it. "But there are croissants and mimosa makings on the back patio."

I followed her through the French door onto the patio. "Are you working the faire today?"

"I believe Benjamin will be there." You had to admire her unflappability. "Oh my." She shaded her eyes with a gloved hand. "I do love watching men ride."

I followed her gaze to the desert, pink and gold with the morning sun. The men rode toward us, Hayden on a tall bay, John Robert on a slightly smaller pinto. They both knew how to sit a horse, especially Hayden, who doffed an imaginary cowboy hat as he pulled up short in front of us, flashed a toothy Kennedy-esque grin, then wheeled around and trotted toward the corral.

Once they got the horses settled, John Robert excused himself to use the bathroom, and Hayden sat down between Jackie and me. "That was some pretty fancy riding," I said in my regular voice. "Where'd you learn to ride like that?"

"I spent summers on my uncle's ranch in Lone Pine. It's a little town in California, just east of the Sierra Nevada."

"That's where you're from?"

"No. LA born and bred. Still stay there between gigs, but I'm on the road most of the year."

"Really? How is that, the traveling? Do you get lonely?" I told myself I was asking as a detective, not as an actor who was trying to decide whether to give up her home for the traveling thespian life.

"Sometimes." Hayden gave me a slow smile. Oh no. He thought I was hitting on him.

"You two should go riding sometime," Jackie said. I wished I were sitting next to her so I could kick her.

"All right, ladies and gents!" John Robert burst out of the French doors, his enthusiasm preceding him like a parade. "I realized I had it all wrong yesterday."

"Had what wrong?" I asked in my Marilyn voice.

"*Kennelot.*"

"So you're changing the name?"

"No, no, no, love the name. No, I was all wrong about the direction of the show."

Phew. When we left him, he was thinking about using the missiles as a not-very-subtle metaphor for JFK's male appendage.

"So...It's a comedy!"

"*Camelot*? A comedy?" I asked.

"They did it with *Spamalot*, so why not this?"

Jackie coughed delicately into a gloved hand. "It seems to me that the Kennedy story is more...tragic?"

"No, a comedy! Like one of those British sex farces."

"Except American, of course." Hayden had a wicked gleam in

his eye.

"Exactly. A British-style American sex farce. For example, Jackie will find you two in bed." John Robert paced excitedly, his arms windmilling as he talked. "But there will be a lot of slamming doors and people in their underwear."

"Not me," Jackie said, "I'm the straight man, or woman as it were."

"Of course," said John Robert. "We'll add a butler..."

"Maybe Merlin could be the butler?" said Hayden. I elbowed him.

"No, not the butler..." said John Robert. "But we do need a Merlin..."

"How about J. Edgar Hoover?" asked Hayden. "You could put him in a dress part of the time. Sort of like Jack Lemmon in *Some Like It Hot.*"

"Stop it," I whispered.

"Of course!" John Robert's hands waved like two happy birds. "The Marilyn reference from *Some Like It Hot* is perfect. A cross-dressing J. Edgar, slamming doors and everyone running around in their underwear. Everyone except Jackie." She smiled graciously at John Robert and he grinned back. "How can it not be a hit?"

Chapter 47

The rehearsal was a rollercoaster. The lowest point was when John Robert decided to add a cheer about missiles (he obviously had a thing about missiles). Yes, a cheer: "Trojans, Trojans, we will never break!" Yes, really.

The pinnacle of the rehearsal was some pinnacle, though. "Just want to let you know we've got a new backer," he said. "Not only is he thrilled about the idea" —he was?—"but he thinks we may be able to workshop it at the Kennedy Center for the Performing Arts on the way to Broadway. Now, they don't typically do workshops, but he has some pull with...the Kennedy family! Can you believe it?"

It *was* hard to believe. It was also exciting. I mean, if you had to choose between being on Broadway in a clunker, or not being on Broadway at all, which would you choose?

After rehearsal, I stopped at the 7 Eleven to change. The clerk at the cash register was turned away from me, long black hair down her back. I slipped into the bathroom and out again, clad in my multitude of filmy scarves. I grabbed a power bar and took it to the cashier. Just seemed polite to buy something in exchange for the use of for their bathroom/dressing room. But the clerk was not a woman. It was the same guy I'd met on Tuesday, just wore his hair down today.

"Ren faire again, huh?" he said, ringing up my purchase.

I fastened the veil across the bottom half of my face. Maybe he'd remember the costume, not the face...Arghh. Sure he might remember the costume, the *costumes*. And they were just unusual enough that he might mention it to someone—a woman going from

Marilyn Monroe to a belly dancer. I was going to have to find another place to change.

"Pretty popular place, the faire. That guy goes a lot too." The clerk pointed with his chin to a customer pumping gas outside. I nodded my thanks for the change he gave me, and headed to my car. The Ren fairegoer, who was now on his way into the store to pay for his gas, smiled at me with a sort of "Hey, you too?" smile.

I froze. I'd seen that smile just a few minutes ago. It was John Robert.

No flash of recognition in his eyes. The wig and scarves and contacts must've done their trick. But now what? I couldn't follow him right then—I'd promised Jasmine I'd check in with her before the fair opened, and true to the period, she declined to carry a cell phone.

Maybe I could get ahead of him. I raced to the faire, jumped out of my truck, ran to the stage where Jasmine was setting up, checked in, grabbed my ass-sign and raced back out to the entrance, arriving just as the faire was opening. Lots of cars already parked. I made a loop around the parking lot. I'd noted the make of John Robert's car (a Land Rover) and license number (HDB1008), but didn't see it there. Maybe he stopped on the way? I waited at the entrance for a few minutes, turning around every so often to show my sign to folks coming in. I kept an eye out for John Robert, who'd been wearing the same short, hooded cape I saw him in the day of the joust. Of course I didn't see him. Why didn't I just let Jasmine wait? What had I been thinking?

Actually, I hadn't been thinking, at least not about John Robert. I'd been focused on the suspects from the faire, and yes, sidetracked by the thought of Broadway. Arghh. I was easily distracted by nature, and there were too many facets to this investigation, too many ways to go.

"Here you are."

"Aah!"

It was just Jasmine. "Scared the bloody life outta me," I said. I was a little grouchy over losing John Robert.

"My apologies, milady. I should have told you, but standing by the entrance—"

"You mean wigglin' me arse near the entrance." Yep, a little grouchy.

Jasmine put a finger to her lips. "As I was saying, my *mute* friend, you'd better move on. People are so overwhelmed when they first arrive that they're not as likely to remember you. Keep to the inside of the faire."

And miss John Robert. Still I nodded and moved on. What else could I do?

I didn't see him, of course, not with billions (okay thousands) of people milling about the faire. But I did see someone who jogged an important memory. "I've got the money I owe you," I said to the fortuneteller. "Let's go inside." Once inside the crimson caravan, I took thirty dollars from a pouch on my belt and handed it to the crone. Then I pulled out another twenty, holding the extra cash just out of reach. "How did you know about William?" I said. "And how did you know to warn me? And how did you know about the storm?"

"When was this we talked?" The old woman's eyes crinkled in concentration.

"Tuesday."

"Ah. The haboob I knew because I have a weather app on my phone—don't tell anyone I have my phone on me, all right? The warning, well, spies are never well-liked." Ouch. "But William...what did I say about William?"

"You didn't say anything, but the card you drew for me was the Magician, upside-down."

"I see." She frowned. "The cards aren't usually that literal..."

"Do you know anyone who might want to harm William?" I watched her closely, employing a trick I'd learned from Uncle Bob. He'd told me that people usually gaze one direction when telling the truth and a different direction when telling a lie. The woman had looked slightly right when telling me about the weather app, which seemed like a truth.

"William? No." Her eyes looked slightly right.

"How about Angus? Do you know who hurt him?"

"No," she said, closing her eyes. Dang.

"Do you think the cards might have an answer?" I didn't really believe in tarot—or at least I didn't think I did—but she might tell me something of use again. She shrugged and began to shuffle the cards.

"Just one card again," I said. "It's all I have time for."

"That's not a good complete reading, but if you insist." She held out the deck to me. I pulled out a card, placed it face up on the table and then wished I hadn't. The card showed a tall tower being hit by lightning. It was on fire, flames bursting from the roof and licking out of the windows. Worst of all were the figures—a man and a woman—falling head first toward the ground, tongues of fire chasing them down. "Please tell me that's not as bad as it looks."

"No card is good or bad, but the Tower...Hmm..." The woman tapped the card with an arthritic finger. "It signifies destruction, great upheaval, perhaps a crisis."

Was this another warning? "What kind of crisis? Is there something I should avoid?" Though I wanted to solve this case, I didn't want to end up leaping from a burning building.

"You can't avoid it. All you can do is learn from it."

"Wow. Okay. Thanks, I guess." I handed her the money. "You'll let me know if you hear anything else?"

"It depends."

"On what?"

"On whether you survive your Tower experience."

Chapter 48

Great. Now I was looking over my shoulder as well as looking for John Robert and trying to hear gossip about Angus, and Bianca, and Riley, and William. I kept trying to tell myself that the woman was just an actor trying to scare me off my investigation, but I was the one who picked the Tower, and it was one scary card. I was shaken enough that I nearly missed the hooded figure in my peripheral vision. John Robert? No, another hooded man. Another familiar one.

"Thought you were on a diet," I said to the monk sitting at a picnic table. He was chewing on a ginormous turkey leg.

"I have it on good authority that turkey is diet food," said Uncle Bob.

I nodded at his pewter tankard as I sat across from him. "And the beer?"

"Fooled you." Uncle Bob tipped the stein toward me so I could see its contents. "Just water, for now. I'm allowing myself one beer at the end of the day. Hey," he waved his drumstick at the crowd in the street or maybe at a pirate. "This is great. Why didn't you bring me here before?"

Was he teasing me? No, my uncle's face looked as earnest as one stuffed with a turkey leg could. "It's not like theater," he said. "It's more like a different world. And I get to be part of it. I love it here."

Uncle Bob a Rennie. Whoda thunk it?

I looked around to make sure no one was listening, then leaned across the table. "Do you have your phone?" I whispered, leaning across the table.

"Yes," he whispered back, taking his phone out of a pocket in his robe.

"I want you to Google a photo."

"Why are we whispering?"

"I'm really not supposed to use a phone."

"You're not supposed to be talking either."

Oops.

"And it's okay if *I* use the phone, right?"

"Yeah." I stopped whispering and sat back. "I'm not thinking straight. I'm a little freaked out." I told him about the Tower card.

"Wow," he said, looking at his phone. "You're right. That is one creepy card."

"Oh, I didn't mean you should look up the tarot card. Try to find a recent photo of John Robert Turner."

"The playwright guy you're working with?" He tapped on his screen. "I've been wondering why you hadn't said much about him. Thought he was off your radar."

"Only because I was blinded by Broadway."

"So you still suspect him?"

It was at this moment that I realized something. Uncle Bob had let me take the lead on this investigation. And I was screwing it up.

I pushed away the guilt so I could do the work I needed to. "He's got kind of a teddy bear face. And today he's wearing a short brown hooded cloak."

"Sounds like an Ewok."

"That's John Robert. Cuddly-looking but possibly dangerous." Uncle Bob turned his phone toward me so I could see the photo he'd pulled up. "Yeah, that's him. If you see him, follow him." I tried to sound professional so Uncle Bob wouldn't know how lost I really was with this investigation. "I'd be especially interested to know if he talks to Bianca, or any jousters." I remembered that John Robert himself could ride. "Or any armor makers."

"There are armor makers here? This is the greatest place ever," said Monk-le Bob. "You want to hear what I learned today?" I nodded, and he told me about hanging out at the jousting arena, asking questions. "The most important thing I came away with is that jousting is really specialized. You have to be strong, a good rider, and you have to practice."

"So our suspect has to be a jouster."

"Pretty much. They said a cowboy might be able to pull it off. They probably wouldn't be able to do all of the things jousters do, like putting a lance tip through a wooden ring—man, that was impressive—but you said the imposter basically just rode toward Angus and knocked him off his horse, right?"

"Right."

"Yeah, a cowboy could probably do that."

"Or a cowgirl." I thought of Bianca.

"Egads," said Uncle Bob.

"Egads?"

"Thought I'd try some Ren faire speak. Is that Ren faire speak?"

"Not sure. That's why I'm a mime."

"Basically what I meant was, crap. Just when I thought we'd narrowed down our suspect list."

Chapter 49

But we *had* narrowed down our list. How many jousters or cowboys/cowgirls could there be at one Ren faire? Now to figure out who exactly they were. I made a note to ask Doug. He might know.

As I wiggled and jiggled my way through the faire, I realized I'd dropped another investigative thread: William's accident. I had the feeling that his OD and Angus's death could be connected, but how? William had seemed troubled that night—and he'd said something about an appointment. Could someone have given him some bad drugs on purpose, maybe some 'devil weed'?

And something else connected the two men: Bianca. She was conveniently nearby when the accident happened, by herself in the dark empty fairegrounds. Could she have had something to do with William's accident, and then changed her mind when she heard me shouting for help?

No one from the belly dance show was around, so I ducked into the falconry stage. "The average human male has a gripping strength of ninety pounds," Bianca's amplified voice floated toward me. I wanted to talk to her in private this time. "Owls like Snowy here have a gripping strength of a *thousand* pounds." Maybe if I waited backstage. "Snowy is a barn owl. We got him after he'd been hit by a car." Ah, one of the doors to the mews was open. "All of our birds came from wildlife rehabilitation facilities or zoos and for one reason or another, were deemed unfit to be returned to the wild." I slipped backstage. "It's illegal to keep a wild bird as a pet or to sell it. Owls like Snowy here are endangered. It's all of our jobs to make sure they thrive."

I hurriedly searched the backstage area for any sign of drugs. Nada. The cages were all empty, the birds all out with Bianca and her assistants, flying and diving and doing cool bird-type things. The big cage in the back still had the sheet thrown over it. Ah ha. I walked toward it. Something inside the cage rustled. Was it really a bird? Was it still sick? I crept closer to see, and *Aaah!* Something flew at me, wings beating in my face. Everything was blackness and feathers and horrible shrieking and—

"On her head!" Bianca's voice cut through the tumult. The black maelstrom lifted, but not far. I felt claws on my scalp, even through my wig.

"Nevermore," said the raven on my head. "Nevermore."

"What are you doing here?" said Bianca.

"Sorry." I glanced at the big cage. Still covered. Edgar was my only attacker. "Oi fought your show wasn't over until Edgar and you had dinner onstage."

"We have more than one show. What are you doing here?"

"Oi wanted to see how you were doin.' It's the first time Oi had a chance to talk to you after the fing with William."

"The fing?"

"The in-ci-dent."

"You could have talked to me outside."

"Oi'm supposed to be silent in public. Besides, Oi just love birds, Oi do. Had a pet budgie when I was a tyke. They're a bit like fairies, yeah?"

"Fairies who'll rip your scalp off." She didn't have to remind me that I had a large bird on my head. His talons were sharp. "But not Edgar. Though he does make a pretty good watchdog. Come here, boy." She held out a hand, and Edgar blessedly left my head to fly to her. "Sorry. I'm just a little jittery after everything's that's happened. If I'd known it was you, I wouldn't have sent in the cavalry. I really appreciate you helping William. God knows what would've happened if you hadn't found him when you did."

"He's going to be okay, roight?"

"Yeah." The light was low, but I saw tears gather in her eyes.

"He's a good man, you know."

"Seems like it. Was it an OD?"

"Sort of." She bit off the words, as if to tell me that was all she'd say.

"Lucky you were about, yeah?"

"And you."

"I was headin' back to me car." I waited.

"It's really none of your business, but I was letting some of the owls hunt before the storm came up. Don't want to take all the wildness out of them."

"Sure. And Oi didn't mean to be so nosy." Yes, I did. "Thanks for fillin' me in."

"No worries. But next time you want to talk to me, wait outside, okay? I don't like people in the mews."

"All righty then. Toodle-oo." I walked out of the mews and into the crush of the faire, thinking not about John Robert or William or even Bianca, but...

What was in that cage?

Chapter 50

Riley would probably know, but I couldn't call him. I'd just have to wait to ask him until tomorrow morning. I didn't like it. I was not a patient person.

I was also a pretty sucky investigator. I circled the faire several times, but couldn't find John Robert. How had I lost him? An even better question: How had I lost sight of the fact that John Robert was a suspect? He might have been able to pull off the joust, given the way he rode that pinto this morning.

And Hayden rode too. Rode well. And he was at John Robert's ranch. Could he be a suspect? I couldn't see any connection between him and Angus, but that didn't mean there wasn't one.

Since Matt had told me he wasn't sure we'd be able to talk that night (a church supper), I'd planned to hang out at the afterhours faire party tonight, but it was a vague plan: I just hoped to pick up a little more information. But I needed to be proactive if I was ever going to solve this case. First on my to-do list: See William.

I went to his onsite wizard tent near closing time. William looked fine, sitting straight and tall on his throne, smiling at the fans who were lined up waiting to talk to him. After everyone had left, I slipped inside. "Hiya."

When he saw it was just me, William slumped back in his carved throne, the powerful wizard turning into a tired middle-aged man before my eyes. "Prudence, isn't it?"

"Oi was just stoppin' by to see how you're doin'. After the incident and all."

"As well as can be expected." Dark purplish shadows under his eyes. "Which means I should really go rest."

"O' course, o' course. Oi'll leave you to it. It's just I was 'specially concerned, seein' as how it was me who found you."

"Was it you? My thanks. And my apologies. I really don't remember the night at all."

"Nothing? Not even talkin' wif me while you were smoking like Gandalf?"

William shook his head. "Not even that."

"Word is maybe you got some bad stuff. That stuff you were smoking, maybe."

"Possibly."

Arghh. Could he be more vague? Maybe if I made him worry for me. "Is there someone that Oi should uh, avoid...buying from?"

"Prudence." He used his wizard voice as he stood up. "You should avoid buying. Period."

Well that was a bust. I left William's tent and walked through the now-closed faire to my truck, where I used my cell phone to call Uncle Bob. He picked up on speakerphone—he'd already left and was on his way home. No, he didn't see John Robert and no, he wasn't going back to the office but I was welcome to, and if I did could I make sure not to leave anything stinky in the trash?

I went home, changed out of my belly dancing costume and into street clothes, and drove to the office so I could use our computer and databases. It was time to start acting like a detective.

Before going down the research rabbit hole, I emailed Doug. "Could you give me a list of any faire people who jousted in the past? And maybe any cowboys you know of?"

Doug must have been working late, because his reply came right away: "Have no idea who may have jousted in the past. And cowboys I know of: Roy Rogers, John Wayne and Clint Eastwood. Hope that's helpful."

I never did like sarcasm. But he was right; it had been too much to hope for. I put that puzzle piece aside and picked up the next one: Hayden. I ran him through Duda Detectives's databases, Googled him, and looked him on IMDB.

Huh. Hayden Sanders had quite the resume. He'd appeared in

several TV shows and made a bunch of movies—mostly indies, but still. Ooh, he'd even appeared in an early film directed by Andre (yes, one-name, Oscar-winning Andre).

But...I went on to IMDB to see what I could about the films he'd made, more specifically, where they were filmed. All but one in Southern California. All the TV shows listed in his bio had been shot there too. But Hayden said he was on the road most of the time. On the road where? Doing what?

I searched, but I couldn't find any reason for him to be on the road. Maybe he just liked to travel.

There was a lot more info on John Robert, but nothing that led me to believe he was a jouster or a cowboy or—

Cowboy. Shit. I grabbed my phone and made a call.

"Unless you are calling me to apologize—and I do mean apologize with a capital A and drinks involved at a later date—I am hanging up on you." Loud country music blared in the background.

"Timothy—"

"You are speaking to Anita." Timothy's drag name. "To Anita Mann, the second-place winner in the Arizona Gay Rodeo's Wild Drag Race, which *someone* promised to watch."

"I know and I am so sorry."

"You should be. You didn't get to see my new Cher costume—a bellbottom jumpsuit with rhinestones."

Of course there were rhinestones.

"And you'll never get see it either, because it's white. *Was* white. I didn't even think about it until I was being dragged through the dirt."

"I'm sure you looked fabulous."

"I did, and you missed it."

"I'll make it up to you. And there will be cocktails involved."

"And hors d'ouvres."

"And hors d'ouvres."

"All right." Timothy finally sounded mollified. And I really was sorry I missed seeing him ride a steer in a rhinestoned Cher jumpsuit. "I am only forgiving you because I think this double-undercover thing is eating your brain." I was afraid it was. "So I guess I'll share my tasty little tidbit with you."

"Okay. Good." I had no idea what it could be.

"My friend Frederick came to watch me tonight, like a good friend would" —okay, maybe he wasn't completely mollified—"and guess who he pointed out?"

"Who?" I couldn't remember exactly who Frederick was or why Timothy thought I would know him.

"Benjamin."

"*Oh.*"

"He looked pretty fine, too, in his tight little Wranglers."

"Did you get introduced? Or did you want me to introduce you?"

"*No.* Let me finish my story." He paused, making sure I was going to give him the stage. "He looked fine in his tight little Wranglers, and his pearl snap-buttoned shirt and his black Stetson, *sitting on his horse*." Timothy paused again. "Now you can ask."

"His horse?"

"Benjamin was one of the barrel riders tonight. Took home first place."

Chapter 51

I hung up in a funk. All I wanted was for just one person to not be capable of killing Angus during the joust. Was that really too much to ask for?

Okay, the fortune-telling crone probably couldn't have done it. That was one person. Didn't make me feel better. In fact, it made me think of that Tower card. Maybe it was my investigation that was going up in flames.

And then, as if he knew I needed moral support, Matt called. "We're still at the church, and I can only talk a for a few minutes," he said. "But I wanted to let you know I'm coming home tomorrow night. Mom got admitted to the rehab center today, and between the social worker and the church, Dad's all set up. My flight arrives at nine thirty. Could you pick me up?"

"Of course."

"How's your head today?"

My head? With everything else going on, I'd forgotten all about it. I touched it. Still a little tender, but nothing bad. "Fine," I said. Then I waited for Matt to say something about being more careful, or less stupid. He didn't. Probably because he knew how hard it was for me to have admitted my stupidity to him. And because he wasn't my mother. "Hey, I know you don't have much time," I said, "but can I vent?"

"Shoot."

I told Matt all about my muddled investigation. Talking felt so good that I rambled on, and before he could get a word in edgewise, he had to go. "Dad's fading. I need to drive us home."

I drove home shortly afterward too. I'd done all I knew to do, at least for right then. Matt texted me right before I went to bed. "Can't wait to see you tomorrow night. XXXOOO."

I fell asleep wondering how it might feel to have him next to me every night.

John Robert had given us the weekend off from rehearsal, so I slept in an hour later the next morning. Bliss. I got dressed for the faire while eating a bagel. As I got into my truck I noticed I had cream cheese in my wig. Was this a thing that happened to women with long hair? I decided it was.

Riley called while I was just a few miles from the faire. I was also sitting in a mile-long traffic jam, something I'd managed to avoid when approaching from Harmony Ranch. "Happens every faire day," Riley said. "That's why it's cool to live on site...Oh..." he heaved a big sigh.

Uh oh. I didn't want to ask if he was sighing for not being at the faire, or not having the fifth-wheel, or even being in jail. I didn't have time for sad, which kinda sucked for Riley right now, but would be way better for him in the long run if I could prove someone else killed Angus

"I only have a few minutes—"

"So you think. Those traffic jams are killer, man."

"And I wanted to know if you know what's in the big cage that Bianca keeps covered."

"A bird?"

"Is that a question?"

"I thought you were pulling my leg. Of course it's a bird. What else would she keep in a cage?"

"But you've never seen it?"

"I might have. She volunteers for some wildlife rehab thing, so besides the birds in her show there's always other birds around. She helps them get well, then releases them or gets them to good homes and stuff."

Not anymore, she'd said. So why did she still have a sick bird?

The cars in front of me started to move, and I did too. At about five miles an hour. "Do you think Bianca could've had anything to do with Angus's death?"

"No way. Bianca would never hurt anyone. She's all peace and love and birds."

And wild sex. With bruises on her arms. "Hey, about Angus...Somebody told me they called him 'Charming Bully'."

"Yeah. He was such an asshole, but the kind you want to follow, you know?"

"Like the football player in high school who was mean to all the geeks, but everyone else wanted to be his friend?" I pushed away a few bad memories of being a theater geek in high school. No time for old tapes right now.

"Exactly."

I wished I could see Riley's face right then—I wasn't sure if he'd been the theater geek or the football player. "'Bully' also makes me think of fights," I prompted.

"Hell yeah. Angus was always getting in fights, just for the fun of it."

"With who?" I was almost at the turnoff to the faire.

"Everyone, man. He'd fight the other knights just to see who was toughest."

Dang. Now I had to check out all the non-jousting knights too. "But that's not bullying exactly."

"He did that too. He was especially mean to the gay guys."

"Anybody in particular?" I wanted to ask about Benjamin, but I knew better than to ask a leading question if I wanted to keep an open mind.

"Nah. Pretty much all of them."

Great. Now I had to check out all the knights and all the gay guys. My list of suspects was getting longer by the hour. I pulled onto the dirt road that led to the faire. "Did he ever fight with women? I mean, physically?"

"No." Riley's voice was emphatic. "There's a code of honor among us. Fighting with women is off limits—unless it's like mud wrestling or something." Riley swallowed, loudly enough that I heard it over the phone. "Which is why it was especially bad that I, uh, pushed Bianca. I'm not just a bad boyfriend. I'm a bad knight."

"Riley, I talked to Bianca. She said you didn't push her."

"What?"

"She said she just fell. She also said you're an idiot."

"Really? That's great. Hey, would you, um, tell her I've been thinking about her? That I'm sorry?"

"Sure." I needed to call Bianca anyway. She'd left me a voicemail and we'd been playing phone tag ever since. "Take care, Riley."

I veered off from the line of cars and pulled onto the side road that led to the employee parking lot. Dang. I was definitely late, and I had one more thing to do before I went to work. "Bianca?" I was surprised she picked up since the faire was already open, but then heard the squawking of birds in the background. Must be inside the mews. "It's Ivy. Everything okay?"

"Fine. I just wanted to...You're in touch with Riley, right?"

"Yeah. In fact, he just asked me to tell you he's been thinking about you. That he's sorry."

"...Okay. Let him know we're raising bail. We'll probably have enough tomorrow to get him out."

"We?"

"Lots of people around here. Pretty much everyone thinks Riley wasn't involved with the...accident."

"Pretty much everyone?"

"Yeah. And the others don't really care who did it."

Chapter 52

I was really late. I hurried through the faire to the Gimme Shimmie stage. "Sorry," I said to Jasmine. "Oi got stuck in—"

She zipped her lips, giving the gesture a slightly pissed-off flourish at the end. "It is well and good that you are kin to Doug," she said. "Or you would be looking for other employment." She thrust my sign at me. "Now go."

I did. I went straight to From Hoods to Snoods. Benjamin was at the shop, untangling ribbons from wreaths of silk flowers. I swept past him, crooking a finger to let him know he should follow me to the back of the shop, where a couple of costumed mannequins could hide us from view. "Congratulations," I said. "I heard you won first place last night."

"Thank you." His voice was wary.

"Which means you ride well enough to joust."

"Oh."

"And I heard you and Angus had it out once."

"He pushed my friend into a cactus. You know how much that hurts?"

"Actually, I do. Any other fights with Angus? Or times when he bullied you or your friends?"

Benjamin pressed his lips together but didn't say anything.

I sighed. I didn't want to ask the next question. "Do you have an alibi for the time of the joust? Maybe you were working here?"

His lips stayed where they were.

"No?" I asked. "You weren't working?"

Still nothing from Benjamin, which I took to mean no alibi.

"Well," I said, "thanks for being honest. Or at least not lying. I hope you didn't do it."

I did. Benjamin finally had his dream role, and he was an awesome Jackie. I hoped I wouldn't have to take that away from him.

I'd just left Benjamin and passed the Green Man swaying on his stilts in the middle of the road when...Oh no. Really?

I sidled up to the Green Man. "Cover me?" I whispered. He obligingly bent his leaf-covered boughs around me. I patted his trunk in thanks and peered out between his leaves.

Hayden/JFK was dressed in regular street clothes—a red T-shirt and khaki shorts, and seemed to be alone. He walked leisurely down the road—almost too leisurely, as if he was acting. And he was heading for Benjamin's shop. Had Benjamin told him he was Jackie?

No. Benjamin's shoulders jumped when he saw Hayden. He turned on his heel and headed for the interior of the shop.

"Excuse me." Hayden plucked a cap from one of the displays near the road. "Can you tell me what kind of feather this is?"

Benjamin, still facing away from Hayden, waved another employee over, a young woman. She bustled over to Hayden. "I believe that's a grouse feather, milord."

"Right." Hayden put the hat down. "Thank you." He pulled his phone from a pocket, glanced at it, and left the shop.

This was curious. Why was Hayden there if it wasn't about Benjamin? He didn't seem like the Renaissance-cap-wearing type. Maybe he needed a costume for some reason? He was on the move now. "Thanks for the camouflage," I said to the Green Man. He unwound his limbs from around me and bowed his head slightly. I took off after Hayden, staying hidden in the crowd, in case my belly dancer outfit disguise wasn't good enough to fool someone who'd been looking at me close-up for the past week.

Hayden. This was really weird. Did everyone and their uncle go to the Ren faire? Well, there were twelve thousand people a day, so yeah, maybe they did. Or maybe Hayden had found out I worked here and was looking for me. After all, he was flirting with me yesterday. Or maybe he was blackmailing Benjamin, and Benjamin pretended not to know him because he was afraid I was watching and would find out. It all made my head swim.

And just when I thought things couldn't get more muddled, Hayden turned to his left and made things even worse.

Chapter 53

Yep, Hayden turned left, walked up to the back door of the mews, knocked, and was admitted. By Bianca. Whom he hugged before entering the mews and shutting the door behind them.

I sat down on a bench outside a nearby jewelry booth. Thinking while walking was not my strong point and I needed all the brain cells I could muster for this puzzle. How did Hayden and Bianca know each other? I'd done background checks on both. Bianca was from Pennsylvania. She'd attended community college there for a few years before working in Ren fairs. No links to California or even the West Coast. And Hayden had no links to the East Coast. What the hell?

The mews door opened. I turned my back on it, and watched via a mirror meant for trying on necklaces. Hayden came out while Bianca stood in the doorway. She said something to him. He nodded, then hugged her again. She closed the door and he started down the road. I followed again at a respectable distance, silently thanking him for wearing a red shirt.

I didn't have to follow him for very long. He didn't watch any shows or browse any shops. He just headed for the exit and into the parking lot. I followed him, ducking behind cars, until I saw him get into his Prius and drive away.

I hurried back to the faire, trying to think while walking. Hayden had to be there to meet Bianca. And it must be important—he paid twenty-six dollars for the privilege to enter the faire and didn't even get a turkey leg. I made my way back to Benjamin's booth and again motioned him to the back. "I saw Hayden."

"I know. You didn't tell him? About me, I mean?" Benjamin's

eyes pleaded with me.

"No."

"It was just a coincidence?"

"I think he was here to see someone else. Listen, when did you and he start working with John Robert?"

"I auditioned a day before you did. Hayden was already at the ranch. I had the feeling he and John Robert somehow knew each other."

"Any idea how?" John Robert was from New York–the East Coast-West Coast dilemma again.

"No."

Dang. I said goodbye and walked away from all the hoods and snoods, lackadaisically wiggling my sign. So Hayden knew Bianca. Hayden knew John Robert, and had been at his ranch before the joust. What did it all mean?

The sound of bagpipes drove everything else from my mind (bagpipes can do that). Everything except that it must be noon if the Pulchritudinous Pipes Show was beginning. Arggh, late again: this time for a noon meeting with a monk.

Uncle Bob sat at the same picnic table as before, drinking iced tea. Two other black-robed men sat at the far end of the tab, enjoying fish and chips and big plastic cups of beer. "What's bothering you my child?" my uncle asked in a solemn voice.

"I'm just...bummed and confused. I don't feel like I know anything more than when we started." I filled him in on the latest news.

"You know a lot more. Just not enough. We knew this was going to be a tough gig."

"Yeah." I drew a frownie face in a little puddle of iced tea Uncle Bob had spilled.

"And I think you'll remember that with most cases you've worked, things just sort of come together at the end. Somehow."

"What happens if we don't find out who was responsible for

Angus's death? I mean, I know the client is still supposed to pay, but do they ever stiff you?"

"It happens." Uncle Bob sucked on his iced tea straw, looking longingly at the monks' beer (or maybe the fries). "But that happens with any business. Don't worry about it. And I've got something that could help..." He leaned forward over the table, not an easy task for a man of his girth. "Pink called me last night."

Pink, or Detective Pinkstaff as he was known at the Phoenix PD, was one of my uncle's best friends. "He knows we're working this case. Sent us something from the coroner's assistant he thought we would find interesting." My uncle paused. For someone who wasn't in theater, he sure had a flair for the dramatic.

"And?" I asked, to get the ball rolling.

"He said the body—Angus"—that was one thing I loved about my uncle. No one was ever just a body to him—"had scratches on his face. Not caused by the joust."

"They're sure? It couldn't have been a scrape from the helmet or something?"

"No. They're going to run some tests, hoping there's some more evidence there—but the guy told Pink it looked like the scratches were caused the night before he died."

"Like maybe he got into a fight and someone scratched his face."

"Exactly."

"Huh." I told Uncle Bob about the bruises on Bianca's arms. "But..." I tried to put my thoughts together.

"You don't think she did it?"

"Riley said that there's a code of chivalry here—that men don't fight with women."

"But women might fight with men."

"I don't know. I got the impression the bruises were from..." Have you ever been talking when suddenly all the noise around you went quiet so that your words rang out really really loud? That was what happened as soon as I said "...ROUGH SEX."

The two monks sitting at our table giggled. Yes, giggled.

"Plus," I plowed ahead, pretending that a dozen nearby people were not wondering about my sex life, "though Bianca could have been the jouster, she's the least likely candidate. Being a woman, she probably doesn't have as much upper body strength as the men, and she was at the scene of the accident afterward. She could have dumped the armor and run to the arena, but..."

"Yeah. I see the problem. But she could have planned it."

I nodded. "I know. And about a dozen people—that we know of—could have carried it out. I'm still bummed and confused."

The monks finished their meals and got up.

"God be with you, my friend," one said to Uncle Bob.

"And with you," said the monk who'd taken over my uncle.

"Looks like you've already made friends." I watched the two men walk away, their skirts swishing up the dust in the road. "Cool costumes."

"They're real monks." Uncle Bob grinned. "Everyone loves a Ren faire. By the way, I keep meaning to ask how you're managing to investigate here, since you can't talk and all."

I made series of gestures that were supposed to signify me listening and talking quietly behind the scenes and being a brilliant mime and detective.

"You got a stomachache?"

Maybe not such a brilliant mime. I shrugged, and the little coins on the edge of my belly dancer bra jingled.

"Seems like there's something else on your mind."

"Can't fool a PI," I said. "Matt's coming home today."

"Oh."

"And I haven't decided what to do."

"Ah."

"Remember when you said something about me being a snail in a shell?"

"Yeah..."

"And how Matt drew me out of it?"

"Uh huh."

"Does that mean he makes me a better person?"

"Well, being the crack PI you are, I bet you noticed my sort of non-responses to your last few statements."

"Oh," I said, giving him some of his own medicine.

"That's because you have to make this decision on your own. I can't help you. But I'll listen if you want to talk."

"Even about mushy stuff?"

"Well..."

We both smiled at his non-response. "That's okay," I said. "I don't even know where I'd start."

"How about answering your own question?"

"My own...? Oh. Does Matt make me a better person?" I rested my elbows on the picnic table, and thought. Really thought. About how Matt helped me see Cody as a whole person. How he gave me confidence to audition and investigate. How I was a little braver, a little kinder, a little more open since I'd known him. "Yeah," I said. "He does."

"Does that get you any closer to your answer?"

"Yeah." I echoed myself. "It does."

Chapter 54

I was being a bad detective again. Rather than investigating or looking for clues or even eavesdropping, I just hoped my subconscious would sort things out, and I let my conscious brain spend the rest of the day at the faire thinking about me and Matt. Could I really have love *and* my dream career? It seemed too much to hope for, but I wanted to believe it was possible.

I skipped the after-hours party again (see? Bad detective) in favor of going home and showering before I picked up Matt at the airport. I was on the road home when *Mooooo! Mooooo! Mooooo!* Uncle Bob was right. The cow ringtone was better. Actually kind of comforting. *Mooooo! Mooooo! Mooooo!* I glanced at the display and all the comfort went away.

"Mom?" I said when I picked up. "Is everything okay?" My mother did not call me. Okay, she called probably twice a year. On my birthday and...maybe just once a year.

"I can't get ahold of Cody," she said. "I've been trying his cell phone all day."

Oh. Phew. "He doesn't have one any longer. Remember I emailed you?" My brother had bought a cell phone at the urging of an unscrupulous talent agent. When he got out of his bogus contract, he was left with a phone he didn't really want. Instead of going down to the mall and throttling the guy who had talked him into the exorbitantly expensive plan, I called the carrier and explained the situation, adding that I was sure they wouldn't want a social media campaign about their exploitation of people with intellectual disabilities. They discontinued the service, and Cody kept the phone in case he needed to call 911. "Did you try the group home?" I asked.

"I hate calling there. I always get one of those...boys." My mother had never reconciled herself to the fact that Cody and the other guys who lived at the house were grown men. Actually, she never reconciled herself to the idea of the group home at all, and was still mad that I suggested it to Cody years ago. She'd wanted to keep him at home, even though she didn't really want him there. Matt called it "the mother-martyr syndrome."

"The guys are good at taking messages." Mostly. "Or you could ask to talk to somebody who works there. Or just tell me whatever it is. I'll let him know."

"I just wanted to let him know that your father and I are leaving the country for a while."

"You are?"

"He's taking that job in Italy."

"What job?"

"Didn't we tell you?"

Mom and I hadn't spoken since Christmas. Dad had been better at communicating with Cody and me for a while, but I hadn't heard from him in over a month, and no one ever mentioned Italy. "I think I would have remembered."

"And *I* think we told you when you were here over the holidays. Anyway, it's a consultant job. Pays very well, the village we'll be living in is beautiful, and it's so much cheaper."

"Wow. Nice. Have fun." I managed to say this in a pleasant tone, though I felt like I'd been punched in the gut. Abandoned. Again.

"We'll be gone for at least six months, more if the job works out. You'll tell your brother?"

"I'll let him know."

"And you'll watch out for him while we're gone?"

I always watched out for Cody. I managed his finances. I dealt with Social Security and healthcare and the group home. I saw him in person at least once a week. My mother knew this. She was really reminding me that I hadn't watched out for him when it counted.

"Of course."

"I thought of you the other day." She did? "Read a funny article about actors."

Wow. "Why don't you send it to me?" Maybe Mom was starting to accept my career choice.

"Oh. Well, okay. And you'll give your brother the message?"

"Will do."

"Bye."

The rest of the way home my thoughts swung between "my parents are moving halfway across the world and forgot to tell me," and "my mom read an article about actors and thought of me." By the time I reached my apartment, I decided to focus on the latter. Maybe they had told me at Christmas. There was that one night when I overdid the eggnog.

I showered off the faire's dust and makeup, then sat down with a beer and booted up my laptop to look for Mom's email. I felt hopeful, but guardedly so. Thus the beer.

The email was at the top of my inbox: "Article I told you about." No message in the body of the email, just a link to a clickbait site. I bit.

Oh no. Really? "Top Reasons Why You Don't Want to Date an Actor." Gee, thanks, Mom.

Wait—she'd said the article was funny. Maybe I was taking offense where I shouldn't. Maybe there were some funny photos. I went to the first slide.

No funny photo, just a crack about our weird schedules. But I couldn't help it. I went to the next slide. And the next. I was ready for the stuff Candy and I had talked about—the schedules, travel, lack of money—but the rest...

I got up and got myself another beer. I sat down again and read about actors—how we were moody and insecure due to all the rejection we faced; overly concerned about aging and our appearances; dramatic and needy in our relationships; and dependent on external satisfaction, which was always fleeting. And these weren't the worst reasons not to date us. We were also incapable of real lasting happiness (owing to that external validation thing) and so self-absorbed that other people always came second to us and our careers.

I once fell out of a swing when I was six and hit the ground so hard the wind was knocked out of me. I lay there on the ground, everything hurting, wondering if I'd be able to breathe again. I felt the same way now. Everything hurt: the fact that Mom thought this was funny, the fact that people thought we were actually like that, and the fact that some of the reasons were true. About some actors. About me. I *was* insecure. I was working on not worrying about my appearance, but the aging thing was real: I could hear the clock ticking every day. Dramatic and needy? Maybe. I certainly liked external validation—maybe I was dependent on it. I wasn't sure I was capable of real lasting happiness. Worst of all, I was pretty sure I was self-absorbed. In fact, I was pretty sure that's why my mother thought of me she read the article. It was an accusation I'd heard over and over since Cody's accident.

And it seemed justified. Like yesterday's call to Matt—all I did was vent to him about stupid stuff in my life. Did I even ask about him or his mom or dad? I couldn't remember. Had I sent flowers or even a card? No. Even worse, I'd been considering the "living together" decision by how it would impact me and my career, not how it'd affect Matt. What it'd feel like for him to live with my lifestyle, my insecurities, my general messed-up-ness.

The hurt I felt when reading the article didn't go away. It got worse. I loved Matt. He was a good man.

And he deserved better.

Chapter 55

"My parents are moving to Italy." It was the first thing I said to Matt after he got into my truck outside the terminal. Not "Hello," or "How was your flight?" or even "Sorry I was late." Definitely self-absorbed. And afraid to say what was really on my mind. I pulled out into traffic.

"Italy? Are you kidding? Where?...Hey, car!"

I slammed on the brakes. We skidded to a stop just inches from the sedan I'd nearly sideswiped. "I just realized they didn't say where." I clunked my head on the steering wheel. Such an idiot. "Just Italy. Maybe it's a smaller country than I think."

"God, your parents," he said. "That sucks." Matt leaned over to kiss me, but I turned my head to look for oncoming traffic so I could merge. Also because I thought I'd burst into tears if he kissed me. I slid into traffic and kept my eyes on the road. "Good flight?"

"You know: crowded, a little bumpy, but free Coke." I could feel him looking at me. "You okay? Do you want to talk about Italy?"

"Are you social-working me?"

"What? No."

I knew I was picking a fight to distance myself from him. To make what I had to do hurt less for both of us. So I didn't stop. "Sounds like you are."

"I had enough of that at home," Matt said quietly. "Listen, if you don't want to talk, maybe we can just go back to my place, sit on the couch, maybe listen to music or watch something funny on television..."

"No."

"Oh yeah, you have to work tomorrow morning. At the faire, right? Maybe afterwards you can come over, teach me how to belly dance..."

"No."

"Okay." Matt sounded confused and a little hurt. He didn't say anything more. I didn't either. After what felt like eons, I pulled into his apartment's parking lot.

Matt finally broke the silence. "Ivy, what is it? What's wrong?"

"I can't do this." *To you,* I wanted to add, but didn't. It might open up the conversation and I didn't want to talk. I'd made up my mind.

"Listen." Matt took off his seatbelt so he could turn toward me. "We don't have to move in together. Let's just forget about that for now."

"For now. That's the trouble. I don't know if I'll ever be ready. And with my career..."

"Oh." Matt sounded relieved. "Your career. Don't worry about that. I'd never want you to give that up."

I loved Matt so much. So I had to keep going. "So it's okay if I move to San Diego and then to New York and then who knows where? It's okay if I'm on the road more than I'm home? If I have fake sex with men who aren't you?"

"Well—"

"Let me answer that question: It's not. It's not okay to always put myself and my career ahead of you."

"I don't think you—"

"Yes, I do. I—" I had to stop. I didn't have a lump in my throat—I had a lump that filled my entire chest cavity.

"Ivy, look at me."

I did. Matt was so beautiful. My chest felt like it might explode.

"I thought we were fine," Matt said. "Better than fine. I would have never asked you to—" he shook his head. "I suspect this is really about your parents, and no, I'm not social-working you—so why don't we just talk about it tomorrow when—"

"This isn't about us, or even my parents. It's about me. It's always about me. That's the problem." The lump in my chest turned in on itself, became a giant hole. I was in danger of being swallowed, but I had to do this. "I love you," I said, "but I think I need...some time on my own."

"Really? Are you sure? What if we just—"

"I'm sure."

"...Okay." I didn't look at Matt but I heard the tears in his voice. I felt him leave, felt him step out the door, felt him turn back to look at me, felt him shut the door. Then he was gone, and I tumbled into the black hole in my chest.

Chapter 56

I don't think I slept at all. I must have dozed a little but every time I came to, the same tape was playing in my head. Matt's beautiful face. Matt's voice, cracking with emotion. Matt, whom I was leaving. Had left.

Since I was already up, I got on the road a little early. I pulled into the employee parking lot and *Mooooo! Mooooo!* Not so comforting this morning: I'd almost forgotten my daily call with Riley.

"Hey, Ivy." Riley sounded as bad as I felt.

"You okay? Did you ever get that aspirin? Maybe I can do something about it."

"No, it's just...I'm still here. I miss my life. It was pretty cool, you know."

"Just hang on a little while longer. I think you'll be out of there soon."

"Really? You found whoever pretended to be me?"

"Um, no. I just think you'll get out on bail."

"How? You didn't call my mom, did you?"

"No. Bianca said that everyone at the faire is raising money. She thought they should have enough by today sometime."

"Bianca said that?"

"Yeah."

"She's not mad at me anymore?"

"She doesn't think you did it."

Riley's sigh of relief was so big I swear I felt his breath through the phone. "Cool. That's cool. She's cool."

"And Uncle Bob said you can probably get the marijuana

charge reduced to a misdemeanor."

"He's cool too. Everything's cool. Yeah. Thanks, Ivy." He hung up, and I sat there, wishing everything was cool.

I was just about to stash my phone under the seat when it buzzed at me: a text. I squinted at it, hoping it wasn't Matt—and hoping it was. I was a mess.

Not Matt, Uncle Bob. "Too much sun the last couple days." That monk robe did look hot. "You okay without me?"

No, I wanted to say, I'm not okay. I did the right thing but it hurts like hell. But I said, "Sure. Take care. XXOO."

I went through the day like a belly dancing automaton. Even Jasmine noticed. "You've lost your shine, my girl." Indeed I had. I hoped it would come back.

I was about to wrap up the day and count it as a total loss when I wiggled my way past the Bawdy Buccaneers show. They were leading the crowd in a cheer: "Trojans, Trojans, we will never break!"

The same cheer John Robert had used on Friday. And that fact jogged something else loose in my mind—he'd also used "Might for right"—William's catch phrase. Is that what he was doing at the faire? Stealing ideas?

"Tell your fortune, milady?"

I whipped around. The question wasn't directed at me, but no one else was biting, which was good, because that was one crone who had some explaining to do.

"Inside. Now," I said, walking ahead of her into her stupid bloody caravan. The deck of tarot cards was on her table. I sat in her seat, turned the cards face up, and spread them across the table.

"What are you doing?" She'd followed me in.

"I wanted to make sure these cards weren't all Towers. Or Magicians."

"You think I was tricking you."

"I think you know too much."

"The crone kn—"

"Do not go there," I said. Then I burst into tears.

She let me cry for a while, passing me Kleenex when I needed them. I finally got myself under control. "You knew my life was going to go down in flames."

"I didn't." She spoke gently, dropping the Slavic accent. Her real voice had a Midwestern softness. "I'm sorry."

"But you knew about William." I watched her eyes.

"No."

She was telling the truth. "But before the joust that killed Angus, you said death was near. And you told Riley he was going to be famous."

"Angus was called the Black Death, remember? I saw him standing right behind you; that's all I meant. And about Riley being famous—he's a good jouster and funny and big-hearted. I thought—I think—he'll do well here."

"When you showed me the Magician card, you said something about evil."

"I was talking about Angus. Hated that guy. Listen," the crone said, "I'm just an actress. I really don't know anything. Though I do believe the cards can show us things about ourselves."

"Okay then..." I picked up the card in front of me—a skull-faced knight in black armor with the word "Death" scrawled underneath. "Let's see if they can show us who killed Angus." I placed the card in front of the crone.

"That's not really how it works."

I tapped my finger on a card that showed a woman with bird wings. "There's Bianca, the middle of the love triangle..." I put it next to The Fool card. "There's Riley..." I found The Magician and put it next to them. "William the Wondrous..." I pointed to another card with a man and a woman who looked like twins holding cups... "Benjamin and his alter ego"...then another one that had a man stealing swords from something that looked like a faire "John Robert, and..." I searched for a card to represent my last suspect. I point to a man carrying a sword, with birds in the background for the Bianca connection... “Hayden,” I said.

I watched the crone. I was pretty sure she did know more than she was saying. Maybe her eyes would give her away. But instead of looking at the cards, she looked at me. “Are you sure that’s everyone?”

Chapter 57

Was that a clue? Had I missed someone? The fortuneteller wouldn't say any more, and she wanted me gone. "I have to make a living, you know." She practically pushed me outside.

But what was she trying to tell me? Maybe she was pointing out the fact that I had too many suspects, or maybe...

"Doug," I said, sticking my head back inside the caravan.

The crone laughed, "Doug, joust? I doubt he's ever been within ten feet of a horse."

She was right. Not Doug. Arghh. I did have too many suspects. And a headache. And a heartache.

I told Jasmine I wasn't feeling well, and left the faire early. I went home and tried to take a nap. Didn't work. I lay on my couch and let my mind wander through the investigation, hoping it would show me something I'd missed. That didn't work either. It was as if my brain was trying so hard not to think about Matt that it was too tired to think about anything else. I finally gave up and called Cody. "You free for dinner?"

"Um...Aren't we having dinner tomorrow?"

Our weekly double date night: Cody and Sarah and me and Matt. That was really why I'd called. I could tell Cody about me and Matt while we were at the group home, then take him out to dinner so we could process it. "I don't think that's going to work out."

"Okay. Should Sarah come?"

"Let's just make it you and me this time." I arranged to pick up Cody in fifteen minutes.

This was not going to be fun.

Cody had loved Matt before I did.

They met several years ago. Matt was working at the group home while finishing his master's in social work. He was a quiet force of change in that house, not only insisting that the guys be treated like the adults they were, but giving them goals—like getting part-time jobs—and boundaries, like not sleeping late and missing work. Best of all, by being comfortable with who he was—a slightly geeky, sci-fi-loving college student—he helped them embrace who they were too. Ever since Matt, Cody and his buddies at the home felt free to dance, to tell bad jokes, to have friendly arguments about the best superhero, to be who they were, regardless of society's expectations.

So I expected Cody would be upset about the break-up. I didn't think he'd go ballistic.

"What!?" Cody yelled, loud enough that the guys who'd been in the living room with us scattered. "You did what?" He began to shake, like he did when he was upset. "Why?"

"Well, he asked me to move in with him and—"

"So you broke up with him!?" Cody was wobbling so wildly I was afraid he'd fall over.

"Let's sit down for a minute."

"No. You tell me why."

"It just wasn't going to work out."

"Don't you love him?"

"Yes. Yes, I do. But..."

"Then why?" Cody began to cry. Noisily and hard, his body shaking with each sob.

Then I was crying too. "Because...I'm an actor."

"So?"

"I'm selfish and self-absorbed."

"What? You are not."

"I'm dramatic and needy. I'm always putting myself first."

"You're not. You're wrong. You should call Matt and tell him that—"

"For God's sake, Cody. I am. Look what I did to you."

Cody stopped crying. He looked at me with wet eyes. "What are you talking about?"

"I didn't want you with us, so I ignored you. I let you fall through the ice. I didn't save you." I sank onto the couch. "I let you go."

Cody sat down next to me. "I love you, Olive-y. I love you more than anybody. Even Mom and Dad or Uncle Bob or Sarah."

"I know."

"No, you don't. If you did, you'd know that my accident doesn't matter."

"How can you say that? I don't think you understand what I took away from you."

Cody thrust out his chin. "And I don't think you understand what I have." He stood up. "I like my life. I have friends and a job and a girlfriend. And I have you and Matt. Your life is good, too, and it's better when you're with Matt. And if you can't see that, you're just dumb." A huge insult in this house. "You're the dumbest person I know." Cody turned around and walked out of the room.

I sat on the couch, unable to move. Cody was right. I'd never thought about his life from his point of view. But...didn't that just prove my point?

"Olive-y?" said a distinctive thick-tongued voice. Cody's best friend Stu padded softly into the room. "I heard you fight with Cody." He sat down on the couch next to me. "Sorry." Stu patted my knee. "But he's right. You're really dumb."

Chapter 58

I felt worse than dumb. I felt bad. A bad sister. A bad detective, which in turn meant a bad niece. A bad person.

I felt bad all the way home. I felt bad when I opened the door to my empty apartment, and bad when I grabbed a beer from the fridge. *Bad.* I really wanted to talk to someone, but who? Not Matt, Cody or Uncle Bob, since they were the people I was feeling bad about. Not Candy, who didn't need my pity party right now. Timothy? Right—after I didn't tell him I got the *Camelot* gig, forgot about his dream theater company, and stood him up at the gay rodeo. Add "bad friend" to the list.

But, said a small voice inside me, *you are good at something. You are good at acting.*

Thank God I still had that.

The next morning, I stepped through the French doors onto John Robert's patio. "I need coffee," I said in Marilyn's breathless voice. "Lots and lots of coff—oops!" One of my kitten heels caught on the threshold and I stumbled into Hayden.

He caught me and I righted myself. "Oh my." I patted my wig to make sure it was in place. "I may have had a bit too much last night."

John Robert's face scrunched up in worry. "No, Marilyn. You really mustn't. With your history of substance abuse, you..." He stopped, maybe because he realized he was speaking to me as if I was the dead star, or maybe because it was impolite to remind someone how they died.

"I really do need coffee." The usual OJ and champagne glared brightly at me from a side table next to Jackie, but there was no coffee on display. Just as I'd hoped. I smiled at John Robert. "Is there a pot in the kitchen?"

"I'll get it," he said.

"I'll join you." It was all going as planned. Last night, when I realized I had put all my eggs into the acting basket, I realized something else: I needed to help this play. And the first step was to protect it. I had to talk John Robert out of using other people's ideas. Even if the material wasn't copyrighted, anyone could go on the web and watch the Ren faire shows, and that could be more than embarrassing for John Robert—and the show's backers.

"So," I said once John Robert and I were alone in the kitchen, "I've been meaning to talk to you."

"I know." He hung his head like a bad dog. Had he recognized me at the faire? Was he about to confess to stealing ideas? Or maybe something worse? "It stinks," he said. "*I* stink. I don't know why I thought I'd be better off, but—" He made a choking sound and threw his arms around my neck. "I made a horrible mistake and I don't know what to do."

"Um," I said into his hair. "Which mistake are you talking about? I mean, what mistake?"

He pushed himself away from me and wiped his eyes. "Leaving Lewis, of course. He's not just my partner and the love of my life, he's my muse. I can't work without him. Well, I can, but I'm awful. I even resorted to stealing ideas from entertainers at the Ren faire—can you believe it? I wouldn't need to do that if Lewis was here. We're so much better together. I can't explain it, but when I'm with him the ideas fill the room like butterflies. I just reach out and one lights on the back of my hand. And then Lewis makes the idea better. He makes everything better." Echoes of my "love talk" with Cody.

"Why did you break up?" I used my real voice. It seemed wrong to play a character when talking about such a serious subject.

"Because I was stupid. I wanted the glory all to myself. I didn't want be part of the team Turner and Toe, I wanted to be John

Robert Turner, the Broadway sensation. I don't know why I thought I had to break up with Lewis in order to prove myself. I even picked a fight with him." Oh boy, more echoes.

"Maybe that was the only way you could strike out on your own," I said.

"But I don't want to be on my own. I want Lewis. Oh God, I miss him." John Robert hung his head. "I'd give up anything for him. My career, even."

"Have you told Lewis what you just told me?"

"What?" said John Robert. "Go crawling back on my hands and knees?"

"What have you got to lose?"

"Besides my ego?"

"Yeah, besides that. I think egos are..." I tried to think how Uncle Bob would say it. "You know how they talk about 'bruised egos'? They never say that egos are 'bloody' or 'critically ill.' I think that's because they're sort of superficial. Sure, they hurt when they get poked, but they're not really a big deal, and they heal pretty quickly."

John Robert nodded slowly. "And no one's really been poking it beside myself."

"We do that to ourselves."

"Yes. You're right. I should tell him. Call him. Today." As he talked through his decision, John Robert's red tear-stained face—his funny froggy face—became beautiful, like it was lit from within. Amazing what love will do for you.

He poured me some coffee, and I got milk out of the refrigerator. I started to sniff it out of habit, then stopped. Did millionaires' milk go sour, too, or did their maids check it daily? I decided it was impolite and took a chance, pouring the milk sniff-free into my coffee. "So," I said casually, "What's your connection with the Ren faire?"

"My connection?"

"You said something about it earlier."

"Oh, yeah." He turned toward the counter and wiped up a drop of spilled coffee. "It's not really a connection."

"I thought I saw you there a few days ago."

He glanced at me over his shoulder. "You were there?" His eyes were wide. Surprise? Fear? "Isn't it great?" Maybe it was delight. "It's what gave me the idea to reimagine *Camelot*. I'd been wanting to do something about the Kennedys anyway." He turned away again, staring out the window over the kitchen sink. "I was reaching, I guess, but *Hello Dolly Madison* did so well, and I do love the Kennedys, but...I don't think it's going to work." He snuck a look at me over his shoulder, probably hoping I'd contradict him.

I didn't. I couldn't. John Robert was a nice guy, but his *Kennelot* concepts...Hey. He'd distracted me. "You said something earlier about, um, stealing ideas. Did you work with someone there?"

"No." John Robert's face fell. "I just hung around the entertainers with the biggest crowds. I wasn't planning to steal outright—I'd make the ideas my own eventually. I was just so desperate for inspiration."

"I, uh, heard that horse that was here was from there." I hoped my vagueness sounded like I was at the end of the gossip chain, not just poorly spoken.

John Robert's face brightened again. "Wasn't that lucky? That poor horse. What if he hadn't found my swimming pool?"

How *did* the horse find the pool? "Did you get the reward?"

"No. I don't need the money. I would have given it to Juan if he'd told the faire the horse was here, but...I just let it go. I heard the performers raised the money themselves. They don't make much, you know." John Robert's face went from bright to dark again, like he was experiencing a fast-moving storm. Maybe he was, but I didn't think it had anything to do with the horse. "Oh God," he said. "I really want to call Lewis but..."

Yeah, not about the horse. "Fear is stupid, and so are regrets," I said, quoting John Robert's favorite dead movie star.

"Oh, Marilyn," he said. "I'm going to miss you."

Chapter 59

I walked slowly back to the patio, my mind's wheels spinning. Not going anywhere, mind you. Just spinning. John Robert was going to miss me. That didn't sound good. Not only that, I didn't learn squat about the horse, or about John Robert and the Ren faire.

I stepped onto the patio. Jackie was nowhere in sight. Maybe I could turn my detective luck around, find out what was really up with Hayden and Bianca and the faire.

Hayden beat me to the punch. "What's wrong?"

So many things. I chose one, just to start the conversation. "I talked John Robert into calling Lewis. And I get the feeling that *Kennelot* is...over." As I said the words, I felt their truth. Oh no. And I helped push it into the grave.

"Ah." Hayden poured himself some orange juice. "Probably."

"You don't seem that upset."

"I saw it coming. Come on, didn't you?"

"Yeah, but..." *Broad...way*...The tune in my head became a dirge. I blocked it out.

"And I've got something else lined up."

"Cool." Okay, Ivy, this is where to start prodding. Forget about Broadway for a minute and get back to detecting. "What is it?"

"A film. With Andre."

"Andre? Wow." I acted like I didn't know Hayden had worked with him before. "How in the world...?"

"I've known Andre since his student film days, even acted in one of them when I was in college, pre-law school."

"You're a lawyer?" Finally, some information.

"Nah. Only went for a year. I decided there were better ways to use my talents."

"Like?" Give me something. Please please please.

"Acting, of course." He smiled at me, but his eyes narrowed a bit. "Don't you want to know about the movie?"

"Of course." *Act like an actor, Ivy, not a detective.*

"It's a biopic." Hayden flashed his boyish JFK smile. "About the Kennedys."

"But..." Uncle Bob had always maintained that coincidences were seldom, well, coincidental. My mind flashed on John Robert and Hayden returning from their ride in the desert, looking awfully buddy-buddy. "Wait, did you know John Robert before this? Is he involved in the film, too?"

"He doesn't have anything to do with the movie, but yeah, he knew me. Sort of. He and Andre are friendly. They were on the phone a couple of weeks ago when Andre mentioned the script he was planning to direct. John Robert got all excited and asked if he'd be stealing his thunder by trying *Camelot* with the Kennedys and Marilyn." Another borrowed idea. At least John Robert asked to use this one. "Andre said sure, go for it."

"Because he thought they'd cross-promote each other?"

"Because he never thought John Robert would go through with it, at least not without Lewis."

I was still having trouble making all the connections. "And you?"

"Andre's been planning to use me as Kennedy all along. When John Robert told him he wanted to workshop his idea with actors, Andre suggested me. Thought it'd give me a chance to perfect my JFK persona."

"Wow." My mind was seriously spinning now. Hayden and John Robert were connected. Hayden and Bianca were connected. John Robert and Riley's horse were connected. I almost felt dizzy. I sat down, just as Jackie came through the French doors. "Everything okay?" she asked.

And Jackie and Hayden were connected, through *Kennelot* if nothing else. Arghh. This investigation sucked. "I may have just sunk our Broadway boat," I said. That sucked too.

Jackie sat quickly, as if she were felled by an axe, her perfect facade cracking. I felt for her/him. Sure I wanted to work with John Robert and get to Broadway, but playing Marilyn wasn't a lifelong dream for me, like Jackie was for Benjamin. His lip trembled a little.

I explained my conversation with John Robert. "I'm sorry." I touched Benjamin on the arm. "I know how much this meant to you."

"Aw, buck up, you two. You'll have this workshop on your resume, and I wouldn't be surprised if John Robert recommends you for something else," Hayden said. "And if not, there's always the Ren faire."

Jackie stiffened. I felt my body doing the same. Was he talking to both of us?

"Or your PI work."

Shit. He was talking to me.

Jackie shook her head almost imperceptibly—she didn't tell. Hayden was grinning at me openly. No use in lying now. "Who knows?" I asked.

"All the Ren faire people know. That's one reason they made you be silent—trying to keep you from asking too many questions." I slid a glance at Jackie. She affirmed the fact with her eyes.

"But how did they figure it out?" I'd been so careful.

"First of all, there was the way the administration foisted you off on the belly dancing troupe..."

Jackie gave me an "I told you so" look.

"Plus the bad accent..."

"Oi!" I said. "It weren't that bad."

"The fact that no one is named Prudence anymore."

"Come on, there have to be some Beatles fans somewhere."

"But I guess what clinched it was your outie."

"My what?"

"Seems you wore a short top one day when you were being yourself." Arghh, that damn tied-at-the-waist-Marilyn-shirt. I wore it the day I borrowed Riley's armor. "Of course it was on view in your belly dancing costume, too, and I hear that it's...distinctive." Hayden grinned. "Which makes me want to see it." He reached for my shirt.

"*No.*" I clamped my top to my distinctive belly button. "You should have paid attention the day I wore my shirt tied up. Now it's your turn. How are you involved with the faire? Does it have anything to do with the reason you're on the road a lot?"

"Good one," said Hayden. "But just because you've blown your cover doesn't mean I have to blow mine."

Just then John Robert came back outside, beaming. "Something came up, so we'll take today off. I'll give you all a call about tomorrow."

Things felt very final as we walked through the house to the driveway out front. John Robert waved goodbye, then closed the front door. Hayden gave Jackie and me a jaunty wave, got into his Prius, and drove off.

"Did you have to do it?" Jackie said to me. "Couldn't you have left well enough alone?"

"Come on, you know nothing about *Kennelot* was 'well enough.' And yes, I had to. You should have seen John Robert. He was so sad."

"And now you've made the rest of us that way. Thanks a lot." Jackie got into her Cadillac and drove away, literally leaving me in the dust.

I tried to not think too much on the drive back to town, to concentrate on the road and the traffic. I was doing okay until my phone rang. I picked up on speaker.

"Ivy?" It was John Robert. "I wanted you to be the first to know." If the joy in his voice was any indication, I already knew. "Lewis and I are back together. He's flying out. He'll be here this evening."

"I'm so glad for you." I was. I really was.

"I just wanted to say thank you. I'm not sure I would have...Who knows what might have happened if you didn't help me figure this out? I might have blown it forever."

"Yeah." I tried not to think about blowing something forever.

"And about *Kennelot*...I think I'm going to take a break. It's not really working." I wanted to convince him to keep trying for the sake of my career. But I couldn't, because he was right. Oh boy, was he right. "It's not completely off the table. Maybe Lewis will have some ideas."

"Sure."

"I'll keep in touch. Your Marilyn is truly amazing. Truly."

"Thanks." I hung up the phone.

No Broadway.

No undercover job.

No Matt.

The sky above me was clear and blue, but still, a big dark cloud descended on my truck, closing in more and more until it crushed my heart.

Chapter 60

I'd told my uncle I'd come into the office after rehearsal. I knew I should, but I couldn't face Uncle Bob. If I saw him, I'd want to talk to him, and I just didn't have the heart to tell him that my bellybutton blew my cover, or that Broadway was a no-go, or that I broke up with Matt.

So I chickened out and went home. "Now I think *I* got too much sun," I said over the phone. "Do you mind if I take the day off?"

"No problem," said the nicest uncle in the world.

Oh. Dang. My sense of responsibility kicked in. "Wait, maybe I should come in. Hayden said something weird today, about having a cover. He'd also said he was on the road a lot, but I can't figure out why. *And* I saw him with Bianca at the faire. I ran a background check earlier, but—"

"Don't worry. I'll do some digging. You just feel better."

I hung up, lay down on the couch, put a (clean) dishrag over my eyes to block out the daylight, and tried to sleep. I was able to nap, probably because I hadn't had a good night's sleep in ages. But it was a fitful sleep, full of jousting horses and birds of prey and...cows?

Mooooo! Mooooo! I looked at my phone: Uncle Bob. And it was five thirty—after his normal work hours. I suddenly felt wide-awake. "Hey," I said. "Did you find something?"

"On Hayden, no. Just an actor with a trust fund as far as I can tell."

"Any reason he'd be traveling?"

"Maybe just for fun? He's got the cash. But that's not the

reason I called you. Remember how the coroner was going to run some more tests on the scratch on Angus's face?"

"Yeah."

"Well, they discovered something," said Uncle Bob. "That scratch was made by a bird."

After throwing on a black hoodie and some sweats, I got into my truck and headed east, toward the faire. I wanted to surprise Bianca, in case she'd run, and I wanted to do it on her own turf, in case she'd inadvertently give me more clues. I told Uncle Bob I wanted to do this alone—I didn't think Bianca was dangerous and thought I'd get more out of a conversation just between us two women—but I told him where I'd be and I promised to have my cell phone on me.

But how to approach this? "Hi, I can tell by the bird scratches on Angus's face that you had something to do with his death, and must have set up your ex-boyfriend to take the fall?" Maybe a little subtler than that.

I was still mulling over my talking points when I got to the faire. I parked at the far end of the public parking lot so Bianca wouldn't be alerted by the sound of my truck, turned off the ringer on my phone, and pulled my hood over my head to make me a little less visible. I walked into the dark empty faire toward the mews. I thought I'd try that before Bianca's trailer. Yes. A light shone through a small window.

I was nearly there when I remembered something: Bianca knew I'd been undercover. She'd known at least since Thursday, when I was hit on the head. And I was hit on the head *after* she saw my distinctive bellybutton. Probably did it herself. I probably should have brought my uncle along.

Typically, when faced with even a smidgen of danger, I'd feel a little jolt of adrenaline. My heart would beat faster, my muscles tense in readiness for fight or flight. Instead I just felt exhausted—tired of the strain of the investigation, the pressure of making the

Matt decision, the stress of pretending to be someone else all the time. So I wasn't paying a lot of attention to my surroundings.

"Don't move," said a voice behind me. "I've got a weapon. What are you doing here?" Bianca's voice.

"It's just me." Being an actor was a plus when you were trying to sound calm when faced with a potential murderer with a weapon. "Just me, Ivy-the-friend-of Riley slash Prudence-the-belly-dancing-mime. Can I turn around now?"

"Okay."

Bianca stood behind me, Edgar perched on her shoulder. "You have a weapon?" I asked, pulling down my hood.

"I was lying. I thought you were a thief or something."

"Just a bad investigator, but...oh. You do have a weapon."

"No, I was—"

"Edgar. Edgar, your watchdog. Your weapon."

"Edgar isn't a wea—"

"The coroner said there were bird scratches on Angus's face. Recent ones, probably made the night before he died." I motioned toward the mews. "Can we go inside?" I wanted to see Bianca's face when I questioned her.

"Oh. Yeah. Sure."

We walked the short distance and Bianca opened the door for me. It was only slightly lighter inside than outside. "Could we turn on another light?" I asked.

"I'd rather not." Bianca motioned to the cages, all covered now. "They're sleeping."

"Okay. Put Edgar to bed too, would you? Or at least in his cage."

Bianca opened the door to Edgar's cage and he flew in. I made sure she latched the door. I motioned for her to sit in a wooden chair. I stood in front of her, like a prosecutor. It felt wrong. I dragged another chair over and sat facing her. Better.

"You said 'belly dancing mime,'" Bianca said. "You're blowing your own cover?"

"Seems my outie outed me. I figured you told Hayden, who's

not who he pretends to be, either." Of course I didn't know who that really was. I was hoping Bianca would give me a clue.

"Thank God for that. We'd be in big trouble without their lawyers."

Their lawyers. "What's the name of Hayden's group again?"

"You mean the Winged Army?"

"How come I've never heard of them?"

"They operate under the radar."

"So when did you contact Hayden? Before or after the joust?"

Bianca raised her chin and looked at me. "I think you're pretending to know more than you do."

"I know you hit me on the head."

"Sorry. But I didn't mean to knock you out, just knock you down. I still think you fainted. And I did make sure you were okay afterward."

"Did you hit Riley on the head too?"

"See what I mean about pretending to know things?"

"Okay." I stood up. "This is what I know: I know you were in a love triangle with Angus and Riley—"

"Not sure I'd call it love."

I walked as I talked, hoping that it looked like I was pacing. "I know you hit me on the head."

"And helped you afterward."

"I know you were suspiciously close by after William's 'accident.'" I was almost in place.

"And probably saved his life."

I was right where I needed to be. "And I know that *this*"—I tore the sheet off the mystery cage—"is part of the reason that..." I stopped. Inside the cage was a bird, nearly two feet tall, with a white dappled chest and darker wings. Its beauty was marred by blue tape on one wing and a creepy leather hood that covered its head. "It really is a sick bird." I draped the cloth back over the cage. "I'm sorry." And to my surprise, I began to cry.

"Um..." Bianca walked over to me. "Do you want to talk about it?"

"I don't know. I don't know anything. That's the problem."

"You know I hit you on the head," she said. "That's something."

"Omigod, this is so unprofessional." I swiped at my eyes. "But...it's been a hell of a week."

"I know."

We just stood there for a minute, drawing strength from silence. Once I stopped crying I walked back to our chairs and sat. Bianca followed, sitting opposite me. "You said you weren't sure you'd call it love," I said finally. "You didn't love Angus?"

"No. I thought I did, but it was just sex and..." Now Bianca's eyes filled with tears. But if she didn't love Angus, why? Were the tears for Riley?

"I know what it feels like to screw up a relationship," I said. "And I think Riley will forgive you. Already forgives you." Bianca nodded, but I could tell from her face that wasn't why she was crying. "And I know what it feels like to be responsible for a...loss. To have caused an accident that took someone's life away from him."

"You do?" Bianca's eyes searched the air for an explanation. "Omigod." Her eyes met mine. "Your brother. Riley said he was...That he had..."

"A brain injury. From an accident I could have stopped."

"Oh." She let go a big breath. "Oh. Maybe you can understand. I am responsible for an accident, and probably a death—deaths. But not Angus's."

Chapter 61

"I found out about everything the night before Angus died," Bianca said. "We'd made love here in the afternoon after one of his jousts, up on top of one of the turrets."

"On top of a turret?"

"There's a small flat space where we stand to release the birds. You're hidden if you lie down, but it's still sort of public so it feels dangerous and Angus liked—" She must have sensed my discomfort. "*Anyway*, that evening I realized that he'd left his helmet there, so I came back—thought I'd get it and drop it off at his RV before he had to joust again."

"Or before anyone else found it."

"Yeah. So I got here, but Angus was already here. But not to get his helmet. He was messing with Morgana there." Bianca pointed at the sick bird's cage. "She's a gyrfalcon. She came here from a wildlife rescue place, like most of my birds, and I thought...I thought..." She took a deep breath. "Let me back up. Angus and I got together about six months ago. One of the things that drew us together, besides the sex, was the fact that he loved birds. He knew everything about them. Said he was working with the Winged Army, helping them find places where injured birds could be rehabbed before releasing them back to the wild."

"The Winged Army is the wildlife rescue organization Hayden works with?"

Bianca nodded.

"And they're 'off the radar' because..."

"They don't want to be well known. Their methods are sometimes...unorthodox. Nothing really bad, but they might release a captive bird from time to time, without the permission of its 'owner.'" She made air quotes. "Angus asked if I could help the cause, just keep a bird for a month or two. I was thrilled. He brought me five birds before Morgana." She shook her head. "I should have suspected something. The birds all seemed healthy. He said it was just their final stop: a time to rest and get strong before being released. But..." Bianca's tears started up again in earnest. She bit her bottom lip so hard I thought she might break the skin. "But then that night, I came back to get his helmet and found him..." She wiped her eyes. "Do you know what seeling is? With a double 'e'?"

"...Yeah. The term's used in *Macbeth*. Comes from when they used to train falcons by sewing their eyes...oh no." I shut my eyes against the grisly sight I imagined.

Bianca struggled to talk, like she had to force the words out of her mouth. "At first I thought he was getting Morgana ready to go—I'd forgotten she was leaving that night. And he was getting her ready, but not for...He was holding her and she was too quiet, because Angus had already taped her up, even her beak. Used packing tape. I guess that way she'd fit into the mailing tube. 'Hey, babe,' Angus said when he saw me, like what he was doing was okay. 'Morgana's flying airmail.'

"I lost it, screaming my head off, and Edgar attacked Angus. Scratched him up pretty good. And with me screaming and Edgar shrieking and Angus yelling, well...somebody heard us. That...person pulled Edgar off Angus, but I couldn't calm down. How many birds had he done this to? Do you know that only ten percent of birds smuggled like that survive? I helped Angus kill the birds. All those beautiful birds." Bianca covered her face with her hands.

"You didn't." I stroked her bowed head. "You didn't know. You were trying to help."

She raised her head. "And then, while I'm standing there sobbing and trying not to scream, Angus had the balls to say, 'So you found me out. I'll give you both a cut.' Like it was about money.

Money." She spit the word out.

"There was a lot of money involved?"

"I guess he got something like a hundred thousand per bird."

"*A hundred thousand*?"

"Falcons are a big deal in Arabian countries. But Angus only got that if they were...alive on delivery. All those deaths were worth it to him if just one hundred-thousand-dollar-bird paid off." She closed her eyes. "I was so stupid. All this time I thought we were doing something good together, that Angus actually cared about the birds...and about me." She hugged her knees. "So much of this is my fault. I was pissed off at Riley for taking me for granted. I was beginning to think he was with me so he didn't have to sleep in a tent. And then Angus started coming around, and he could be so...charming."

Charming Bully.

"He'd sweep into the mews and sweep me up too, saying he needed me, right then, that he couldn't stand to be without me one more minute..." Bianca swiped at her eyes. "It sounds stupid now, but it was so...I don't know, wildly romantic, someone wanting you that much. But of course he didn't."

"He was just using you as a stopover for the birds, a cover for the smuggling."

"And using me in other ways, too. And I fell for it. Stupid, stupid girl."

"Not stupid. Human. Just human."

"Stupid. And cowardly. Do you know why I didn't turn him in? After he offered me the money and I spit in his face,"—I hoped she really had—"I told him I was turning him in. 'Uh, uh, uh,' he said, and smiled, actually smiled. I would have scratched that smile right off his face if...somebody didn't hold me back. 'You're in this up to your eyeballs,' Angus said. 'As is the faire. Smuggling these babies is a federal offense. No one's going believe that the people around here didn't know, or that you didn't help me. Enough people know we're a couple. 'Of course Bianca knew what we were doing,' I'll say in my defense. 'It was fine with her until she found out I was seeing someone on the side.' And yeah. I've already planted that seed—*really* enjoyed the planting, too. You may be good with birds, babe, but you suck in the sack. Or wait, maybe you're not so good with birds. I mean, look at poor Morgana here. What a mess.'"

The words weren't directed at me and still they felt like blows. "I would have killed him too."

"I didn't. I wanted to, but I didn't. I was afraid."

"So...you planned it with the somebody who found you two fighting?"

"No. It wasn't like that. I didn't plan anything, and Angus was never supposed to be—look, does it matter? It was an accident."

"It wasn't," I said gently. "It was too well-coordinated."

"It *was*. It was an accident, because it was never supposed to go that far. The person who did it didn't know Angus was missing his gorget."

"It was still here in the mews, from the night before?"

Bianca nodded. "The person was just protecting us, trying to make Angus leave. The bastard kept saying he was going to stick close to me—to us—to make sure we kept quiet, like he was going to blackmail us. And when I took Morgana away from him, he said I owed him. He was going to suck us all dry."

"So you didn't plan—"

"No. I found out about it later." Bianca grabbed my shoulders. "It was an *accident*. It will never happen again." Her nails dug into me. "The world is better off without Angus. No one misses Angus. No one. Please just leave it there. Please."

Chapter 62

I left the mews and walked back to the parking lot through the dark fairegrounds. A white glow backlit the nearby mountains, making them look black and sharp. I felt muddled, like I'd been scrambled like an egg. I was sickened by Angus and sorry for Bianca and confused about what to do next. Bianca was right. No one missed Angus. The world was almost certainly better off without him. And lord I was tired. Tired of the investigation, tired of the stupid decisions I'd made, tired of it all.

The full moon crept up over the mountains like a thief, stealing the warmth from the night. I shivered, even though it wasn't cold. I should let it go, give up this investigation. No one cared that Angus was dead, and people obviously did care about whoever had inadvertently killed him. Which was...who? Who was the someone who saw what Angus had done, what he might still do?

I believed Bianca when she said she hadn't done it, or even planned it. And I was pretty sure John Robert was only guilty of stealing ideas. But could Riley have been in on it? Possibly. Maybe he thought he'd get back in Bianca's good graces. And it looked like he had—after all, she was the one who'd collected money for his bail.

Could William have been the jouster? Sure. He'd said something like "most of us who ride have jousted before," and age aside I suspected he was in pretty good shape under those wizard robes.

Benjamin? Yes. He rode well enough to win the barrel racing competition and had a history with Angus. Plus, even if he wasn't the someone who interrupted the scene at the mews, he could have found out about the bird smuggling from...

Hayden. Who rode so well it was as if he and the horse were one. Who loved birds so much that rescuing them was part of his life mission. Who must have known that Angus was using his beloved Winged Army as cover for smuggling. So, yeah, Hayden could have done it too. I had four suspects, all of whom I liked, all of whom seemed to be good men.

That was it. I was giving up. Cold blue moonlight cast twisted shadows through a nearby mesquite tree. I started walking to my truck, my moon shadow stretching grotesquely in front of me. I hated this. I hated giving up. It felt like failure, even when, as Bianca said, it wouldn't happen again. There wouldn't be any more violence. Angus was inadvertently killed because someone was protecting—

Protecting them. Bianca had said that someone was protecting the faire from Angus, who was going to "suck them dry." Someone was kindly escorting the psychic vampire from their midst. William. It must be William.

I stopped walking so I could think. Yes, there had been clues, subtle but there. The crone's Magician card. The gossiping woman who had blanched when I asked her if the killer was named Billy. The jousters around the campfire saying that everyone knew it was an accident—because they knew William never intended murder.

But there was William's drug overdose. I didn't think it could be intentional or his friends would have been more worried. They wouldn't have let him out of their sight, maybe not even out of the hospital. So was it accidental, or...? What if it was really an attack on William? What if someone actually missed Angus and decided to revenge him?

I made a one-eighty and picked up my pace. I wasn't giving up. I was going to talk to William.

I walked toward Tin Can Alley to find William's RV. I felt lighter for some reason, maybe because I had a direction, or maybe because I wasn't giving up on—

Splash!

I stopped. A splash? The fairegrounds weren't used after dark, so the only light came from the moon and some security lights mounted on buildings. I looked for some sort of movement or maybe the glimmer of light on a puddle. Nothing but a few bats catching the edges of the light. I started walking again, then stopped. The sound bothered me. This was the desert. There were no splashes in the desert. Maybe squelches in the mud pit or...

The Undersea Grotto. It was right across the street. Maybe the after-hours party had moved there? Maybe not. It looked awfully dark. I jogged toward the Grotto. Huh. No one outside. I stepped inside. Still dark. No laughter or splashing or undersea party. Empty, the ropes that kept people in line snaking through the darkness. I started to go back outside, but as my eyes adjusted to the darkness, I noticed something in the tank. A fish? No, too big for a fish, though it had silver scales.

Oh no.

I hung onto one of the ropes and closed my eyes. It didn't help. I was back in Spokane again, eleven years old again with snowflakes freezing on my cheeks. Then, a *crack* and shout, and Cody's blonde hair floating out from his head like a halo, slowly sinking in that icy pond...He was...and I couldn't...

Oh no, oh no, oh no. I couldn't breathe, like I was the one was shocked into paralysis by the cold, who didn't have time to even gulp air, who felt the water pressing against my nose and mouth...

I forced open my eyes. He was still there, in the tank, underwater. Long blonde, no, *silver* hair twisted in the water like strands of kelp. Amongst all that hair, an eye opened. A chill ran through me. So much sorrow in that gaze. William's gaze.

Omigod, omigod, omigod. It was happening. Again. I still felt like I couldn't breathe and so afraid that I couldn't move. Fear of the water, fear of screwing up, fear of losing someone again. But I had to do something. There was no one else around and no time to get anyone.

I willed my feet to move, and they did, around to the side of the tank, where a ladder stretched to the top. I focused on each rung. *You can do this, you can do this, you can do this*...I made it to the top of the tank and climbed onto the platform that ran around the rim, where the mermaids must sit before diving in to the water. Into the water. *You can do this, you can do this you, can do this...*

Still afraid. Could you die from fear? *You can do this, you can do this, you can...*

I jumped into the water.

Chapter 63

The cold darkness slipped over my head. Then I was somehow Cody, sinking in a panic. I struggled to the top of the tank and gulped air. I made it. Everything was okay. *No.* I wasn't Cody, everything wasn't okay and I needed to go down, not up. I beat down the terror that rose in my throat and kicked my way to the bottom of the tank: pressure in my ears, pressure in my head, pressure in my heart.

William floated upright near the bottom of the tank, weighed down by the fish scales I'd glimpsed earlier—his chain mail. Oh my God. I couldn't think about how much he must weigh with that on. And then, I couldn't think of anything. It was as if I'd entered some sort of mental and emotional vacuum, as if my mind emptied itself—of all fear, all anxiety, of everything except *push.*

Push said my legs, my arms, my chest.

Push.

My whole being became just something that pushed.

PUSH.

And then somehow Cody—*William* was on the partly submerged ledge and we were both breathing blessed, blessed air.

I checked his breathing, hoping hoping hoping I wouldn't have to perform CPR. William sputtered, coughing water. Thank God.

He laid his head back against the wooden platform. I climbed up onto it (I wanted to be all the way out of the water) then collapsed on the wet boards. An odd combination of exhaustion and exhilaration ran through me. I didn't want to move, but adrenaline still shot through my veins, making my heart race and...

Hey.

I did it. I saved William. From drowning. I did it. Oh my God, I did it. I had no idea how, but I did it.

The pounding in my chest became a drum, a happy parade beat. A ball of warmth began to glow inside me, making me warm and light and near to bursting with happiness, like Scrooge when he realizes it's still Christmas; like George Bailey when he realizes he still has his wonderful life.

I did it. I saved him. I turned my head to look at William, and he seemed unbearably beautiful in his humanity. "William," I whispered. "You have got to stop doing those drugs. There were no mermaids singing."

He opened an eye. "It's you." He shut it again, groaning. "No. There are no mermaids. But there is something. At the bottom of the ladder."

I sat up. "What? What's down there?" Evidence that someone else had been there? Could William have been attacked, somehow put in the tank? I didn't think so. It'd be pretty tough to get a stoned guy in chainmail up that ladder. "What is it, William?" But he didn't say any more, just lay with eyes closed, breathing easily, as if he were sleeping. I knew almost nothing about hallucinogens—maybe you got really tired after a trip?

I crept quietly down the ladder, not wanting to wake up William. I reached the bottom. What was the something that was here? I felt around in the dark. My hand touched a piece of paper taped to the side rail of the ladder. Must be a note. But though my eyes had adjusted to the dark, I still couldn't read the writing. I needed to find a light. I stepped outside the Grotto.

Omigod...The world was so beautiful. The full moon shone like a mirror in the clear desert night, bathing everything in blue, turning the stones in the road to silver and casting lacy shadows through the mesquite trees. Everything was *so* beautiful and I was so full, so buoyant with happiness I felt like I wasn't walking but gliding inches above the rocky ground.

I'd saved William. I wasn't who my mother thought I was. I wasn't self-centered. I was good. A good person in a beautiful world. I felt the night's beauty deep inside me: the moon, the mesquites, the rocks, even the bats flitting around the security light.

Which was where I was heading. Right. I walked toward the light, which warmed the night with its yellow halo. Wow. Whatever drug William had taken, it couldn't match this euphoria. Now, what had he written on the note? Something about mermaids? Or magic? Or—

No. I stared at the paper. No, no, no. Not those words.

I raced back to the Undersea Grotto, out of the moonlight and into the darkness. It entered me like a breath, taking up all the space so recently filled by beauty. I willed my eyes to see in the blackness.

There was no one in the tank. "Thank God," I said aloud.

"You should leave now." William's voice from above. He must still be on the platform. "I want to do this by myself. Besides, I suspect it will be... messy."

Messy? I looked up at the platform. William was sitting up now. And he was holding a gun. "Stashed this up here," he said, breathing hard. "Hedging my bets."

"I read your note," I said carefully, calm on the outside while my insides whirred like a blender. "If what you wrote is true, Angus's death was an accident. You were just trying to scare him. You didn't know he wasn't wearing his gorget." Keeping close to the tank and out of William's sightline, I crept to the ladder. Maybe I could get the gun away from him. Or maybe he'd shoot us both. It didn't matter. I had to try. "You can't hold yourself responsible."

"Ah, but I can. I do. Though I only planned to knock Angus off his horse—which is bad enough—in my heart I wanted him gone forever. And now he is. I was trying to save us all, and instead...I've ruined everything. I don't deserve to live."

I wanted to say something, no, to shout something, anything that would make William understand that taking another life wouldn't make up for Angus's death. But I didn't want him to know I was climbing the ladder, so I kept silent.

"I have no family except these people..."

I reached the edge of the platform.

"And now I've betrayed them."

I peered over the rim. William sat at the far end, legs dangling into the water, gun in the hand closest to me. No way to sneak up on him now.

"I murdered Angus. Killed our futures. Destroyed any love they had for me."

"Destroyed their love?" I stepped onto the platform. "You can't be serious. You're one of the most loved men I know." I still sounded calm, but felt as if I was on the bottom of the tank again, pressure against every inch of my being. And fear again, fear that I couldn't save him this time.

"Not now. Not after this. I killed Angus. *Killed* him. And by doing so, I put everyone I love in jeopardy. I preach kindness, but I allowed people to lie for me. I let Bianca cover for me. I nearly forced Riley go to prison, for God's sake. 'Might for right'—I'm such a hypocrite."

I had to stop him, to make him see the way people loved him, the good life he had. What he had. Cody's words rang in my head. "William." I moved close enough to put a hand on his shoulder. A mistake. He jerked, then raised the gun to his temple. I swallowed hard. *Don't panic, don't panic.*

"You can't imagine it," he said. "You can't imagine taking a life through your stupidity, trying to live with that every day, reminded by everything around you. It...crushes me. I can't live with it." A *click* as he pulled back the hammer on the gun.

Help, help, help, I prayed. Then, a miracle. That ball of warmth grew inside me again, smaller but there—all goodness and love and light. I felt as if I'd swallowed the moon. Impossibly, it was inside me and it was silver and it divided itself into bubbles that rose to my mouth and turned into words. "Actually I can...I can do more than imagine what you're going through. I've been where you are. It seems...impossible to go on." It didn't feel like me talking. "Impossible to ever be whole enough or good enough to be loved, ever again." William stared into the darkness, his eyes focused on nothing. "But here's the thing: people love us anyway. They love us not just in spite of our imperfections, but even because of them. Being imperfect makes us human. Touchable. Lovable. I don't even know you, and I love you. You somehow saved me."

He looked at me then, lowering the gun just a fraction. "I saved you?" Cynicism in his voice—but also a little hope.

"Yes, you did. You helped me see that I haven't really been living, that I've been afraid to open up to anyone, that I actually might be able to love and be loved."

"I didn't do that."

"You did. Saving you saved me. It was like a film was lifted from my eyes, one I didn't even know was there." I'd been running blindfolded half my life, running away so I wouldn't get hurt again. I'd kidded myself that a career could make up for connection. That the adulation of an audience could replace real love. "And now, I can see the possibility of life and love—the possibility that I saw for the first time tonight, thanks to you—and I can face my fears. I can connect to this beautiful world.

"I won't lie to you," I continued. "It's not easy to step out in faith. It's taken me years—until just a few moments ago, I guess. And I don't know how you'll get there, but here's what I do know." I looked William in the eye. "There are people who will help you through this." I saw the faces of Uncle Bob, Cody, and Matt.

"You did something wrong," I continued. "You're imperfect. You caused an accident. But you are loved. And worthy of love," I held out my hand for the gun, "and life."

I saw it, deep in William's eyes: Hope grew. He lowered the gun from his temple, then stretched out his arm in front of him. My throat tightened. Was I wrong? Was he turning it on himself again? No. William opened his hand and let go of the gun, dropped it into the water. It sank beneath the surface, carrying his sorrow, and all my bad years, with it.

Chapter 64

Riley flew into the mews, nearly breaking down the door in the process. "Bianca! Is everything all right? Bianca!" He stood at the door panting. "Thank God," he said when he saw her on the other side of the room. "But what's going on?" He pointed out the door, where a police car was parked on the dirt road near the mews, its lights flashing blue and white in the dark desert night.

"Everyone's okay," I said. "They arrested William."

"William? Oh man. That sucks." Riley's face took on an unusual expression: He looked like he was thinking. "So *he* hit me on the head and posed as me. Probably why he helped raise the reward money for my horse." Riley shrugged, forgiving William immediately. Not the type to hold a grudge. "But why are the police here at the mews?"

"William wanted to wait for the police here."

After we left the Undersea Grotto, William insisted I call the police. He wanted to confess, to make amends, especially since Riley was still under suspicion. My phone had gone into the mermaid tank with me, but a light still shone in the mews so we went there. "This is good," William had said as we knocked on the door. "I can apologize to Bianca too."

"Apologize?" Bianca opened the door—must've been right on the other side. "You...you don't...you're a very silly man." She drew William into a big hug. "And you're all wet." She looked at me. "Both of you."

"We had...a sort of baptism," I said. "And now it's a new life."

William continued to hug Bianca, his eyes closed. "A new life," he said.

Now, about a half hour later, I was dry (desert air, you know), and Riley stood awkwardly near the mews door. "Hey." He walked toward Bianca. "I, uh, got out last night."

"I know," she said.

"And I wanted to say thank you. For raising bail."

"You're welcome." Bianca stood still as Riley approached.

"But I wasn't sure if that meant...you know, if you forgave me."

"Riley, you didn't push me. There's nothing to forgive—on my end." They were just a few feet apart now. "I'm sorry," Bianca said to him. "For everything. It was like I lost my mind for a while. I just...I couldn't tell if you were with me just so you could live in the fifth-wheel."

"What? No. I mean, it's a sweet RV, man, but no. It's all about you. I love you."

Bianca opened her arms and Riley went to her, lifting her off the floor in a big bear hug. When he set her down, she made a face, wrinkling up her nose.

"What?" Riley said, then sniffed the air. Then he lifted an arm and smelled underneath. "Whoa, is that me?" He clamped his arms down by his sides and smiled at Bianca. "Hey, do you think if we'd never invented soap we'd like the smell of B.O.?"

"That's why I love him," Bianca said to me. "He's so deep."

The elation I'd felt after saving William had necessarily abated while I saved him a second time and had to turn him in to the police, but it was back. I walked to my truck through the dark faire, feeling like a buoyant light, a moonbeam, part of that wide starlit sky. I was looking up at those stars, which is why I didn't see the figure hiding in my truck bed until it leapt out of the truck in front of me. "*Aah!*" I screamed.

"*Aah!* You scared me."

"*I* scared *you*?" I said to Matt.

"It was a pretty impressive scream."

"I've had vocal training. And you jumped me."

"It was supposed to be romantic, in a Three Musketeers sort of way."

"In a *scary* Three Musketeers sort of way."

"Not romantic?" He took a tentative step toward me.

"Well, the fact that you're here is romantic." I took a step closer too. "Driving all the way out to the edges of the desert to find your lady love this time of night...Hey..."

"Uncle Bob told me where you were."

I loved the fact that he knew what I was going to ask.

"I wanted to talk," he said. "I was going to surprise you."

"And you did." I pulled him close to me and kissed him. "And now I'm surprising you."

"You are," he mumbled through the kiss. "It's a very nice surprise."

After a minute or two, we let each other go. Now Matt sniffed the air. I resisted sniffing my armpit. I'd showered that morning. "Why do you smell like chlorine?" Matt asked.

I unlatched my tailgate, hopped onto it, and patted the space beside me. "Let's talk."

I told him about Bianca and Angus and Riley. About the bird smuggling. About William. "Wait, you jumped into the tank?" he asked.

"Don't forget the gun part."

"But you jumped into a twenty-foot-deep tank of water? In the dark?" Matt knew me well.

"Yeah." I didn't want to talk about it. There were other things I needed to say. I started off by telling Matt about John Robert and Lewis and no Broadway.

"Did you know you were shooting yourself in the foot when you convinced John Robert to call Lewis?"

"Yeah, but he was so miserable. Like me. I think listening to him helped me see what life might be like...without you." Matt didn't say anything. Just watched me, listening. "When I was talking to him, I realized that I didn't have to choose, either, that you'd always supported my career." And what I'd realized in talking with William was that I needed to choose Matt's love. To be open to it. And worthy of it. "But I really thought I was doing the right thing, that I was saving you from me, because I was so messed up that we could never work. That you'd be stuck with a self-absorbed actor who was never going to be happy."

"And now?"

"Well..." I'd saved William even though I was terrified. That seemed pretty unselfish. And those moments of happiness I'd experienced in the last few hours felt like a window into possibility. "I think we can work out the rest."

"I do too," Matt said. "That's what I drove out here to tell you. That I wasn't letting you go without a fight. But..."

My heart constricted. "Yeah?"

"Ivy, you can't keep shutting down. You can't keep running away. You have to be open with me, to tell me what's going on with you, whether it's a paper cut or a chance to go to Broadway."

"You really want me to tell you about a paper cut?"

"And you have to stop deflecting me like that," Matt said. "At least when we're having a serious conversation. I'm not saying I don't love your sense of humor—I do—but sometimes you use it to keep me at a distance. You don't have to be afraid of getting close. I'm not going to abandon you like your parents. You have to believe that or it won't work. You have to believe you're loved. That I love you and you love me and that it's a good thing."

I felt elated and scared at the same time. My palms began to sweat. Could I do this? Did I really believe that this was love, and that it could be good? I thought about Matt—how he supported me in my acting and talked me through my PI cases. How he helped me to really see my brother. How he encouraged me to open up, not to just to him, but to life in general, and like I'd told William, to understand that I was worthy of love and life. Yes. Matt made me a better person. "It is good, and it is love," I finally said. "Cody was right."

"I'm so glad." Matt took my face in his hands and kissed me tenderly. "Now what's this about Cody?"

We called my brother on speakerphone, using Matt's cell. I was afraid he might not come to the phone if he knew it was me. "Hi Cody," said Matt. "I wanted to let you know I'm back in town."

"I know. I mean, thank you."

"And I wanted to let you know something else."

"I think I know." Cody sounded depressed.

"No," I said. "This is good news."

"Olive-y? Is that you? Are you with Matt?"

"Yes and yes."

"Does this mean you're back together?"

"Yes again."

"Ohhhh..." Cody groaned with relief. "I'm so glad," he said. "I knew you weren't dumb."

It was getting late, so we said goodbye to Cody pretty quickly, promising to see him in the next few days. Then I decided to try out my new straight-talking persona. "When do you want to start looking at apartments?"

"I think we have one more thing to talk through first."

Uh oh.

"I know you're not going to Broadway—at least not with *Kennelot*—but you need to know that I don't want you to give up your acting career."

"A career is wonderful, but you can't curl up with it on a cold night." A Marilyn quote. Matt frowned at me. "Sorry, deflecting again."

"Yeah. I don't feel like you've ever completely believed me about that, but it's true. You wouldn't be Ivy if you weren't an actor."

"I'd be Olive Ziegwart."

"You're that, too. You're Olive Ziegwart the detective, and Olive-y the sister of Cody, and Ivy Meadows the actress. And here's the thing: I love all of them."

"Wow. This straight-talking thing isn't so bad if it means I get to hear things like that." I leaned in closer to him.

"I don't know how it's going to work," Matt said. "All I can say is that we'll make it work."

"I may have an idea about that."

"You do?"

"Have you ever thought about Dolly Parton's husband?"

Chapter 65

I stayed the night with Matt. Even got up and had breakfast with him the next morning at seven o'clock. It was definitely love.

Freshly brewed coffee was waiting for Uncle Bob when he got in the office at nine. "What's this?" he said. "I smelled the coffee when I was coming up the stairs. Nearly went across the street to the jail to get a cop, but then I realized I'd never actually heard of a coffee-brewing burglar." He poured himself a cup. "I'd ask what we're celebrating, but I think I know."

"You do? Did Matt call you?"

"That too?"

"Too?"

Uncle Bob grinned. "Guess you haven't listened to yesterday's messages."

"I may be awake, but I still can't claim to be a morning person." I dialed Duda Detective's voicemail number and listened to a message from our law firm clients. Franko, Hricko, and Maionchi; one from an insurance company offering us a fraud job and...

"Omigod!" I hung up the phone so I could dial using the office landline. My cellphone was drowned. "When did this come in?"

"Last night," said Uncle Bob. "I was working late. She called here when she couldn't reach you. I guess you didn't have your cellphone on, even though you promised—"

I waved at him to be quiet. "Vicki," I said when she picked up. "I just got your message. You're not teasing me, right?"

She wasn't. "So I'll need to fly to LA on Friday for the screen-test," I said to Uncle Bob after I'd peeled myself off the ceiling. "I still can't believe it. I mean, the part isn't big, just two scenes, but it's *Marilyn*."

"And Andre," said Uncle Bob. "Even I know who he is."

I called John Robert and thanked him and then I called Hayden and thanked him. "It was especially nice since I sort of suspected you," I said.

"No problem. I was sort of suspicious."

"That traveling you do—it's with the Winged Army?"

"The who?" Hayden said, but the smile in his voice confirmed my suspicions.

"So did you recommend Jackie for the film too?"

"No," he said. "She's a great actor, but there's something not quite right about her."

Dang. Jackie had looked so devastated yesterday. I hung up the phone and stood there a minute. Yes, I was standing. I was still way too excited to sit.

"Hey, we need to talk about that message you left me at home last night," said Uncle Bob. "About the whole thing with William. And maybe you want tell me why you called me from Matt's phone?"

"I think you know why I called you from Matt's phone, since you told him where I was, and I'll tell you about William in just a sec. I have something I need to do first."

"What?"

"We are all of us stars, and we deserve to twinkle."

Uncle Bob frowned. "Is that Shakespeare? It doesn't sound like Shakespeare. Who said that?" It was Marilyn, of course, but I'd let him figure it out. I dialed the phone again. "Timothy? I know it's way too early, but—" I told him the news about Andre. Mostly to wake him up. It worked.

"Aaaaaah! You are going be a star! A star, baby!"

"Maybe. Isn't it cool!? And speaking of cool—" now for the real reason I called. "I have a great idea for Boys Will Be Girls. You said you're still figuring out a season, right?"

"Yeah..."

"Remember when we were shopping at Re-Dud you said something about being Henry Higgins?"

"Yeah...Omigod, *My Fair Lady.* That would be fab—those costumes!"

I thought this might work. Timothy loved costumes. "And I know the perfect actor to play Eliza Doolittle."

Once I was sure Timothy would pitch *My Fair Lady* with Benjamin as Eliza, I hung up the phone and sat down. "Okay," I said to Uncle Bob. "Here's what happened last night..."

"I can't believe you could do that," he said.

"I know. William must've weighed a ton with his chainmail on and everything."

"No, I meant that you were able to jump into that tank of water." Uncle Bob knew about my water phobia, had even been on the receiving end of a few freak-outs when I was younger. "That's really something, Olive."

"I...uh...thanks. I just...had to do it. Though I still don't know how I lifted him. Adrenaline, I guess."

"That, and..." My uncle tapped a few keys on his computer keyboard. "Water displaces weight, so..." He read from his computer screen, "If you had a hundred-pound person, he'd displace eighty-nine point two-eight pounds, so his effective weight in water would be...ten point seven-one pounds." Oh. I'd kind of liked thinking I had super human strength. Uncle Bob must have noticed my crestfallen face. "But I'm sure William weighed more than a hundred pounds," he said.

"Plus there was the chain mail."

"Exactly. And I meant what I said about you saving him from drowning, Olive. I'm proud of you." Uncle Bob blushed a little. None of us in my family were used to straight-talking. "I'm still not sure I get all of this, though," he said. "So William was the mysterious jouster. But what did he have to do with John Robert or his gardener?"

"Nothing. When William was planning the prank, he looked at Google Earth to find the nearest water to the jousting arena."

"The pool at John Robert's ranch."

"Exactly. William rode out of the arena, dumped the armor, rode Thunder to the ranch, walked a ways, and then hitched his way back to the faire. It was only when he got back that he realized how seriously he'd hurt Angus."

"When he OD'd earlier—was that a suicide attempt?"

I shook my head. "No. He said he just got some bad stuff. The OD did give him the idea to kill himself, but he kept that to himself. He said if anyone at the faire had even suspected they would have put a watch on him, wouldn't have let him out of their sight."

"Protected him, like they tried to do by getting you to drop the case."

"Yeah. Even the fortuneteller was in on it—kept giving me red herrings. I guess they really do treat each other like family."

"Egads," said my uncle. "I love the Renaissance faire."

Chapter 66

The rest of the day was a blur. I talked to the police. I talked to Vicki again. I talked to Cody and Candy and called a bunch of my other friends too. I talked to Doug, who was ponying up the cash for one of Phoenix's best criminal defense lawyers for William. I must have sounded surprised when he told me, because he said, "What can I say? This lawyer thinks he can get the charges reduced enough that William will only be...away from us for a couple of years. We need our wizard. Wouldn't be the same without him." I think that was Doug's way of saying he loved William too.

And of course I called Matt. Even better, I met him at his apartment after work. I took a change of clothes and my toothbrush. After kisses and beer and take-out Chinese, he sat down on the couch and I flopped down beside him, laying my head in his lap. Finally, a chance to think, to process everything that had happened in the last few days.

I guess I was uncharacteristically quiet, because Matt said, "What are you thinking about?"

"*Hamlet*."

"Really?"

"You know, the famous scene where he's thinking of killing himself."

"To be or not to be."

"Yeah. That one."

"Because of William?"

"That and..." I nodded slowly, trying to get my thoughts in order. I wanted to say it right. "I realized that in thinking about us, I've been thinking a lot about life, about what it's meant for, if it's worth it."

Matt's thighs tensed underneath me.

"No, don't worry, I wasn't anywhere as despondent as William was. I was just...lost. I was looking for something and I didn't know exactly what it was."

"You're not alone," Matt said.

"And what I realized is that for me, Hamlet's question isn't quite right—when he asks if it's nobler to stay alive and suffer the slings and arrows of outrageous fortune. I don't know about "nobler," but I do know that's it's worth it. After all, life *is* outrageous fortune, with all its messiness and quick turns and heartaches and love. But we—*I*—have to be open to it, to be willing to experience those things—even to suffer..." I turned to look at Matt and his beautiful, beautiful face. I couldn't believe I'd almost given him up. "Marilyn said, 'We should all start to live before we get too old.' I'm ready now. I want to face all those slings and arrows, and I want to face them with you. After all, to love and be loved is the greatest gift life can offer."

"Shakespeare again?"

I shook my head.

"Marilyn?"

"No." I kissed him. "Ivy Meadows.

Reader's Discussion Guide

I rewrote this book three times (!). I always write several drafts of each book and rewrite each of those several times, but this book changed more than any of the others since *Macdeath* (a first book almost always needs lots of drafts). I'd wanted to set a book at a Renaissance faire for years, ever since the opening jousting scene planted itself in my head, and *Camelot* seemed like the obvious choice for a play that would fit into the world of the book. In each of Ivy's books, I like to make part of the plot parallel the theme of the original play. How to do that with *Camelot*?

In my first draft, I concentrated on the play's love-versus-romance theme (after all, Guinevere does love Arthur even as she betrays him with Lancelot). I think it's not uncommon for us to mistake romance for love, and the problem certainly adds conflict, but when I tried to use it, I ended up with a love triangle between Ivy, Matt, and Hayden. Ugh.

I took out the love triangle and moved on to the play's theme of the death of a dream (the destruction of the "brief shining moment" that was Camelot). I used that theme as Ivy's conflict—in choosing one of her dreams (love or an acting career), she'd have to destroy the other (or so she thought.) Then I made the threat to the Ren faire part of the killer's motive. Better.

But something was still missing, and one day it came to me. It was Cody. Ivy had always thought she'd destroyed his dream (a "normal life"), and she needed to deal with that. So, another draft. And *finally*, the book you have in your hands. I hope you like this insight into how it came to be and enjoy Ivy's Camelot adventure.

- Cindy Brown

Topics & Questions for Discussion

Have you ever had to choose between dreams? What were they? How did you make your decision?

If you could dress up to go to a Renaissance faire, what would you wear? Traditional garb, or something more fantastical?

Ivy nearly gives up on her investigation. Have you ever been about to throw in the towel only to have something change your mind?

What communities do you voluntarily belong to (neighborhood groups, religious organizations, social groups)? How far would you go to defend them?

The Kennedy era has often been referred to as America's Camelot. What do you think would have happened if he hadn't been assassinated?

Enhance Your Book Club or Class Discussion

Visit a Renaissance faire! You can find one near you by going to therenlist.com (and not all of them are as expensive as the fictional Phoenix Ren Faire).

Listen to *Camelot*. I think the Broadway version definitely outshines the film in terms of music—after all Broadway had Julie Andrews singing the role of Guinevere.

Watch the film. It's a little outdated, but it was filmed at a Spanish castle, and you can watch Vanessa Redgrave (Guinevere) and Franco Nero (Lancelot) fall in love. After meeting on the set in 1967, they had a son together, broke up, and then reunited and married in 2006, when they were in their 70's.

Read books about the legend of King Arthur. You can choose from *The Once and Future King*, which inspired the musical; *The Mists of Avalon*, which tells the legend from women's perspectives; or if you're up for a challenge, you can check out the earliest written account of King Arthur by reading *Le Morte D'Arthur* (1485) by Sir Thomas Malory.

Watch *Some Like It Hot*, or other Marilyn Monroe films. Google the famous "Happy Birthday Mr. President" scene and watch it too.

Try the food! You can go with a Medieval feast (Renaissance faires typically straddle Medieval and Renaissance themes) of fish or poultry, fresh bread, honey mustard, eggs (like deviled eggs, but with yep, honey and mustard), chilled strawberry soup—and no forks (they weren't invented yet). Spoons and knives are okay. If you'd like to use all of your silverware, you could try an Italian Renaissance meal of melon, roast chicken, mushrooms, and a stuffed pasta (like ravioli).

According to *The Smithsonian Magazine*, "Wildlife trafficking is thought to be the third most valuable illicit commerce in the world, after drugs and weapons." You can help by:

- Educating yourself and others. Eighty percent of Americans are unaware of the wildlife trafficking happening in the U.S. Learn more at www.stopwildlifetrafficking.org.
- Asking where animal products come from (remember Hayden asking about the feather?).
- Donating or volunteering to the many non-profits who are working to stop animal trafficking.

Visit cindybrownwriter.com to learn more about me and my books, and to sign up for my Slightly Silly Newsletter, an irreverent look at mystery and drama (with a smidgen of book news).

Photo by AJC Photography

Cindy Brown

Cindy Brown has been a theater geek (musician, actor, director, producer, and playwright) since her first professional gig at age 14. Now a full-time writer, she's the author of the Agatha Award-nominated Ivy Meadows series, madcap mysteries set in the off, off, OFF Broadway world of theater. Cindy and her husband live in Portland, Oregon, though she made her home in Phoenix, Arizona, for more than 25 years and knows all the good places to hide dead bodies in both cities.

She'd love to connect with readers at cindybrownwriter.com.

The Ivy Meadows Mystery Series
by Cindy Brown

MACDEATH (#1)
THE SOUND OF MURDER (#2)
OLIVER TWISTED (#3)
IVY GET YOUR GUN (#4)
THE PHANTOM OF OZ (#5)
KILLALOT (#6)

Henery Press Mystery Books

And finally, before you go...
Here are a few other mysteries
you might enjoy:

MURDER ON A SILVER PLATTER

Shawn Reilly Simmons

A Red Carpet Catering Mystery (#1)

Penelope Sutherland and her Red Carpet Catering company just got their big break as the on-set caterer for an upcoming blockbuster. But when she discovers a dead body outside her house, Penelope finds herself in hot water. Things start to boil over when serious accidents threaten the lives of the cast and crew. And when the film's star, who happens to be Penelope's best friend, is poisoned, the entire production is nearly shut down.

Threats and accusations send Penelope out of the frying pan and into the fire as she struggles to keep her company afloat. Before Penelope can dish up dessert, she must find the killer or she'll be the one served up on a silver platter.

COUNTERFEIT CONSPIRACIES

Ritter Ames

A Bodies of Art Mystery (#1)

Laurel Beacham may have been born with a silver spoon in her mouth, but she has long since lost it digging herself out of trouble. Her father gambled and womanized his way through the family fortune before skiing off an Alp, leaving her with more tarnish than trust fund. Quick wits and connections have gained her a reputation as one of the world's premier art recovery experts. The police may catch the thief, but she reclaims the missing masterpieces.

The latest assignment, however, may be her undoing. Using every ounce of luck and larceny she possesses, Laurel must locate a priceless art icon and rescue a co-worker (and ex-lover) from a master criminal, all the while matching wits with a charming new nemesis. Unfortunately, he seems to know where the bodies are buried—and she prefers hers isn't next.

CPSIA information can be obtained
at www.ICGtesting.com
Printed in the USA
BVHW061311051118
532196BV00012B/230/P

9 781635 11430